KNOW YOUR
PLACE

Also by Shelly Ellis

The Branch Ave Boys
In These Streets

Chesterton Scandal series
To Love & Betray
Lust & Loyalty
Best Kept Secrets
Bed of Lies

Gibbons Gold Digger series
Can't Stand the Heat
The Player & the Game
Another Woman's Man
The Best She Ever Had

Published by Dafina Books

KNOW YOUR PLACE

SHELLY ELLIS

KENSINGTON PUBLISHING CORP.
www.kensingtonbooks.com

DAFINA BOOKS are published by

Kensington Publishing Corp.
119 West 40th Street
New York, NY 10018

All Kensington titles, imprints, and distributed lines are available at special quantity discounts for bulk purchases for sales promotion, premiums, fund-raising, and educational or institutional use.

Special book excerpts or customized printings can also be created to fit specific needs. For details, write or phone the office of the Kensington Sales Manager: Kensington Publishing Corp., 119 West 40th Street, New York, NY 10018. Attn. Sales Department. Phone: 1-800-221-2647.

Dafina and the Dafina logo Reg. U.S. Pat. & TM Off.

ISBN-13: 978-1-4967-1897-6
ISBN-10: 1-4967-1897-6
First Kensington Trade Paperback Printing: May 2019

ISBN-13: 978-1-4967-1898-3 (ebook)
ISBN-10: 1-4967-1898-4 (ebook)
First Kensington Electronic Edition: May 2019

10 9 8 7 6 5 4 3 2 1

Printed in the United States of America

To Andrew and Chloe . . . without you,
this doesn't work. Thanks for making it all worth it.

Acknowledgments

For me, each book is a new, scary but exciting journey, no matter how many books I've previously written. I usually start with an overall idea, write a few chapters, write a synopsis, write a few more chapters, progress to a chapter outline, and then set about finishing my novel. But the truth is, no matter how much I plan out the plot and think I know the characters, I never *really* know where each book is going until I reach the end. (Hence, the "scary but exciting journey" bit.) Inevitably, I'll have a few twists and turns I hadn't anticipated; my latest novel, *Know Your Place*, was no exception. I hit a few brick walls this time around. (I wasn't quite sure how Derrick would evolve as a character. And when it comes to writing a book series, you never know which book will be the last, so it's always a negotiation with my editor with just how many cliffhangers I should leave at the end that may or may not be addressed in the follow-up.)

There was more than one point in the course of writing this work where I was staring at the ceiling, ready to rip my hair out, and I had the usual people around me ready to talk me down. One of those people is my husband, Andrew, who always tells me, "You'll get through it. You always do," instilling me with the confidence I need to make it to the end. My other supporters are my parents, who provide babysitting duties for my five-year-old, allowing me time to catch up on my writing. They also lend an ear to listen to my laments. Thanks for always supporting me. I also want to thank my rock star agent, Barbara Poelle, and my editor, literary diva Esi Sogah. My books are my babies, so when I entrust them to someone, I don't do it lightly. Thank you for your care, dedication, and professionalism. You guys are great at what you do, and I deeply respect you for that.

Thanks to all my author buddies who share advice, praise, and jokes with me. Thanks to all my readers who plunk down their money to buy my books. I feel blessed to do what I do and even more blessed that you appreciate and like my work!

Chapter 1

Derrick

Derrick Miller stared down at the two open suitcases in front of him, closed his eyes for a few seconds, and slowly opened them again.

It was insane but, in the back of his mind, he had hoped they would disappear. Maybe the suitcases—one filled with multiple stacks of hundred-dollar bills bound neatly with multicolored rubber bands, the other stuffed with packs of white powder that was more than likely cocaine—were figments of his imagination, mini mirages right here at the Branch Avenue Boys' Youth Institute dormitories.

But of course, they weren't; the suitcases didn't shimmer then disappear like a waterfall floating in the desert. They were still there with their lids yawning open, and what they contained was bared for all the world to see.

This was real, *too* real for Derrick's liking.

"Come on, man! We gonna be late," someone shouted in the hallway, shaking Derrick out of his stupor.

His eyes darted to the dormitory's open door as two boys jogged by, probably on their way to their morning classes. Derrick's eyes snapped back to the suitcases. He couldn't leave them here. He certainly couldn't let any of the boys at the Institute see them. He didn't know whom they belonged to, but he suspected Cole, the student who was assigned to the bunk where he'd found the suitcases, knew who the owner was. He'd talk to Cole later, but his first mission was to find a place to hide these damn things.

Derrick quickly flipped both of the lids closed, zipping each of them with shaking hands. He grabbed the handles and yanked them off the bed. They landed on the linoleum floor with a thud. They had to weigh about a hundred pounds each.

Derrick gritted his teeth as he lifted the suitcases and lugged them to the door, one in each hand. He walked straight down the hall to the stairwell. A few students eyed him curiously. Several boys had a questioning look on their faces, probably wondering what the Institute's director was doing, carrying luggage down the hall in the middle of the day like he was heading to Ronald Reagan Washington National Airport fifteen miles up the road.

"Hey, Mr. Derrick!" one of the boys—dark skinned and stocky—called out as he held open the stainless steel door for him. His dark eyes dropped to the suitcases. "Damn, those look heavy! You need some h—"

"No!" Derrick barked between bursts of breath.

The boy's ready smile disappeared.

"I mean . . . I mean, no. I-I got it. Th-thanks for asking though," Derrick stuttered with a slight grimace.

The boy nodded just as Derrick disappeared into the stairwell and made the slow trek down the stairs to the floor below. With each step, the suitcases felt heavier and heavier. Sweat erupted on his forehead and rolled down the bridge of his nose. The short bursts of breath came out faster, making a faint whistle between his clenched teeth. The tendons and muscles in his arms started to jitter. His heart was beating fast from the stress and the strain. When he finally pushed the steel door open and reached his office, he didn't lower the suitcases to the floor as much as hurl them.

He shut his office door behind him, locked it, and looked around frantically for a place to hide the suitcases. The office didn't have a storage closet and the suitcases certainly wouldn't fit in any of his cabinets or shelves. The only spot where they could possibly fit was a corner beside his file cabinet. He shoved them both into the dusty, dark space.

By now, not only was his brow sweaty, but pools of sweat had also formed under his armpits. His palms were slick with it. Sweat even dripped down his back and the crack of his ass.

When Derrick finally finished shoving the suitcases into the hiding space, he dragged across the floor a potted fiddle-leaf fig tree his fiancée, Melissa, had given him for his birthday to add a little softness to his sterile office. He set it in front of the suitcases. He then stood back and surveyed his handiwork.

It was a questionable hiding job—the plant barely provided any coverage—but it would have to do for now.

He flopped back into his rolling chair and let out a slow, long exhale. It took another ten minutes for his heart to finally return to its normal pace, for his hands to stop shaking.

How the hell did those things even get here?

How had the boys managed to smuggle something so heavy and massive into the dorms, right under the noses of the instructors and security guards? When had they done it? It must have been recently because the suitcases certainly would have been noticed during their weekly inspections of the boys' bunks and lockers. Had someone else brought them?

Cole knows all the answers, he thought, staring at the fig tree. *And that boy better tell me the damn truth!*

"Cole!" Derrick called out as he saw the boy stroll toward one of the classrooms. He cupped his hand around his mouth like a megaphone. "Cole!"

Cole glanced over his shoulder at him and rolled his eyes. For a split second, he looked like he was going to pretend he hadn't heard Derrick and continue on his way, but he turned on his heel and walked toward him anyway. An expression of pure contempt was on the young man's face.

Derrick knew that Cole was angry at him. The boy obviously had a crush on Morgan Owens, the new carpentry instructor at the Institute. Cole had come to her defense before when another student had sexually harassed her in class, and he probably felt he was taking up for her again, against Derrick this time, after seeing her cry. But Cole didn't know the full backstory of Derrick's complicated relationship with the beautiful instructor, nor did Derrick care to share it with him. That was between him and Morgan. Besides, the suitcases were of bigger concern right now.

"What do you want?" Cole snarled with a curl in his lip, drawing closer to him.

"I want you in my office—*now!*"

"Can't," Cole said with a shrug, casually shoving his hands into his jeans pockets. He painted on a fake grin. "Gotta get to class. Sorry, Mr. D."

Derrick's jaw tightened as he watched the young man turn back around. "It wasn't a question, Cole. I said come to my office."

Cole started to stroll away.

"I found them! I found them under your bunk!" he

called out, making the young man stop in his tracks. "You didn't even do a decent job of hiding them. Why?"

Cole faced him again. He didn't look smug anymore. He looked alarmed—and annoyed.

"Come to my office. I'm not gonna tell you again."

Finally, Cole sucked his teeth and nodded.

A minute later, Cole walked into Derrick's office. Derrick stomped in after him, slamming the door shut behind them.

"What the hell . . . *what the hell* were you thinking, bringing some shit like this into my school?" Derrick yelled as Cole flopped into one of the armchairs facing his desk.

Cole sat in sullen silence with his arms crossed over his chest, glaring at nothing in particular.

"Your mother begged me . . . she got on her damn knees in this very office and begged me to let you into this program so that you wouldn't have to go to jail, and this is what you do?" he asked as he charged around his desk to face Cole. The young man still refused to meet his gaze. "This is how you repay her? *Repay me?*"

"Man, I don't owe you shit," Cole muttered, still staring at the wall in front of him defiantly.

"Oh, is that what you think? Then how about I just send your ungrateful ass to jail then?"

Cole didn't reply.

Derrick shifted the potted fiddle-leaf fig tree out of the way and pointed to the suitcases. "Give me one . . . give me *one* good reason why I shouldn't call the damn cops, tell them about what I found, and have your ass thrown in prison right now."

Cole finally shifted his eyes and looked up at him.

"'Cause you ain't that stupid," Cole answered in a voice that was both glacial and hollow. "'Cause you don't wanna get your shit fucked up. That's why you ain't callin' the police."

"Shit fucked up by who? Whose suitcases are these? Who the fuck do you work for?"

"It ain't none of your damn business," Cole said, shaking his head.

"When you bring that shit here—yes, it is! This shit *is* my business now! You were low-key about it. I'll give you that. But the boys still know the truth. Word got around, right? They know who you work for . . . 'who you fuck with,' don't they? That's why they've all been going out of their way to kiss your skinny little ass! If you don't tell me, I'm gonna find out." He sat on the edge of his desk. "Who do you work for? Whose bags are those?"

The office fell silent. Finally, Cole sucked his teeth again. "They're Dolla Dolla's. All right?"

Derrick felt an icy chill snake its way up his spine. They belonged to Dolla, his best friend Ricky's business partner. The drug kingpin's empire stretched far and wide in D.C. Hell, Dolla Dolla's grubby, blood-stained fingers had even touched Ricky's upscale restaurant, Reynaud's, providing the money Ricky needed to start it. But Derrick never would have guessed that Dolla would reach here, within the Institute's walls. Derrick never thought Dolla could taint a place he held so sacred.

"It's his bags," Cole continued. "It's his shipment. He usually keeps it somewhere else but they had to move it quick. They asked me if I could keep it until they could move it again. I told them no one here would touch it."

"Why . . . why would you do something like that?" Derrick sputtered. "Why would you bring that here? You know who Dolla is! Cole, he could—"

"Look, he ain't gonna do nothin'. This shit will be gone in a few days . . . maybe a week," Cole assured him. "You ain't gotta worry about it."

"No, I do have to worry about it because you're putting me and every single teacher and boy at the Institute at risk with this bullshit!"

"So you gonna snitch and tell the cops? Is that what you telling me?"

"No, what I'm telling you is—"

Derrick's words were stopped short by a frantic knock at his office door.

"I'm busy right now!" he called out.

"I'm sorry, Mr. Miller, but your fiancée just called the front desk," a muffled voice replied through the closed door. "She said she's been trying to reach you all morning."

Derrick frowned, reached back, and opened one of his desk drawers. He pulled out his cell phone, which he had tossed inside the drawer more than an hour ago. He saw that there were several text messages from Melissa.

What the hell is going on, D? the most recent message read. **Call me back!**

When he saw it, his heart sank. Did this have something to do with Morgan?

When he told Morgan that very morning that he had to break off their affair because he'd decided to get back with his fiancée, Morgan hadn't taken the news well—as he'd expected. He hadn't seen her since then. He'd assumed that she had either gone off to lick her wounds, or had decided to ignore her anger and go about her workday. He had not anticipated that she might try to reach out to Melissa, that she might tell Melissa what had gone down between them.

"Your fiancée asked if you could call her back ASAP, Mr. Miller," the muffled voice explained. On cue, his cell began to buzz. Melissa's name popped up on the screen.

"Okay, got it. Thanks!" Derrick called back distractedly, then took a deep breath. He glanced at Cole. "I've gotta take this. We *will* finish this conversation later though. This ain't over."

Cole pushed himself to his feet, not looking remotely intimidated. He walked toward the door and swung it open. "Just leave your office door open later so I can move them again," he called over his shoulder. "They'll be outta here in a few days. I told you, you ain't gotta worry about it."

Derrick opened his mouth to reply, but Cole shut the door before he could. Derrick's frown deepened. A heavy crease formed in the center of his brow.

All morning he'd felt like things were teetering wildly off kilter and threatening to topple over. First, he'd had to break things off with Morgan and got her explosive response. Then he'd stumbled upon the suitcases. And now, Cole was acting like he was running the Institute, like *he* was giving Derrick orders—not the other way around. Derrick felt like he was losing control of his life.

Or I never really had it, he mused, as he pressed the button to answer his cell. Maybe it had been an illusion all along.

"Hey," he answered hesitantly, wary of what his fiancée was about to say to him. He braced himself for accusations and recriminations, for an endless stream of four-letter words.

But instead she said, "Where have you been, Dee? I've called you about six times! I even sent texts!" Melissa shouted, sounding panicked. "You never called me back!"

"I'm sorry, baby. I left my phone in my office. I just saw your messages."

"Have you read them though? Did you see the link I sent you? The one from Fox 5?"

He slowly shook his head, now confused. "No. No, I didn't see it. What's up? What's wrong?"

"Ricky's club was raided last night. The news story said his restaurant was too!"

Derrick hopped off his desk. He shot to his feet. "*What?* What do you mean, it was raided?"

"There was like a half dozen raids last night, all around the city and a few in Virginia and Maryland. They said lots of people were arrested. Have you . . . have you talked to Ricky? Have you heard from him since last night?"

Derrick shook his head. "No," he said weakly, now feeling numb with shock, "I haven't."

"Oh, God, Dee! Do you think Ricky got arrested? Do you think he's in jail right now?"

Derrick shook his head again. "I don't know, Lissa. I don't know."

Chapter 2

Ricky

Ricky Reynaud leaned back in his chair and squinted at the track lighting beating down on him like a hot July sun.

His neck ached. His back ached. A dull throb had spread across his temples. He was starting to feel out of it. He had been up for almost twenty-four hours straight, unable to sleep in the loud, crowded holding cell they had kept him in for most of the night and morning since the raid at his strip club. He was still wearing the same clothes from the night before. The smell of his signature cologne, Gucci Guilty, had long since faded and was now replaced with a rank body odor he was sure followed him around like a stink cloud.

The cops hadn't let him make any phone calls—not even to his friends or his lawyer. He had been sitting in this all white, bare room alone for fifteen minutes . . . or thirty minutes . . . or maybe even an hour. He didn't know how long anymore. He was starting to lose track of time.

All he knew was who had put him here, who had gotten him in this situation in the first place.

Simone.

That is Patrol Officer Simone Fuller of the Metropolitan Police Department—his former lover.

Every impulse had told him to stay far, far away from Simone. From the moment she had told him her story of woe about her little sister, Skylar, being turned out by his business partner, Dolla, alarm bells had sounded in his head. Even Derrick—Mr. Goody Two-shoes—had warned him against helping her. But Ricky had pressed forward anyway, despite his instincts telling him to do the opposite. He had helped her by finding her sister and trying to rescue the wayward girl. He had even fallen in love with Simone, and he could honestly say it was the first time in his life he had ever fallen that hard for a woman. He had risked his life for her. And how had she rewarded all that love and sacrifice? By ratting him out to the cops, by having his businesses raided and his property seized.

I was so fucking stupid, he now thought, sadly shaking his head.

It had all been a hustle—an easy hustle, at that. She'd probably never remotely felt anything for him, certainly not love. She'd turned on the tears when convenient to gain his sympathy. Then she spread her legs and sucked his dick when the tears no longer worked. Maybe she had been undercover this whole time, something she had denied from the beginning. Maybe the whole thing had been a setup. Maybe her real objective wasn't rescuing Skylar, but taking down Dolla Dolla all along, and Ricky had just been the pawn on the chessboard she'd used to help capture the king.

Either way, it left Ricky sitting here alone in this room, in handcuffs. Either way, he had likely lost his restaurant, his home, and his livelihood. He also was probably going to jail for a very, *very* long time.

I'mma kill her. I'mma fuckin' kill her, he thought for the umpteenth time. He didn't know how. He didn't know when, but as soon as he got his hands on Simone, she would feel his rage.

The door to the room finally swung open and two men strolled inside. They looked like plainclothes police officers. At the sight of them, Ricky pushed back his shoulders. He sat upright in his metal chair despite the ache in his back and shoulders.

"Hey!" one said with a smile, like he was greeting an old classmate on the street.

He was the shorter of the two and had a sizeable beer gut. He wore wire-rimmed glasses and an ugly striped tie. He had a bald brown head that glistened under the overhead lights; it made him look like the Mr. Peanut mascot.

"How you doing, Mr. Reynaud?" Mr. Peanut said.

"I'm not answering any questions or sayin' shit without my lawyer present," Ricky answered in a monotone.

"You need a lawyer present to say how you're doing?" Mr. Peanut asked with a chuckle. "Damn! It's like that, huh?"

Ricky didn't respond. Instead, he eyed the two men guardedly.

"My name's Detective Ramsey. This is Detective Dominguez." Mr. Peanut, who he now knew as Detective Ramsey, gestured to the man standing beside him.

The other detective had a full head of wavy, graying hair, was a couple of inches taller and several shades lighter than his counterpart. Rather than speak, he dipped his pockmarked chin at Ricky and grunted.

"You've been here for a while, haven't you? At least since midnight. I bet you're pretty damn hungry, ain't ya'?" Detective Ramsey tossed a plastic-wrapped honey bun onto the table. He set a bottle of orange juice beside it. "Go ahead. Eat!"

So that was it? They thought they could get him to snitch for a one-dollar dessert and some orange juice?

Ricky watched as they both pulled out folding chairs on the opposite side of the table and sat down. He glanced at the food sitting inches in front of him.

"I'm not a honey bun kinda dude," he muttered dryly.

"Well, that's all we got on the fuckin' menu, so you can either eat that—or eat air," Detective Dominguez growled, making Ricky cock an eyebrow.

So it was obvious which one was going to be the good cop and which one was going to be the bad cop. He just wondered what their objective was. What would they try to trick him into saying?

"You had a rough night, Ricky . . . can I call you Ricky?" Ramsey asked, inclining his head. "Haven't eaten. Haven't slept. We'd like to get you out of here and home to your own warm bed as soon as possible—if we can. But we're—"

"But we're gonna need you to cooperate," Dominguez interrupted. "Don't give us any bullshit, or your ass could be in here until next year!"

"I want to speak with my lawyer," Ricky repeated slowly and firmly, narrowing his eyes at them.

He knew what they were trying to do, to trip him up and get him to confess something incriminating. But Ricky wasn't just some "around-the-way nigga" they'd picked up off a street corner with a dime bag in his pocket. He knew his rights, and he knew they were violating them by not allowing his lawyer to be present during questioning.

"You're facing quite a few serious charges, Ricky," Ramsey continued as he flipped open a manila folder he had brought in with him, pretending like he hadn't heard Ricky's request. "Drug possession . . . money laundering . . . racketeering . . . and if the feds get involved, you can probably look forward to tax evasion too."

"The way I count it, that adds up to *a lot* of time behind bars," Dominguez murmured with a smirk. "You could be an old man pissing in a diaper, eating mashed-up peas by the time you're free. Or you could just die in jail."

"You don't want that, do you, Ricky?" Ramsey asked, now frowning, doing an almost comical impression of concern. "You're what . . . thirty? *Thirty-one?* You're still a young man! You've got a lot to live for and look forward to. Before this, you didn't even have a real criminal record . . . a few misdemeanors and speeding tickets, but that's about it. And like we said . . . you're facing some pretty serious shit now. Don't go down like this! Help us out so we can help you out. Tell us what you know about Dolla Dolla and maybe we can . . . I don't know . . . maybe we can work out a deal with the prosecutors to get some of your charges reduced or even dropped."

"I didn't waive my right to an attorney. I want my goddamn lawyer!" Ricky shouted.

"You think that piece of shit feels any loyalty to *you*?" Dominguez asked, leaning forward. "You think he wouldn't hesitate to send all of you motherfuckas to jail if it meant saving his own ass? You know the old saying, Ricky. No honor among thieves. He'd name names . . . point fingers. He'd do it in a cocaine heartbeat. You're one dumb son of a bitch if you're willing to sacrifice your freedom for him!"

"Just talk to us, Ricky," Ramsey pleaded, squinting at him from behind his bifocals. "Tell us all that you know. You don't have to worry. We can protect you!"

Ricky barked out a laugh, making Dominguez's grimace harden and Ramsey's mask of concern disappear.

"Damn, y'all are laying this on thick," he said with a weary shake of the head. "It was a good performance up until that point. 'We can protect you.'" He chuckled. "Get the fuck outta here! Y'all couldn't protect shit! Just stop playing, and let me talk to my lawyer."

The room fell silent. Detectives Ramsey and Dominguez exchanged a glance.

"Fine," Detective Ramsey muttered, closing his folder and pushing back his chair. "Fine. Have it your way."

Dominguez pushed back from the table too, adjusting his tie. "Told you it was a waste of time, Eddie. These motherfuckas are all stupid!"

Both men rose to their feet and strolled toward the door.

"So that's it?" Ricky called after them. "I get to speak with my lawyer now, right?"

"Yeah, we'll let you call your lawyer," Ramsey said as he reached for the doorknob, then paused as if he'd forgotten something. He turned back around to face Ricky. "Oh, by the way, your friend Dolla Dolla is being questioned right now too, a couple of doors down. Should I tell him you said hi?"

Ricky stilled.

"Or maybe I could pop in and tell him just how loyal you really are. Maybe I should tell him that the only reason why we were able to conduct all those raids yesterday is because you sold him out to a patrol officer with the Metro Police," Ramsey continued, now smiling. "I wonder if he knows what kind of guy you really are, Ricky. I wonder how he'll react when he finds out what you did to him. You think your lawyer would be able to help out with that one?"

This time, Dominguez laughed, hearty and loud.

Ricky swallowed. He started to shake. His stomach clenched as the panic threatened to make him throw up right there in the bare white room. He watched helplessly as Detective Ramsey turned the knob and both men sauntered into the hall.

"Wait! Wait!" he shouted, making them pause again.

"Yeah?" Ramsey asked, raising his brows.

"Shut the door," he said, lowering his eyes to the table-top. He let out an unsteady breath. "I'll help you. All right? Just . . . Just tell me what you wanna know."

Ramsey grinned. "Now we're talkin'."

Chapter 3

Jamal

Jamal Lighty stepped out of the shower, wiped himself down with a towel, and wiped the condensation off his bathroom mirror. He paused after wrapping the towel around his waist and stared at his reflection, taking in the angle of his brow, the bristle of hairs along his chin, and the light sprinkling of freckles along the bridge of his nose, which he'd inherited from his mother. He then gazed into his dark eyes, wondering if he could spot anything there—some flicker or glimmer . . . some sign that showed he had changed, that he was no longer the man he'd been a week ago. But he didn't see anything.

"Humph," he grunted before reaching for his toothbrush.

For some dumb reason, he'd expected that he might look a little different. He thought after agreeing to accept bribes to keep the mayor of D.C.'s dirty secrets, after becoming complicit to crime and corruption, he'd have metamorphosed into someone else.

Maybe I'll grow a long, pointy mustache that I could

start twirling like Snidely Whiplash, he thought with a sad chuckle as he squeezed toothpaste onto his brush. *Or my eyes will start glowing red like some damn vampire.*

But of course he knew the truth; nothing would happen. Jamal didn't look any different and probably never would. He didn't *feel* any different either, though he waited for a wave of guilt or self-loathing to overwhelm him.

After all these years of trying to play the good guy and earn other people's respect, he had finally embraced who he really was: a "ruthless motherfucka" according to Ricky, his former friend. Or better yet, a "low-down, shady fuck."

That's the insult that Melissa, Derrick's girl, had lobbed at him when he'd kissed her. She'd said he'd betrayed her man by doing it. Of course, part of him still rebelled against her accusation. When he'd kissed her, he'd done it out of a long-held love of Melissa, one he'd harbored for almost twenty years. He hadn't meant nor wanted to stab Derrick, his former friend, in the back. What he'd felt—what he'd professed to her that night—wasn't about Derrick at all. He'd wanted to defend himself, but another part of him thought, "What difference does it make?" Why should he care what Melissa thought of him? She'd probably gone back to Derrick anyway, though the two would never make one another happy in the end. Why should he care what *anyone* thought of him? He was his own man. He made his own decisions. He had no reason to be ashamed of his choices.

"I am what I am," he muttered before he began to brush his teeth and prepare for the work day.

Jamal arrived at the Wilson Building a little more than an hour later, sipping coffee from his travel mug. When he stepped into his office, he was immediately met by his assistant. She didn't wait for him to remove his coat before she stood from her chair, rounded her desk, and handed a folder to him.

"Good morning, Mr. Lighty. Mayor Johnson told me to give this to you as soon as you arrived, sir. He said you can read it on the plane," she chirped perkily, making Jamal squint in confusion.

"*Plane?* What . . . what plane?"

"The flight you're taking today."

When he continued to stare at her blankly, her eager smile disappeared. "You weren't aware you had a trip this week?"

Jamal shook his head.

"I'm so sorry, sir! I thought you and Mayor Johnson had planned this." She pursed her lips and lowered her brown eyes. "Though I did think it was odd that you were disappearing to Chicago for a couple days when you hadn't mentioned any of it to—"

"Wait." Jamal held up his hand, making her eyes snap back to his face. "Back up. I'm taking a trip to Chicago?"

She nodded. "That's what the ticket says. You guys are taking a 10:55 flight on American Airlines to Chicago. First class." She shrugged her slender shoulders as he finally took the folder she held out to him, juggling his travel mug and briefcase all the while. He flipped it open and saw the boarding pass along with several stapled stacks of paper detailing some mayoral summit. "I'm sorry I can't give more information, Mr. Lighty. Mr. Johnson's assistant wasn't big on details when she sent me the paperwork and flight info. Hopefully, it's all explained in your packet." She gestured to the glossy folder again. "I'm clearing out your schedule for today and tomorrow as she instructed though. Hope that helps, at least."

"Th-Thank you, Sharon," he said weakly. "I'll just . . . I'll just pop in the mayor's office to find out . . . you know . . . what's going on."

She laughed. "That's probably a good idea!"

It didn't take him long to find Mayor Johnson. The older man was striding down the hall toward him, heading in the same direction that Jamal had just come from. Johnson was throwing on his wool coat and tying a scarf around his throat as he walked. When he saw Jamal, his brown, wrinkled face widened into a grin.

Jamal had heard of the phrase "the banality of evil," and Mayor Vernon Johnson embodied it. He was an unassuming black man, medium stature, wearing a navy-blue pinstripe suit, but to Jamal he oozed sleaze and contempt. He had threatened Jamal's life and the life of his ex-girlfriend in an attempt to get what he wanted. Jamal suspected that the mayor would've followed through with that threat if Jamal hadn't agreed to keep his secrets.

"Ah, Jay! There you are. Glad I caught you! I was just going to ask my assistant to call you and tell you to meet me downstairs. My driver is waiting to take us to the airport."

"Yeah, uh . . . about that, sir. I didn't know I was going to Chicago today. I certainly didn't know I was headed there . . . well . . . uh . . . *right now*."

"Are you saying you don't want to go? This is a pretty big summit. I heard quite a few overseas dignitaries might make an appearance. Rahm is even throwing a cocktail party tonight, to which we've been invited." He tilted his head. "But if you want to skip the summit, that's up to you."

"No, sir, it's . . . it's not that I don't want to go! I just had no idea that I was leaving in a couple of hours! I would've like some heads-up or—"

The mayor leaned toward him, still sporting his saccharine grin. But now he fixed Jamal with a penetrating gaze that made the younger man uneasy.

"Jay, was it not you who only a week ago told me you wanted to be at my side from now on when I go to these functions? That you want a more prominent role in my administration? You said you wanted more prestige. That was part of our deal, wasn't it?"

Jamal cleared his throat. "Y-yes . . . yes, sir. I-I did say that. I just—"

"And I'm holding up my end of the bargain," Mayor Johnson said, clapping him on the shoulder. "But if this is too much for you then I could—"

"No." Jamal quickly shook his head. "No, sir! It isn't too much. I can . . . I can make it work."

"Glad to hear." He clapped Jamal on the shoulder again. "So I guess we'll be on our way then?"

Jamal glanced down at the travel mug he still held in one hand and the briefcase he held in the other. He hadn't gotten to finish his coffee yet, or even use the bathroom. He hadn't packed any clothes. He didn't even have a damn toothbrush, and now he was about to board a flight for an overnight trip to Chicago? But he guessed this was his life now.

If you wanted to play with the big boys, you had to keep your sneaks handy and be ready to get it poppin' at a moment's notice.

He loudly exhaled. "Sure, sir. Lead the way."

They walked toward the elevators that would take them to the mezzanine level. The mayor pressed the down button and glanced at Jamal.

"I'll be honest, Jay. I'm rather looking forward to this trip. Things have been . . . well . . . tense as of late, now that our mutual friend has managed to get himself into trouble," he whispered, glancing over his shoulder.

Jamal knew Johnson was referring to Dolla Dolla. The drug kingpin had been secretly in business with the mayor for years. Dolla Dolla had even helped fund Johnson's campaign. Though few, besides Jamal, knew of the mayor's and the high-profile criminal's professional relationship, everyone in town had heard about Dolla Dolla's arrest. It had made the front page of all the local papers, and videos of Dolla Dolla's perp walk kept appearing on the news in constant rotation with Dolla Dolla gazing menacingly at the reporters and cameras. Jamal had also heard that Ricky's restaurant and strip club had been raided. He'd wondered if his old buddy had been arrested too.

More than once in the past few days he had dialed Ricky's number to see if he was all right . . . if the cops had managed to snare him. He would dial, only to hang up before the phone started ringing. Jamal would remind himself that they weren't friends anymore; his intrusion into Ricky's life might not be appreciated. And besides, Jamal had warned Ricky that one day his dealings with Dolla Dolla would drag him into some shady mess. It was bound to happen eventually.

You're one to talk, nigga, Ricky's voice chided in his head, but Jamal ignored it.

"Our mutual friend is in quite the situation," the mayor continued as they waited, "and now I've been tasked with helping him to get out of it, like I'm some goddamn miracle worker. Our friend is—"

"Please stop calling him that," Jamal said, cringing. "He's not my friend. He never was. I don't even know the man!"

The mayor let out a rumbling chuckle, deep and throaty, that made his chest quiver. He sounded like a movie villain. "Oh, Jay, quite to the contrary! He's my friend . . . and now he's *your* friend too, thanks to our deal. He's our mutual benefactor. His fate, unfortunately, may be connected to ours." He glanced at Jamal again as the elevator doors finally opened. "Don't ever forget that. Don't ever . . . *ever* forget who your friends are. Or you might live to regret it."

At those words, Jamal audibly swallowed. He then followed the mayor into the elevator, feeling a sense of disquiet even as he did it.

Chapter 4

Derrick

"Where you going, baby?" Melissa called out to Derrick, making him pause.

He had been about to head into their hallway, but turned back around and strolled into their kitchen instead. He saw his fiancée standing at the granite counter, humming softly as she chopped shallots and green peppers while their calico cat, Brownie, sat purring at her feet on the tiled floor.

She paused from chopping vegetables and glanced up at Derrick as he walked toward her. "I was just making dinner. Don't tell me you're heading out now," she whined playfully and pouted.

Derrick leaned down and kissed her neck, making her lower her knife to the chopping block, turn, and raise her lips to his for a sultry kiss.

He had missed moments like this; he had practically yearned for them. Those several months when he and Melissa had been fighting and could barely look at one another, let alone speak to one another, had been some of the most painful months in his life. Now their relationship was back to what it had been, what it should be. He didn't have to worry about touching her and watching her shrink away from him. She no longer cooked dinner, silently made her plate, and disappeared into their home office, shutting the door behind her. They ate dinner together and watched a movie afterwards or made love. They were connected again.

He didn't want to go back to those dark months, but he knew they very well could. If Melissa ever found out about Morgan, if she ever found out about the affair he'd had during their months of silence, she would leave him. He was sure of it.

But there's no reason for her to find out, he thought, as he held her close.

Morgan still wasn't speaking to him. Now *she* was the one ignoring him or answering him in monosyllables whenever they were forced to speak with one another at the Institute. He doubted she would say anything to Melissa; she would've done it by now.

Of course, there were times he wished Morgan would speak, that he could confide in her like he once did. He still wasn't sure if the suitcases Cole had brought to the Institute were still hidden somewhere or whether Dolla Dolla had finally ordered his minions to move them somewhere else. He'd tried to ask Cole, but the young man had only given him cryptic answers.

"I'm takin' care of it. Don't worry about it," Cole had told him earlier that week before walking off.

It was obvious he didn't think Derrick was on a need-to-know basis. But he knew Cole would tell Morgan the truth if she asked him. The young man had a thing for her, after all. But Derrick couldn't even talk to Morgan.

Melissa pulled away from Derrick and smiled, but when she gazed up at him, her smile faded. "What's the matter? What's with the frown?"

He shook his head. "Nothin'." He kissed her again, this time giving her a quick peck as he wrapped his arms around her. "Just thinking about stuff."

She raised her brows. "Oh? Thinkin' about what stuff?"

About how you'd look at me if you ever found out what I did. Thinking about the mess I'm still dealing with, he mused, but said instead, "I'm heading out to meet Ricky. That's why I can't stay for dinner. He texted me a couple hours ago and asked me to meet up. I'm seeing him for the first time since he got out. It's . . . it's gonna be rough. I'm bracing myself for what he's gonna say . . . what he might be feeling."

"It sucks what Ricky's dealing with."

"'Sucks' is putting it lightly, bae."

"But you know he was on this path. He's been on it for a long, *long* time. He knew what he was doing and—"

"Lissa, stop."

"Baby, I'm just saying—"

"I *know* what you're saying," he replied firmly, cutting her off. "And yes, Ricky isn't perfect, but he didn't deserve this. He's losing everything . . . *everything*, Lissa, and now he's facing some serious jail time. He didn't commit a crime. He—"

"No, he just covered for men who did."

Derrick pursed his lips. "Look, I don't want to argue with you. We've done enough arguing." He kissed her forehead. "Life's too short. I don't want to do it anymore."

She gradually nodded. "You're right. I'm sorry."

"You don't have to apologize. I know how you feel about Ricky."

"No, you don't. I like Ricky, Dee. I always have! I just don't like the decisions he makes. But I know he's your friend. I know he's been good to you. So give him my love, all right?" she said softly.

Derrick's heart warmed at her words. "I will." He then unwound his arms from around her and walked out of the kitchen.

"And Dee!" she called after him.

He turned back around to face her.

"You're right too," she continued, "about . . . about life being too short. I've thought about it for a while now, and . . . and I think . . . I think it's finally time to reach out to my dad."

His eyes widened in surprise. Of all the things for her to say, that was the last that he'd expected. He'd been trying to convince her for years to finally talk to her dad. But she had shut him out of her life after he came out of the closet and moved in with his boyfriend, Lucas.

"You really mean it, baby?"

"Yeah, I don't know how Mama will feel about it, but it's worth a try." She shrugged. "I figured we can't keep pretending like he doesn't exist. I'm not saying that he and I have to go back to what we were before . . . well, before everything happened, but I thought we could try to build some type of a relationship again." She inclined her head. "What do you think? Should I ask him to meet up for coffee, maybe? So we can talk?"

Derrick smiled and nodded. "I think that would be really nice, Lissa. I know your dad would love to meet up with you."

"Okay, I guess I'll text him today or tomorrow and try to set something up."

"Do that. Do it before you lose your nerve," he said

while pointing at her and strolling back into the hall. He headed to their hallway closet to grab his coat. "I'll be back in a few hours, all right?"

"All right! Bye, baby!"

Derrick tapped the horn once, then twice. Finally, Ricky spotted his gray Nissan Sentra parked along the curb. When he did, he jogged down the sidewalk toward his car. Derrick squinted out the windshield as his childhood friend approached.

The sun was setting, so the light wasn't that good, but even from here, he could see Ricky had bags under his dark eyes, like he hadn't slept. He looked beat. Ricky hadn't been in jail for long—only two or three days—but he seemed haggard, like he had been in there for years.

You look like shit, bruh, Derrick thought.

But considering what Ricky was enduring, who would look good in this situation?

When Ricky tugged the door handle and swung the passenger-side door open, Derrick pasted on a grin. He resolved that they wouldn't talk about jail tonight, or Ricky's charges. They wouldn't talk about the raids at Reynaud's and Club Majesty. Whatever was weighing heavy on his friend's mind, they would try diligently to ignore it tonight.

"What's up, nigga?" he asked, taking on a casual tone as Ricky climbed inside and slammed the door behind him.

"What's up?" Ricky echoed with a sigh.

"Not much," Derrick said as he pressed the accelerator and turned the wheel. The car pulled onto the roadway. "Same shit at the Institute that I'm always dealing with," he lied. "You know how it is."

"Yeah, but it could be worse," Ricky said morosely while gazing out the window.

"But I'll tell you what . . . forget what happened this week, because we about to get lit, bruh! First, we're going to the pool hall and have some beers. I might even let you whip my ass at a couple games. Then we're headed to Ray's, where—"

"I don't wanna do that, Dee," Ricky interrupted.

Derrick made a right-hand turn. "That's cool! If you don't want to go to Ray's, we can try the place on F Street that—"

"I don't want to go to the place on F Street either. I want to go to Reynaud's."

Derrick tore his eyes from the road and whipped around to face his friend. "What? Why the hell do you want to go there?"

"I just do," Ricky answered quietly. "I haven't been there since I got out. I want to see it. I want to see what they did to it."

"Are you sure though?"

Ricky nodded. "Yeah, I'm sure."

Derrick turned the wheel again. "Okay, bruh! If that's what you really want to do."

It wasn't a long drive to Ricky's restaurant, even in evening traffic. They arrived there twenty minutes later, circling the block a few times before they found an open parking space.

As they approached the building, they could see the lights were off inside and yellow police tape was looped through the entrance's brass door handles. When they walked up to the locked glass doors, Derrick felt a knot tighten in his stomach. He had no idea what awaited them inside the restaurant, but he was almost certain it wouldn't be good. He glanced at his friend.

"Are you *really* sure you wanna do this, man?" Derrick asked yet again.

Ricky sighed as he ripped off the yellow police tape from the door frame, letting it flutter to the ground and then down the sidewalk toward a subway grate. "Why not? I've got to do this shit anyway! At least for insurance reasons."

"But why *today*? You just got out only a couple of days ago!"

He didn't know why his friend was so eager to see, up close and personal, everything that he had once loved and worked hard for, now in shambles.

Don't let it smack you in the face. Not this *soon,* Derrick thought, but didn't say it aloud.

Ricky stuck his key into the lock. "Because today is as good as any." He shoved one of the glass doors open and they were hit with a vague stench that smelled like rotten food. "Because I knew we were meeting up, and . . ." He paused.

"And what?"

Ricky grimaced. "I knew with you here, I . . . I wouldn't have to . . . to do this shit alone."

Derrick blinked in surprise.

Ricky wasn't one to show vulnerability, even when they were kids. He had always put on a brave front, a bravado that made it seem like nothing ever fazed him. If Ricky was showing even a hint of vulnerability now, Derrick knew his friend had to be at an all-time low.

They didn't hug; they just weren't those kinds of dudes, but at that moment, Derrick wanted to give his friend a re-assuring hug. He wanted to let Ricky know he was here for him, so he clapped a hand on Ricky's shoulder and squeezed.

"Then let's do this, bruh."

Ricky nodded and stepped inside the restaurant, and Derrick immediately followed. He watched as his friend walked toward a nearby wall panel and flicked on a series of switches, making the restaurant blaze with light. When Derrick saw what lay before him, he winced.

Almost every table and chair had been overturned. Broken wineglasses and dishes along with silverware lay strewn on the floor; he and Ricky could hear the glass crunching underfoot as they weaved their way among the tables. Derrick even saw a smear of food on some of the walls, as though dishes had been thrown at them purposely. It was an abstract painting, both colorful and sticky. And the smell . . . the smell in the room was awful, almost nauseating.

Derrick tried to recall the posh restaurant that Reynaud's had been only a couple weeks ago. Looking around him, he couldn't.

"Shit," Ricky said in one exhalation, stopping in the center of the room and scrubbing his hands over his face. He slowly turned in a circle. "Goddamn."

"Those motherfuckas," Derrick whispered in disbelief, shaking his head with outrage as he surveyed the disarray. "Those motherfuckas! They didn't have to do this. They didn't have to fuck your shit up like this!"

"Yes, they did."

"What?"

"That's how they treat niggas like me. That's how they teach *us* a lesson," Ricky said in a hollow voice that almost didn't sound like himself. "You're poor and don't have shit your whole life. You finally . . . *finally* hustle your way into something good, something real—and they smack you down! 'Nice try, nigga! Your black ass goes back to square one!'" He bent down, picked up a broken wineglass, then roughly tossed it aside. "I tried to do it the legit way. I *tried* getting a business loan. I went to eleven different banks and they all said the same damn thing: I was too much of a risk! My business plan was too much of a risk! I tried to get a loan to rent this goddamn spot and they turned me down for that too. Dolla was the only nigga that would help me—who would give me the money to open Reynaud's. I didn't have any other choice!" he bellowed, his voice echoing off of the high ceilings. "And now I'm getting punished for doing business with him. The same system that kept turning me away is now punishing me for going around it!"

Derrick fell silent. He lowered his eyes.

"But I expected some shit like this from them! I didn't expect it from her."

"Her?" Derrick squinted. "Who are you talking about?"

"About her . . . about Simone. *She* did this! She set me up!"

"*Simone?*" The name sounded vaguely familiar and suddenly Derrick realized why it did. He pointed at his friend. "You . . . you mean the cop you were helping out? The one you were helping find her . . . her . . ."

"Her little sister, Skylar," Ricky said, finishing for him. "That's the one."

"But I thought you said you were cuttin' her off . . . that you told her to kick rocks."

Ricky loudly grumbled. "Well, I did . . . kinda. Then she just showed up at my place. Next thing I knew, we were fuckin' almost every night."

"The next thing you knew? Like you slipped and fell into that shit." Derrick closed his eyes. "Oh, come on, man! You really let your dick set you up like that?"

"It wasn't just fuckin', Dee. I poured my heart out to that bitch. I . . . I loved her, and she played me! She probably had been playing me all along—from day one!"

So he was in love with her. That would explain why Ricky had been so trusting and stupid, which was totally out of character for him.

I knew this would happen, Derrick thought.

The moment Derrick had caught wind of the female police officer, he had sensed she would be trouble for his friend, and unfortunately, his worst suspicions had come true.

He slowly opened his eyes. "Ricky, I get that you fell in love with her and love can . . . well, love can make you stupid." His thoughts swung back to his old dilemma with Melissa and Morgan, but he dragged them back to the present. "But you knew what was at stake. I don't understand how you could . . . ."

He stopped when Ricky held up his hand.

"Don't! I don't wanna hear it, Dee! I know I was dumb. I know I fucked up. But I'm handling it. And I'm gonna handle her ass too!"

"Handle her? What the hell does that mean?"

"What the hell you think it means? When I see her, I'm gonna choke the shit out of her, and I'm not gonna stop until she's dead!"

"She's a cop, Ricky. I know that you're mad, but you can't go after—"

"I *can* and I will! The moment I get my hands on her, I'm fuckin' killing her! I don't care if it's the last thing I do before they lock me up. I'm killin' her ass! If it wasn't for her, I wouldn't have lost my restaurant or Club Majesty. If it wasn't for her, my ass wouldn't be facing jail time. If it wasn't for her and the fucked-up situation she's put me in, I wouldn't have to . . . to . . . ." His voice drifted off.

"Have to what?"

"Never mind," Ricky spat. He turned back toward the entrance. "Come on. Let's get out of here. I can't take it anymore. It fuckin' stinks in here!"

Derrick, unsure of how to help Ricky out of his present dilemma, watched as his friend trudged past him, back toward the glass doors.

Oh, who the hell am I kidding? I can't even figure out my own shit, he thought as he followed him.

Chapter 5

Ricky

"Raise your shirt."

"Huh?"

"I said to raise . . . your . . . *shirt*," the man enunciated slowly.

Ricky let out a loud sigh, then begrudgingly tugged the hem of his shirt out of his jeans. He watched as the tech taped a dime-sized mike to his chest.

"There aren't gonna be a lot of wires, right?" Ricky asked anxiously as he watched the tech wind a black wire around his torso and kneel behind him, snaking it to his belt, where a two-and-a-half-inch battery pack was taped to his lower back, tucked into the waistband of his boxers. "I told y'all I can't walk around with all this shit hanging from—"

"We know! Jesus! We heard you the first five hundred fuckin' times," Detective Dominguez barked from his perch on the windowsill.

Ricky eyed him threateningly.

He'd had just about enough of Detective Dominguez and his mouth, and if he wasn't facing twenty to thirty years for his criminal charges, he might take a swing and try to silence the gruff detective. But he had to play the good boy, according to his lawyer. That was the only way the deal he had settled with the prosecutors would work.

If someone had said a year ago that Ricky Reynaud would become a police informant, he would've called them a damn liar. He hated cops—and he hated snitches even more. Derrick wouldn't have believed it either, which was one of the reasons why he couldn't tell even his best friend that he was now working with the Metropolitan Police Department, that at this very moment he was getting miked in the back room of a vacant office building before his scheduled meeting with Dolla Dolla, who had been released from jail earlier that week.

"Are you out of your damn mind?" Derrick would ask him.

Probably, Ricky now thought as the tech rose from his knees and Ricky lowered his shirt back into place. *No, I'm* definitely *out of my damn mind!*

Here he was, putting his life on the line yet again and working with the police because he knew what would happen if Dolla Dolla found out he had betrayed him. Death would be inevitable, but he knew Dolla Dolla wouldn't make it quick and painless. Whatever he did to Ricky, it would also have to set an example to all those who even thought about betraying him. It would have to be something for the streets to remember. Ricky just hoped Dolla Dolla never found out and exacted his punishment.

"All right," the tech said before walking to a laptop that sat open on a nearby table. He held a set of headphones up to one of his ears as he squinted down at the screen. "We need to test this. Can you say 'Testing one, two, three,' please?"

Ricky rolled his eyes. "Testing one, two, three," he grumbled.

The tech nodded and gave a thumbs-up.

"Okay, Ricky," Detective Ramsey said, stepping forward and adjusting his tie, "here are the ground rules. We need you to ask him about—"

"Nah," Ricky said, shaking his head, "there are no 'ground rules.' To hell with that shit! I'll give y'all the info you're looking for, but I gotta do it the way I do it."

He knew that though the police had enough information on Dolla Dolla to put him in jail for a long time, it seemed they also wanted to use the drug kingpin to ensnare his partners: those who were supplying him with not only drugs, but also the young women who seemed to be part of a prostitution ring that went beyond just Dolla Dolla himself. For years, Ricky had made it his job not to know those names. He wasn't interested in the criminal side of Dolla Dolla's enterprise; he was happy to be the legit public face of his business, Club Majesty. Now he had to stick his nose into shit that wasn't his business and more importantly, do it on the low. He didn't trust whatever advice these detectives had to offer; they'd likely blow his cover.

"Yeah, well, don't waste our fuckin' time," Dominguez said as he rose from the windowsill and strolled toward Ricky. "Because if we find out you have no intention of holding up your end of the bargain, then we'll just dump your ass back in jail." He slowly looked him up and down and snickered. "Nice-looking guy like you is bound to make *a lot* of friends in prison. A lot of good cell buddies, I'd imagine. You don't have a gag reflex, do you, Ricky?"

Once again, Ricky felt the overwhelming urge to knock the smile right off the detective's face, to knock out his crooked teeth, and leave him bleeding and begging for mercy. But he knew what was at stake. He had already made several bad decisions in the past few months. There was no reason to add yet another bad decision to the list.

"We done here?" he snapped, turning away from the detective and walking across the room.

"Yeah, we're done!" Ramsey shouted after him before side-eying his partner. "We'll be tailing you there and listening outside. Just make sure you don't get too far out of range. We need to hear what you guys are saying. Okay, Ricky?"

"That means nothing over a thousand feet," the tech called out to him.

"Meet us back here when you're done," Ramsey said. "We'll go over—"

Ricky didn't give him a chance to finish. Instead, he grabbed his wool coat from the back of a chair and walked out the door, leaving the police officers and the technician to scramble after him.

Fifteen minutes later, Ricky pulled up to a stoplight. He glanced in his rearview mirror and saw a van idling in the right lane, two cars behind him.

Though the side panel of the navy-blue van advertised a plumbing company—even displaying a business number where you could call for "24-Hour Service, Day or Night"—he knew it was fake. Instead of two burly plumbers sitting in the front seats, the detectives and technicians were inside the van, setting up their equipment. They were following him to Dolla Dolla's place in the Kalorama neighborhood.

Ricky tried to focus on the road in front of him, but he couldn't. Every mile that he drew closer to his destination, his anxiety got worse. He was starting to sweat beneath his coat. The battery pack tucked in his belt seemed to jab into his back, making him shift uncomfortably in the driver's seat.

"Stupid," he muttered, not caring if the eavesdropping detectives heard him. "This is so goddamn stupid."

It was not just stupid; it was also incredibly dangerous. If Dolla Dolla realized he was wearing a wire, he was a dead man.

The light finally turned green again and Ricky accelerated through the intersection. As he drove, he had to resist the urge to turn the wheel, make a U-turn, and head in the opposite direction, to floor the accelerator again and go speeding down the roadway, dodging around cars and running red lights. He had to fight the urge to drive straight to Simone's apartment and start pounding on her door.

After all, she was the one who had gotten him into this mess, who had put him in such a precarious position.

He'd meant what he'd told Derrick a few days ago: Whenever he finally got his hands on Officer Simone Fuller, he was going to kill her—or at least come damn near close to it. He didn't care what deal he had worked out with the prosecutor. If her murder added more years to his sentence, so be it.

Unfortunately, that bitch was nowhere to be found. He had gone to her place multiple times in the past week or so, pounding on her front door, only to get no answer. He had sat in front of the townhouse where she rented her basement apartment, staking it out, waiting to catch a glimpse of her and confront her on the street if he had to. But she never showed up. He'd waited until late at night, snuck around the back of the townhouse, and peered through the windowpanes, only to see that her place was empty.

All her furniture was gone. Random wires protruded from the walls and a few empty boxes sat abandoned on the floor. Her efficiency apartment looked as if she'd left in a hurry, and he bet he knew the reason why. Simone knew he'd be looking for her. She had to know the threat he'd given her on the night of his arrest wasn't an idle one.

Your ass can run, but you can't hide, baby, he now thought as he pulled to a stop in front of Dolla Dolla's apartment building. *Not from me.*

He'd find Simone eventually, but for now, he had to focus on entrapping his business partner instead—and surviving long enough to do it.

Ricky watched in his rearview mirror as the navy-blue plumbing van pulled up to the curb on the opposite side of the roadway. He unbuckled his seat belt, took a deep breath, climbed out of his Mercedes, and shut the door behind him. He slowly walked toward the gilded doors, feeling his feet grow heavier with each step. He walked through the lobby toward the elevators, wondering if he looked conspicuous with the battery pack at his back and wires taped on his chest.

Nobody can see it, he told himself. *You're just being paranoid.*

He pressed the up button and waited for the elevator to arrive. When the elevator finally dinged, signaling its arrival, he almost jumped out of his Nikes. An elderly white woman wearing a sable hat and a camel wool coat stepped out, wrinkling her nose at Ricky and pulling her Marc Jacobs handbag closer to her side as she passed him. He was too distracted to be offended. He'd barely noticed her at all since he was too busy cursing under his breath, telling himself that he was making a huge mistake.

He boarded and pressed the button to the top floor. The doors closed and he watched as the elevator ascended, as the numbers ticked away on the digital screen above.

He's going to find that mike, the voice of panic in his head insisted. *He's going to find that battery pack. You're stupid to walk around carrying that thing.*

He closed his eyes.

Take it off. Take that shit off before you get caught, the voice urged.

Ricky opened his eyes again and stared at the digital display, feeling his stomach turn.

TAKE IT OFF! TAKE IT OFF WHILE YOU STILL HAVE A CHANCE!

As the elevator neared the penthouse level, Ricky quickly lifted his T-shirt and ripped the mike from his chest, wincing as the tape took a few chest hairs along with it. He then reached around and yanked the battery pack from his jeans. He just barely managed to shove them both into his coat pocket as the elevator doors opened.

He stepped into the penthouse lobby and frantically looked around him. He spotted a trash can sitting several feet away from the elevator. He shoved the mike and battery pack inside it, then turned and headed to Dolla Dolla's apartment.

He didn't know if he'd made the right decision by dumping the surveillance device, but at least his heart wasn't racing anymore. A few seconds later, he knocked on Dolla Dolla's door.

Melvin, one of Dolla Dolla's bodyguards, swung it open seconds later.

"What's up, Mel?" Ricky said.

Instead of responding with a greeting or a joke, like he usually did, Melvin only nodded. His expression was indecipherable. He was a three-hundred-pound sphinx guarding the door to Dolla Dolla's home.

Ricky wasn't offended by Melvin's silence; he knew Melvin's boss probably was in a dark mood and might be taking it out on his staff.

Melvin stepped aside to let Ricky inside the penthouse apartment. Ricky stepped through the doorway and started to head to the living room, where he assumed Dolla Dolla was waiting for him, but he was stopped short by Melvin, who shut the door behind him and placed his hand on his chest.

"Nah, man," Melvin said, shaking his head. "Take off your coat and face the wall."

Ricky blinked, wondering if he'd heard Melvin correctly. He gave a nervous laugh. "What?"

"You heard me, nigga," Melvin said, his voice sounding harder than steel. "I said take off your coat, and turn and face the wall. Put your hands up. I gotta search you."

"But I'm not carrying."

"Just turn and face the damn wall! I'm not gonna tell you again."

Ricky gritted his teeth. He shrugged out of his coat. Melvin yanked it out of his hands, tossed it onto a nearby console table, and began to dig through the pockets. He took out his cell and his wallet, and set them both on the foyer table on top of his coat.

"You'll get all these back after," he said, then motioned to the foyer wall.

Ricky slowly turned and faced the wall like Melvin ordered, bracing his hands on the textured wallpaper. Melvin then began running his hands along his chest, where the mike had been only a minute earlier, and his back, where the battery pack had been. He then patted down his legs and inner thighs, running his hands along his crotch. Gradually, he made his way down to his ankles, lifting the hems of his jeans to see if he had anything tucked inside his socks. When he was done he rose back to his feet.

"Okay, you done," Melvin said.

Ricky was badly shaken by the whole exercise, but he tried his best to mask it. He took a steadying breath and turned back around to face Melvin.

"Want me to open my mouth and raise my tongue too?" he asked with a sneer. "I'm surprised you didn't do a full cavity search."

Melvin sucked his teeth. "Don't take this shit personal, Ricky. I gotta do it to everybody now."

Ricky didn't reply, but he was very grateful he'd dumped the mike, wire, and battery pack when he had the chance. Turns out his voice of panic wasn't that paranoid after all.

He walked toward the living room, where Dolla Dolla sat at the center of his sectional, looking dark and massive against the white leather. Behind him stood two of his bodyguards. Flanking him to his right and left were a half dozen of his men, including his prized emissary, T. J., who looked as sullen as ever. When Ricky walked into the room, Dolla Dolla's eyes zeroed in on him.

"What's up, Ricky?" he said, tugging a cigar from his thick lips. "How you been?"

Ricky shrugged. "Probably about as good as you. Just got out about a week ago." He glanced over his shoulder at Melvin, who stood a few feet behind him with his hands linked in front of him. "That little pat-down at the door brought back some memories though," he said sarcastically.

"Yeah, well, I can't be too careful no more," Dolla Dolla said, clamping his cigar between his teeth. "Gotta make sure nobody got any shady shit on them . . . a recorder or somethin'. That shit that went down at my house . . . at Club Majesty, only could've happened if I had a snitch around here, someone who's been talkin' to the police." He glanced menacingly around his living room at the men assembled. "And I'mma find out who the fuck it is."

"It wasn't me!" T. J. cried, adjusting his jeans at his waist. "Shit! You won't catch me talkin' to no police!"

"I know it wasn't you, T. You loyal. But I think I know who *did* do it," Dolla Dolla said before taking a puff from his cigar.

Ricky could've sworn Dolla Dolla's dark eyes shifted to him again through the haze of smoke. Ricky took a step back, then another, ready to shove Melvin aside or punch him in the face and bolt for the front door, though he knew he would probably never make it there before he felt the bullet in his back.

"I let those bitches in my house and the next thing I know the cops rain down on me!" Dolla Dolla boomed, stopping Ricky in his tracks.

Ricky knew what "bitches" Dolla Dolla was referring to. He meant the harem of girls he used to keep for his own pleasure and then eventually pimped out. One of those girls had been Simone's little sister, Skylar.

"Never had a problem with no po-po until they came along. Now every one of them bitches is gone. They got rounded up with the rest of them. One of them bitches talked to the police to set the ball rollin'. Maybe more than one. I don't know! But I'm fittin' to find out who, and make sure they don't talk no more. And I'm gonna need y'all help."

Several of the men nodded. Ricky mimicked them and nodded too.

"We gonna track these bitches down. We gonna find each and every one of them. And if they talked, find out what the fuck they said. I don't care how y'all do it." Dolla Dolla yanked the cigar from his mouth and stamped it into the glass ash tray sitting in front of him, sending up a plume of smoke and ash. "Y'all feel me?"

All of the other men in attendance nodded, and again, Ricky was the last to nod.

"All right. That's it," Dolla Dolla said, waving his hand dismissively. "Y'all can get the fuck on outta here."

The men slowly rose to their feet and made their way back toward the door.

"Hey, Ricky!" Dolla Dolla called out, making Ricky pause in his steps. He turned to find Dolla Dolla beckoning him forward. "Come over here."

Ricky slowly walked toward him.

"Have a seat, bruh," Dolla Dolla said, leaning back on the sofa sectional.

Ricky sat down, taking a cushion across from him.

"I heard what those cops did to your restaurant. Sorry they shut that shit down. The food was good too. Better than my grandmama's, and she can throw down in the kitchen."

Ricky exhaled and gradually nodded. "Yeah, it was . . . it was fucked up."

Dolla Dolla leaned over and slapped Ricky's knee. "Don't worry, bruh. I'm gonna take care of that shit for you."

"Uh, thanks, Dolla."

"Whoever did this is gonna pay. We ain't goin' down without a fight."

"No doubt," Ricky said, trying his best to sound earnest and not scared.

"Look, I know you ain't a gangbanger like the rest of these niggas. You ain't into busting heads to get shit done, and you don't have to be. That ain't why I keep you around. But I'm gonna need your help in figuring this shit out, too. I need you to pay attention. Keep your ears open. Even see if you can track down one of these girls. You a smooth nigga. One of them bitches would talk to you. She'd spill her guts. I know she would. Then you bring her to me. I'll take care of the rest."

Ricky swallowed the lump in his throat. "I'll do all that I can."

Dolla Dolla nodded again and slapped his shoulder. He smiled. "I'm countin' on you, Ricky. I'm countin' on every one of y'all. Don't let me down."

"I won't."

"You son of a bitch!" Detective Dominguez bellowed as Ricky strode through the office doorway an hour later.

The tech looked up from his open laptop. His face was grim. Dominguez leapt from his chair and jabbed his finger at Ricky. Detective Ramsey grabbed his partner's arm and tugged him back, holding him with all his might.

"You son of bitch!" Dominguez shouted. "You played us, didn't you?"

Ricky vehemently shook his head. "I didn't play you, man. I did what I had to do! They were checking for bugs . . . for wires. They—"

"Bullshit! You ripped off that mike so we wouldn't hear what you two were talking about!" Dominguez insisted, sending spittle flying from his mouth. His teeth were bared, making him looked like some rabid dog. "But I'm on to you, you son of a bitch!"

"Come on, Mateo," Ramsey murmured, still holding his arm. "Calm the hell down."

"No, I'm not calming the fuck down! He's been playing us this whole time, making us think he was gonna flip and work with us, when he's really still working for Dolla. He probably told him about the whole investigation!"

Ricky inclined his head. "You really think I would do that shit? Tell him that I've been talking to the cops this *whole* time . . . that I'm just *pretending* to be an informant like I'm some damn double agent? What kinda movies have you been watchin'?" He curled his lip. "That would be the dumbest fucking thing in the world for me to do!"

"You're full of shit, you fucking liar!" Dominguez yelled, charging at him again. "We should just dump you! Throw your ass back in—"

"Stop!" Ramsey said, holding up his hands and standing between them. "Enough! Enough, all right? This doesn't solve a goddamn thing!" He turned to Dominguez. "And what do you mean, we should just dump him? Stop acting like we've got limitless choices! This thing is too big to screw it up, and right now, he's the only lead we got."

At that, Dominguez finally quieted. He turned away in disgust and stalked off to a corner, kicking a chair out of his way as he went.

Ramsey loudly groused and dropped his hands to his hips. He looked at Ricky again.

"I'm sorry my partner went off on you like that, but you understand our situation here, don't you?" Ramsey asked. "We send you in there with a wire and you come back with nothing."

"And I explained to you that I had to dump it. They gave me a pat-down as soon as I walked in there. They even took my goddamn phone away! His bodyguards are checking all of us now. I can't wear a wire and y'all are just gonna have to accept that shit."

"If you can't wear a wire then what the fuck do we need you for, huh?" Dominguez shouted from the corner. "Why the fuck should we even bother?"

Ricky narrowed his eyes at him. "Because your partner said it himself: I'm all you got. No one knows Dolla's businesses and has an in with him like I do. *Nobody!* Y'all know it. I know it. And I also know what his plans are. I know what's up next."

Ramsey raised his brows. "What's up next?"

"He's starting to track down witnesses so that he can shut them up. And I hope y'all can get to all of them before he does."

Chapter 6

Jamal

"Welcome to the Horchow Hotel, gentlemen!" the doorman said with a slight Spanish accent after swinging open the door to their Lincoln Town Car.

It was a little after one o'clock and Jamal and Mayor Johnson had just arrived in Manhattan. The duo was traveling again—this time to a governance conference. It was their fourth trip in the past two weeks. The mayor was certainly living up to his end of the bargain by making sure Jamal was at his side when he went to these events. Jamal was starting to feel like he had replaced Mayor Johnson's wife, Brenda, as his plus one.

As Jamal and the mayor climbed out of the sedan, Jamal looked up at the skyscrapers, at the hundred or so people walking or milling about on the busy city sidewalk. He heard the sound of honking horns, car engines, and steady thud of heels on cement.

Though he'd spent most of his life living in the big city, surrounded by people, buildings, and noise, nothing . . . absolutely *nothing* compared to New York, in his book.

And it wasn't just the sights: the Empire State Building and the Statue of Liberty, Times Square and Central Park. It was the people. All their hopes, dreams, and fears were crammed into three hundred square miles. They created a palpable energy that he swore he could feel even through the car's tinted windows as they drove into town. He felt the buzz even stronger now, standing on the curb.

"Our first meeting is scheduled for two thirty, right?" Jamal asked.

"It is indeed! Giving us just enough time to freshen up in our hotel rooms. Maybe grab some room service." The older man glanced down at his Movado wristwatch. "Meet me in the lobby at say . . . oh . . . two p.m.?"

Jamal nodded. "Yes, sir."

They left the hotel at two o'clock, on the nose. The rest of the day was a whirlwind of activity, and Jamal struggled to orient himself. He shook hands with mayors, deputy mayors, and council members. He mused over crackers and canapés with federal government undersecretaries and corporate CEOs. He might have even taken a few photos with a foreign minister from Japan, though he couldn't say for sure; he couldn't remember the man's name or title. The whole time, Jamal kept his polite smile locked in place and his answers surface-level and brief—as the mayor had instructed.

"Let me do the talking, Jay," he'd told him tightly during their first trip together to Chicago.

At the time, Jamal had joined a conversation between Mayor Johnson and a few council members from San Francisco about the District's new business incubator program, something Jamal had personally taken the lead on. But his intrusion had obviously upset Mayor Johnson.

"I'll let you know if I need your assistance, but remember, *I'm* the mayor," he'd told him.

"Yes, sir," Jamal had replied, feeling chastised.

But even though Jamal had agreed to the mayor's demand, it annoyed him.

When he'd told Mayor Johnson that he wanted to have a higher profile as deputy mayor of planning and economic development for the District, this wasn't exactly what he'd meant—zipping around in airplanes to summits and conferences, shaking hands and taking pictures. He'd wanted to show people that he was insightful and articulate, that he was smart and eager to learn. He wanted to show them that he could be a real leader—maybe even mayor himself, someday. Instead, he resembled a grinning robot only capable of giving automated answers. He was no better than an electronic mall kiosk, giving directions to Lord & Taylor and the Gap.

When the Town Car arrived back at the Horchow Hotel at around eight p.m., Jamal rode the elevator to the forty-second floor, inserted his key card into the lock, shoved open the door, and flicked on the lights, revealing a loveseat, coffee table, queen-size bed, dresser, and flat-screen television. He took off his suit jacket and tossed it onto the sofa and walked across the room, grabbing the remote as he went. He flicked on the television and fell face-first on the bed, not even bothering to take off his shoes.

He was exhausted and looking forward to a quiet evening alone in his hotel room, watching pay-per-view, eating room service, and maybe enjoying a couple of mini bottles of vodka and a box of M&M's from the minibar.

By ten o'clock he was already in pajama bottoms and a T-shirt, eating shrimp linguini and flipping channels when he heard a knock. He frowned and rose to his feet. He walked across the room and looked through the door's peephole, surprised to see the mayor standing in the corridor. He quickly unlocked the door and opened it.

"Yes, sir?"

Mayor Johnson looked him up and down. "Don't tell me you were already going to retire for the evening. Not a young man like you!"

Jamal glanced at his pajama bottoms. "I thought we had an early start tomorrow so I—"

"Not *that* early! Besides, how often are we in New York nowadays with our busy schedules? You should enjoy yourself. You've been working so hard and doing such a good job, Jay. I've been so impressed with you!"

Jamal's eyes widened. "You . . . you have?"

"Don't sound so surprised! You've been representing the District well. And I feel like we've developed . . . I don't know . . . a sort of friendship between us . . . a level of trust now. Would you agree?"

"Uh, sure. Sure, I trust you."

About as far as I can throw you, Jamal thought sarcastically, but didn't say it aloud.

"Good! Because I'd love to let you in on a little secret of mine. One that I'm sure you'll enjoy!"

"What secret, sir?"

The mayor laughed. "Well, you certainly can't find out the answer standing here in your pajamas! Throw on some clothes—one of your suits would be perfectly fine—and meet me downstairs near the elevator in about fifteen minutes. That's doable, right?"

Jamal started to respond, to tell the mayor that he wasn't feeling up to going out tonight and just wanted to rest, but the older man turned and walked away before he could. So instead, Jamal closed the door and scrambled to throw on some clothes and some cologne in the next fifteen minutes.

He arrived downstairs to find the mayor waiting for him in the lobby, where he was chatting up one of the bellhops.

"Let's be on our way," the older man said before strolling to the hotel's automatic doors.

Let's be on our way.

That seemed to be a favored phrase of the mayor's. Unfortunately, each time he said it, he didn't seem to find it necessary to explain where the hell they were going. They walked into the chilly night and found another Town Car waiting for them. The driver held the door open and the mayor automatically climbed inside, but Jamal hesitated. He didn't know where they were going or what they were doing. Mayor Johnson still hadn't elaborated. What the hell was going on?

"I didn't take you for being a timid one, Jay!" Mayor Johnson called out to him playfully. "Get in! The night is wasting away, my friend."

"Can you give me a hint where we're headed though?"

"It wouldn't be a surprise if I did!"

Jamal hesitated a few more seconds, then sighed.

In for a penny, in for a pound, he thought. Once again, he climbed onto the back seat and reluctantly went along for the ride.

The car pulled off and the mayor began to yammer into his cell phone. Meanwhile, Jamal gazed out the tinted windows at the dark sky beyond the outline of brightly lit buildings as they drove. He didn't know New York well enough to say exactly where they were headed, but after a while, he figured they were somewhere in the East Village based on the landmarks like Little Tokyo. They pulled up in front of a nondescript brick building, circling to the back entrance, where two large men stood in front of a rusted steel door.

What the hell, Jamal thought for what seemed like the hundredth time that day.

Once again the driver stepped out and opened the car door. The mayor headed out first, buttoning his wool coat as he did. Jamal slid out after him, stepping into the blustery cold of the dark city night.

"Come on, Jay! You're about to have the time of your life, brotha," he murmured, his breath sending a mist into the air as they walked toward the steel door. "How you doing this evening?" Johnson called up to one of the bouncers with an easy familiarity, as though he had been here many times before.

"Good, sir," the bouncer said as he held the door open for the mayor and Jamal.

"Is this some sort of club?" Jamal asked, dropping his voice to a whisper.

The mayor laughed. "Just you wait and see, my friend."

The two men walked down a darkened corridor, where their footsteps echoed off the cement floor and high ceilings. It didn't look like a club; it looked like a storage facility with boxes and shelves stacked on each side. Jamal glanced around him uneasily. How exactly was he supposed to have the time of his life in here? Was this some kind of a setup? Had the mayor strung him along for weeks, given him some song and dance about business trips and giving him a higher profile, only to have him murdered here in the East Village?

Jamal stared over his shoulder, waiting for some menacing figure to leap from the shadows.

They stopped in front of an industrial elevator where another bouncer-looking type sat on a stool, smoking a cigarette.

The mayor reached into his breast pocket and swiped a gilded card that looked like a hotel room key over a reader sitting next to the elevator. The reader let out a chirp then flashed green.

The bouncer nodded at the mayor, then scrutinized Jamal.

"Uh, he's my guest," Johnson said, never losing his smile. "One allowed per member. Correct?"

The bouncer grunted a yes, then yanked open the wooden gate and the metal grate to the elevator. Jamal followed Johnson inside, watching as the older man pressed the button for the top floor.

"You know, Jay," the mayor began as the rickety elevator lurched into motion with a series of squeals and bangs. "When you do business trips like these, it's easy to get bogged down in the mundaneness of it all. I swear my eyes nearly crossed more than once today with how goddamn bored I was!" He began to remove his coat. "I don't care about interagency agreements and municipal bond ratings and that idiot of a president we have now. But I have to pretend that I care . . . and it can be downright exhausting! Do you get what I mean, Jay?"

"Y-yes, sir," Jamal stuttered, still looking around him uneasily.

"A man has to unwind every now and then! You have to enjoy yourself or you'll implode!" He tossed his coat over his arm and clapped Jamal on the shoulder, startling him. "And that's what we're about to do. Are you ready, Jay?"

Jamal didn't get a chance to respond before the elevator came to a screeching halt. He heard the pounding bass of the music before the gate even opened. When it did, Jamal was greeted by a sight that made him pause yet again, even as Mayor Johnson strolled into the red-hued room, rubbing his hands together eagerly.

It looked like the elevator had spilled them into a warehouse that had been converted into a plush night club, one populated by staid-looking men in business suits and much, *much* younger women. Unlike the men, the women weren't wearing suits or business attire. In fact, some of them had skipped wearing clothes entirely and were nude, save for their high heels.

As Jamal gazed around him, he saw breasts—lots and *lots* of breasts. He saw bare asses. Jamal looked to his left and saw a short Asian man chatting up a blonde at the bar who was wearing nipple clamps and a leather G-string. He saw another man casually sitting in a booth drinking a martini while a buxom Latina with a tiger tattoo on her thigh straddled his lap and grinded on top of him in time to the music.

"Where . . . where are we?" Jamal murmured dazedly.

"You don't need to know where we are," Johnson called back to him with a grin. "Just know that everything here is comped. The liquor, the drugs—*and* the women," he said with a wink. "Consider it a gift from me to you. It's a reminder of what you get when you're loyal to your friends."

Jamal gaped. This was not any gift he'd wanted or asked for, and he was just about to tell Johnson that, but a woman strolled toward them. She was a black Amazon—almost six-foot tall in heels. She was a dark-skinned North African beauty with delicate features and large, medically enhanced breasts. She wore a fur skirt and a bikini top. Her arms were extended like she was about to envelop the mayor in a hug.

"Vern, you came!" she shouted over the pounding dance music. "Where you been, baby? I haven't seen you in months!"

"Been missing you, Jasmine," Mayor Johnson crooned back to her as she wrapped her arms around him. She lowered her mouth to his and gave him a long, wet kiss.

As Jamal watched the mayor and the young woman tongue each other down, he guessed that the mayor's wife probably didn't know about Jasmine. She probably didn't know the mayor was a card-carrying member of a high-end brothel, either.

"Come on, baby," Jasmine said after a minute, tugging

her head away and saucily licking her lips. "Let's go somewhere private so you can show me just how much you
missed me."

The mayor laughed and slapped her ass, making her
giggle. He and Jasmine wandered off, heading across the
club, leaving Jamal standing awkwardly near the elevator.

"Can I take your coat, sir?" a voice suddenly piped up
from behind him.

Jamal whipped around to find a willowy blonde, wearing sheer lingerie, staring at him eagerly.

"No!" he shouted, making her blink at him in surprise.
"I . . . I m-mean, yes," he stuttered as he shrugged out of
his camel wool coat. "Y-y-yes, thank you. But I . . . I won't
be staying long."

She nodded and took his coat from him. "It will be
waiting for you over here, sir," she said before handing
him a paper ticket and walking swiftly to a door near the
elevator.

Jamal turned around, buttoned his suit jacket, and
walked toward the bar. He would wait for the mayor
there, though he had no idea how long he would be waiting. Perhaps if the mayor took too much time, he could
head back downstairs to the Town Car, though he had no
idea if it was still idling along the curb.

He ordered a drink and sat on one of the free stools at
the bar, wondering how he had gotten himself into this
mess. Every now and then, one of the girls would wander
toward him with a seductive smile. They tried to chat him
up. Each time he'd give them polite, succinct responses
like he was at one of the meet and greets with other city
officials again. Except here, instead of discussing trans-
portation and capital improvement projects, he was de-
clining a hit of blow that a pretty redhead had offered to
him and telling another girl that she could stop rubbing his
dick and cupping his balls, because he wasn't interested.

He kept glancing at his watch. One hour passed, then another. He removed his suit jacket and then loosened his tie. He undid his shirt cuffs. He ordered another drink, then the next and another after that. By midnight, Jamal started to feel a little tipsy, which was definitely his cue to go back to the hotel, whether the mayor was ready to leave or not.

Jamal hopped off the stool and stood on slightly unsteady feet. He reached for his suit jacket that was slung over the back of the stool and tipped both to the floor. He bent down to pick up the fallen stool and his jacket, and watched as the cement floor tilted beneath his feet. He dropped to one knee to steady himself, feeling woozy.

"Whoa, there! You okay, honey?" a throaty voice asked him with a laugh.

He felt a hand touch his shoulder and he shot upright. The world tilted again and slowly began to settle into place. When it did, he could see Melissa giggling at him.

No, that's not Melissa, he thought, frowning.

It couldn't be. Melissa wouldn't be working at a brothel in the East Village wearing a black thong, a lace push-up bra, and a long black wig.

He squinted at the woman and saw that, though she bore a striking resemblance to Derrick's girlfriend, it wasn't her.

"You okay?" she repeated, raising her brows.

He slowly nodded. "Yeah, I'm . . . I'm fine. Just lost my . . . uh . . . footing for a second there."

"I can see that!" She reached down and grabbed his suit jacket. "Let me get that for you, baby." She brushed the dust and dirt from his jacket then handed it to him.

"Thank you," he whispered, still staring at her.

He didn't know if it was the alcohol making him see things, but the resemblance to Melissa was uncanny; she even had dimples like her.

"I'm AnnaLee, by the way." She extended a hand to him. "And you are?"

"Umm, Jamal." He shook her hand awkwardly.

"Good to meet you, Jamal. I would ask you what you're drinking and get you another one," she said, glancing at the empty glass he'd left on the bar counter, "but you look like you've probably had more than enough already."

"Yeah, I would be better off with a coffee rather than another drink, to be honest." He glanced over his shoulder to look at the bartender, who was making a cocktail. Jamal held up his hand limply, motioning to get his attention.

"No, no! I'll take care of that, baby." She grabbed his hand and he instantly felt a charge, a thrill when she touched him. Their eyes met and he genuinely smiled for the first time that night.

"I don't . . . uh . . . want another drink, but I can . . . I can get you one," he said.

She let go of his hand and licked her full ruby-red lips. "I'd like that."

They took two of the remaining free stools at the bar. He ordered her an apple martini and he sipped on bottled water as they talked. The charge he felt earlier grew in intensity. Again, he wasn't sure if it was the alcohol or the room, which was filled with naked women and had a wanton atmosphere, that made him feel like he had stumbled into a real-life porno. Or maybe it was the fact that she looked so much like Melissa, a woman who had dismissed and insulted him, but one he obviously still couldn't let go. But for whatever reason, he was definitely vibing with this woman. He didn't care that her name was likely a fake one, along with her hair and the large breasts she kept leaning toward him as she laughed at every inane thing he said. He wanted her.

When AnnaLee leaned over and whispered into his ear after only an hour of them talking—"You wanna go someplace quiet, honey? I could get us a room"—he didn't lurch back on his chair in shock. He didn't tell her no either.

Instead, he gradually nodded. "Uh, o-okay."

She led him by the hand to a corridor toward the back of the cavernous club, excusing their way through the writhing couples on the dance floor. He had seen Mayor Johnson disappear this way hours earlier and wondered where he'd gone. Now he could see a corridor with a series of slate-black doors. As they walked down the hall, they approached one door and AnnaLee shoved it open. He paused in the doorway when he saw a naked woman reclining on black satin sheets. Had they stumbled into the wrong room? He turned to AnnaLee in confusion. She began to laugh again.

"Don't be scared, baby," she said, tugging him into the sparse, dimly lit bedroom with her, then shutting the door behind him. "This is Star." She gestured to the woman on the bed, who slowly rose to her knees. "She's here to help us have a good time."

"Hey, sweetheart," Star gushed in a breathy voice, crawling across the mattress toward them.

Jamal opened his mouth, ready to tell AnnaLee that they didn't need help to have a good time. He wanted her and only her, but AnnaLee brought her mouth to his, shushing his words.

As her tongue danced in his mouth, he could feel his tie being loosened then removed, he could feel his shirt buttons being opened. He tried to kiss her back, to wrap his arms around her, but she abruptly shoved him back onto the bed.

After he fell back onto the mattress, AnnaLee and Star didn't climb on top of him so much as pounce. They were like a wrestling tag team and he was the hapless man in the stands who had wandered into the ring. One woman unbuckled his pants and tugged them off of his legs, the other ripped the shirt off his shoulders. His boxers were yanked down and pulled to his ankles. His wrists were roughly pulled up above his head. AnnaLee tied his right wrist to the wooden headboard with his necktie while Star used pink furry handcuffs that seemed to have appeared out of nowhere and clamped his left wrist to the other side of the headboard. The whole process probably took less than five minutes.

Some men might find this thrilling . . . even sexually adventurous, but once again, Jamal felt like he was caught in a whirlwind, like what was happening to him was beyond his control.

"Are the handcuffs really necessary?" he asked, laughing uneasily and glancing at his wrists. He tugged at them and listened to the metal clink against the headboard.

AnnaLee held a finger to his lips and gave him a saucy wink. "Trust us. You're gonna enjoy this! We're good at what we do."

She started kissing him again, and nibbling his ear while Star licked her way down his stomach and his navel, following the happy trail to his groin. By the time Anna-Lee was licking and nibbling at his chest and nipples and raking them with her sharp nails, Star had his dick in her mouth. Even as Jamal tensed and squirmed uncomfortably, he could feel himself hardening in Star's mouth. His body was being overwhelmed with dual sensations of excitement and repulsion.

He had only known AnnaLee for about an hour and "knew" Star all of five minutes, and he was already having sex with them both? The whole thing was disconcerting, but he couldn't deny how good it felt to have two beautiful strangers toying with him in such a way.

"You like that, baby?" AnnaLee whispered hotly into his ear, glancing down at Star's bowed head as it bobbed up and down.

He groaned in response, making AnnaLee giggle again. She slowly removed her balconette bra, tossed it over her shoulder, and began to rub her breasts over his eyes and his chin, hovering the dark nipples over his mouth until he began to suckle one. That's what he was doing when he came. His body jerked against the pillows stacked behind him. He went limp and his eyes closed as he sank onto the bed.

"Oh, no! Don't fall asleep on us now, big boy!" Anna-Lee chided, slapping his chest, making his eyes flutter open. A naked Star slinked off the bed and strolled to the other side of the bedroom while AnnaLee knelt beside him, wrapped her hand around his dick and started to stroke him again. "We're just getting started."

"Just let me . . . let me get my breath. Let me . . . let me rest up," he whispered tiredly. "Please. Loosen the handcuffs and let me rest."

Between the sex escapades, the alcohol, and the late hour, he was thoroughly exhausted. His body screamed for him to close his eyes and go to sleep, to take a break. He was even starting to feel nauseated, to get the shakes.

"You don't need rest! *We* know what you need, sweetheart," Star sang as his eyelids sank closed again. His head lulled drunkenly to the side. "Don't worry! Me and Anna-Lee will take care of you."

One of them roughly grabbed his face, twisting it toward her. She shoved something under his nose.

"Breathe in, baby," AnnaLee ordered, even as he squirmed. "Come on! Come on, you can do it!"

He followed her command involuntarily, having no idea what he was about to inhale. When he did, his eyes shot open ten seconds later. His heartbeat suddenly accelerated.

"There he is!" Star exclaimed, removing the tiny bottle from under his nose. She and AnnaLee cackled with delight.

"What . . . what did you give me?" he asked, now panicked. He saw the bright blue bottle. It looked like they had given him a popper of some sort.

"Don't worry about it, baby," AnnaLee assured him as she slipped on a condom and climbed on top of him, cowgirl style. "Now let's get this party started!"

By the time Jamal heard the knock at the bedroom door hours later, his head was pounding. He squinted in the darkened room at the doorway and found Mayor Johnson leaning against the doorjamb, grinning down at him. The light from the hallway shot inside the room, more intrusive than the morning sun, making Jamal wince.

"I was wondering where you were!" Johnson exclaimed. "I've been looking all over for you. I was worried you went home. But now I see you stayed and decided to have a good time. I'm proud of you, Jay!"

Jamal shifted a slumbering AnnaLee aside and disentangled Star's limbs from his own. He slowly pushed himself upright on the bed. It was a challenge. His arms were still sore from being handcuffed to the headboard and it felt like someone was banging a sledgehammer on the inside of his skull.

"What . . . what time is it?" he croaked, making an ugly face at the nasty taste in his mouth. He swore he tasted bile in the back of his throat.

"It is almost six thirty," Mayor Johnson said in a booming voice, making Jamal cringe again. "And we should probably get going."

"Wait . . . it's . . . it's six thirty?"

Had he really been in here that long?

"That is correct! Uh, I'll let you get dressed and say goodbye to these lovely ladies, if you wish. I'll meet you downstairs." He then closed the door behind him.

Jamal rose to his feet and turned on a table lamp. He looked dazedly around the room. His eyes lingered on the bed, where AnnaLee and Star were currently snoring. His gaze then drifted to the night table and the floor, where he searched for his discarded clothes. As he searched, he saw the evidence of all the things he and the girls had done in the past six hours. He saw the discarded thongs, the popper bottles, a neon-pink dildo, several opened condom packets, and the remnants of the lines of cocaine he had done with Star. He had never done the drug before in his life—even when Ricky had offered it to him. But he had done it last night.

"What the fuck got into me?" he whispered with disbelief and a hint of disgust.

It couldn't have been just the alcohol and drugs. Last night, he had turned into almost another person. It was like the insidious transformation he had been anticipating had finally taken place.

Fifteen minutes later, he emerged from the steel door to find the Lincoln Town Car waiting along the curb as if it had been sitting there since ten o'clock the night before. Jamal held his hand over his eyes, squinting against the bright sunlight. He almost stumbled toward the car door that the driver was holding open for him.

When he climbed inside, slumping onto the leather seat, the door slammed shut behind him, making him cringe again.

Mayor Johnson glanced at him knowingly. "Having the worst hangover, huh?"

Jamal slowly nodded, careful not to move his head too quickly.

"Lucky for you, our first meeting today isn't until nine forty-five. You've got a few hours to recover."

A little under three hours to be exact, Jamal thought. He had three hours to pull himself together when he really wanted to sleep for twelve. He stifled a groan.

"Word to the wise," Mayor Johnson said as the car pulled off. "Remember to bring sunglasses, caffeine pills, and Tylenol for nights like these. You'll feel much better."

"I won't have another night like this," Jamal muttered, resting his chin on his chest because he could barely hold up his head, making Mayor Johnson chuckle and slap his knee.

"Oh, yes, you will! Once you've had a night like the one you just had, my boy, you can't get it out of your system." He smirked. "You're all in now!"

Jamal got a sinking feeling at the double meaning of those words. He was definitely all in now with Mayor Johnson and his crazy exploits—in more ways than one.

Chapter 7

Derrick

"Okay, everyone. We've officially reached the end of the agenda. Does anyone else have any questions or feel there's something we should address before I adjourn the meeting? I was hoping to get you guys out early today," Derrick said, looking at the dozen or so faces seated around the long table. He then glanced at the clock on the meeting room wall, relieved that he had actually managed to finish a staff meeting at the Institute with five minutes to spare—a small miracle considering how much their conversations could drift off topic.

"Actually, I have something to add," said Ted, one of the math instructors, as he shot his hand into the air like an overeager student. "And I've raised this issue a few times."

The room filled with a chorus of groans and bemused chuckles. Derrick stifled a sigh. So much for finishing early.

Ted was good at his job, but he could also be more demanding than some of the kids who ran up and down the halls.

"I asked for a new chair and desk for my classroom

months ago, and I've yet to receive either. Is it too much to ask to have furniture for a man to sit down in? I mean . . . do I have to grade papers on the floor?" he asked, raising his gray brows.

"Hey, I asked for a new DVD player last year," another instructor interjected and then shrugged. "I didn't get it and just had to pony up for one myself. They reimbursed me later."

"So you're saying I should have to pay for my own chair and desk?" Ted cried.

Derrick shook his head. "No, that's not what anyone is saying, Ted. I've gotten a whole list of furniture and equipment needs from several instructors. You aren't the only one. But . . . I know you're tired of hearing it, but I have to remind you that we are a nonprofit. We don't receive federal funding. We work almost entirely off grants and we have a limited budget, so—"

"I'm not asking for a projector or a Blu-ray DVD player, Derrick! I'm just asking for a damn chair and table. If that's too much to ask for around here, then I don't know—"

"We'll get you a chair and table," Morgan interjected. "I'll make it the next assignment for our shop class. Just give me the specifications. The boys would be happy to build it for you."

Ted frowned. "I don't want anything that'll break apart as soon as I sit on it."

"It won't," Derrick said. "They do good work down there. Morgan will make sure that they do."

He looked down the table and met her bright green eyes. For a few charged seconds they gazed at one another, and the rest of the room disappeared. It used to be like that between them, a silent inside joke that they would acknowledge with a wink, or a promise of a kiss later that he could look forward to in his office. But the moment ended as soon as it began. Morgan abruptly looked away and stared at Ted again.

"The kids could build you something a lot better than the plywood stuff you'd find at Ikea. It seems like the best solution the school can offer you for now. Take it or leave it. Doesn't make a difference to me either way."

Ted looked like he wanted to mount another argument and complain more, but his shoulders sank and he nodded, seemingly defeated. "Fine. I'll take the chair and desk you guys build me, I guess."

"And I'll take that as a thank you," Morgan said. "You're welcome, Ted."

"Okay," Derrick said, looking around him again at the mix of bored and expectant faces. "If no one else has anything to add, I think we're done for today."

Derrick watched as several people around the table rose to their feet and pushed in their chairs. While he gathered his file folders and pen, he noticed one of the social studies instructors murmur something to Morgan, who promptly laughed and smiled. He hadn't seen her smile in weeks. She certainly hadn't smiled at him, but he deserved the cold shoulder for what he had put her through.

"Hey, Morgan!" he called out to her as she neared the meeting room entryway, where several other of the Institute's faculty members were streaming into the hall.

At the sound of his voice, the muscles in her back visibly stiffened through her T-shirt. She slowly turned around to face him. "Yeah?" she asked.

"Uh, thanks for doing that . . . for offering to build the table and desk for Ted, I mean."

"It's not a big deal. I was trying to find a good semester project for the boys anyway. This was an easy solution."

"It took the heat off of me though," he continued. "He's been asking for that chair and desk for months and I haven't found the discretionary budget for it. I thought I might by the end of the year, but I know that's not what he wanted to hear," Derrick rambled as the last person left the room, leaving them alone. "I appreciate you handling it."

She narrowed her eyes at him. "I didn't do it for you."

"I didn't think you did. I was just saying thanks for making the offer."

"You're welcome," she replied flatly before turning back around to face the doorway.

"Hey, Morgan," he called after her again.

"What, Dee?" she snapped, now not even masking that she was annoyed.

He took several steps toward her and nervously ran a hand over his dreads. This was the most they had said to one another in weeks. He wasn't sure if she would lash out, walk away, or just be aloof, but something compelled him to finally try to talk to her again, to talk about what had happened between them.

He drew even closer to her, close enough to whisper. She glared up at him with those arresting green eyes and he wished he could say he didn't feel any longing for her anymore because he was firmly in love with Melissa, but he did. God help him, he still did.

"Look, I know . . . I know it's been . . . tough between us after what . . . well, after all that happened."

She dropped her hand to her hip. The expression on her face radiated *No shit, Sherlock*, but he pressed onward.

"I know . . . I know you're pissed at me and you have every right to be, but I don't want it to—"

Suddenly, his cell phone began to chime and he glanced down at his hip.

"You better get that. I bet it's the wifey callin'," Morgan said, sucking her teeth. She then turned on her heel and walked away from him.

Derrick shoved his hand into the pocket of his slacks and tugged out his cell.

Morgan was right; it was "the wifey" calling him. He had been expecting Melissa's call today, but not at that very moment. She was finally meeting her dad for a coffee date so that they could talk, and she had been nervous at the prospect, had agonized about it all week. Derrick took a deep breath and clicked the green button on the screen to answer.

"Hey, baby!" he said as he watched Morgan stroll into the hallway, feeling like an important moment had just eluded him. "How'd it go?"

"Umm, it went . . . okay."

"Just okay?" he asked with a frown.

"Well, it went as good as can be expected, I guess. It was weird sitting across the table from him the first few minutes. It felt like I was sitting across the table from a stranger, not my dad. I mean . . . he's changed so much, Dee."

"Not that much. He's still your dad, bae. That part hasn't changed."

"He doesn't even dress the same anymore! He got his damn ear pierced. I told him he kinda looks like a black pirate now."

"But after you talked for a little bit, you felt better, right?" he asked as he strolled into the hallway. "It felt more natural."

"Yeah, it did. He started asking me about work and the kids at school and we fell back into a . . . I don't know . . . rhythm. We were laughing after a while. The next thing I knew we had been talking for almost two hours and Dad had to go because he said he had to meet up with Lucas for something."

Derrick couldn't help but smile as he strolled down the empty hall. This was the first time she had referred to Lucas by his actual name and not as "the man my dad is living with now." The coffee date must have gone better than she'd said. The outcome was certainly better than Derrick had expected.

"I'm glad to hear you guys had a good talk," he said as he tucked his file folders under his arm and pushed open the steel door that led to the stairwell. "See? It didn't turn out bad at all. You were worried about nothin'."

"Well, something happened that I'm a little bit unsure about."

"What happened?" Derrick asked as he walked up the stairs back to the second floor.

He listened to her loudly exhale on the other end of the line. "Dad invited us over for dinner. Me and you, I mean. He said Lucas would love to cook for us. I told him maybe. I said I had to check with you first."

"Well, that's good . . . isn't it? That he invited us over?"

"Not really. I just got on speaking terms with Dad and now I'm supposed to sit and break bread with him and his man?"

"Lissa," he began, trying his best to not make it sound like he was lecturing her, "if you're going to rebuild your relationship with the man, you're going to have to accept that Lucas is in his life too. He's a pretty damn big part of his life, in fact."

"I'm *aware* of that, Dee," she replied tightly.

"I know you're uncomfortable being around them. Hell, sometimes it can get weird for me too, and I don't have anywhere near the same baggage about their relationship that you have, but it has to be done. They're a package deal, so to speak. Just think of having dinner with them as a way of getting over your discomfort with their relationship faster. It's like . . . like pulling off a Band-Aid."

"Pulling off a Band-Aid?" She sounded incredulous.

"Yep," he said as he shoved open another steel door, revealing the second floor. "Just rip it off instead of taking it off a little at a time."

He heard her exhale again as he walked down the hall toward his office. "I hope you're right, Dee."

"Of course, I'm right."

She laughed. "Okay. I'll tell Dad we can come over. I'll try to schedule something for next week or the week after. I just hope . . ." Her voice faded.

"You just hope what?"

"I hope I don't regret this later."

"I promise you won't," he said as he looked up and noticed Rodney, the Institute's head security officer, standing at the other end of the corridor. "Look, Lissa, let me call you back. I see someone I've been meaning to talk to and I finally caught up with him."

"No problem, baby. I'll see you when you get home. Okay?"

"Okay. Love you."

"Love you too," she replied warmly before hanging up.

Derrick tucked his cell back into his pocket. He had been meaning to talk to Rodney about a complaint one of the instructors had made about one of the newer security officers. Derrick raised his hand to get Rodney's attention but paused when he noticed a tall, lanky student stroll toward Rodney and tap him on the shoulder. As Derrick drew even closer, he recognized who that student was.

Cole smiled up at the head security guard and began to speak. From this distance, Derrick couldn't hear what they were saying, but the guard and Cole seemed to be having an animated conversation. They were even laughing with one another.

Ever since Derrick had found the suitcases filled with drugs and money under Cole's bunk, he had not only been obsessing over the fate of those suitcases and whether they had really been removed from the school like Cole had told him last week, but also wondering how the young man had managed to get the suitcases into the school in the first place. Derrick knew it was possible for other students to have smuggled them in, but considering the three guards and security cameras they had all throughout the facility, he didn't understand how the students could've done it so inconspicuously.

Or maybe they hadn't. Maybe they had done it in plain sight because someone in security had willingly turned a blind eye to what they were doing.

Derrick didn't want to consider that scenario. He didn't want to believe that the guards who worked there, who were paid to protect the welfare of the staff and students, could be susceptible to bribes. But he didn't see how it was possible to not consider it.

He watched as Cole and Rodney finished their conversation. Rodney gave Cole a congenial slap on the back and looked in Derrick's direction. Cole looked up just as Derrick drew near them.

"What's up, Mr. Derrick?" he asked.

Derrick didn't respond to him. Instead, he turned to Rodney. "Looks like y'all were having a pretty intense conversation over here."

"The Mavericks," Rodney said without hesitation. "This little dude was trying to school me. Told me the Cavaliers were going to take them out next round, but I told him to lick the milk off his upper lip because he's too damn young and don't know what the hell he's talking about."

Derrick continued to stare at them. "Really? That's all you were talking about."

Rodney laughed and tucked his thumb in his belt. He squinted. "Yeah, that's all. What else would we be talkin' about?"

Derrick didn't have an answer to that one. He watched as the young man raised his hand and bumped Rodney's fist. All the while Cole kept his eyes on Derrick. It could have been Derrick's imagination, but he swore the smug little punk was holding back a smile.

"Nice shootin' the shit with you," Cole said as he walked away, carelessly throwing the words over his shoulder at Rodney.

Derrick's eyes stayed on him until he disappeared down the hall into one of the classrooms.

Chapter 8

Ricky

Ricky stared at his rearview mirror, watching as a woman approached his Mercedes with her hips swaying and her long hair blowing around her shoulders in the gusty February wind. She was a sight to see, drawing appreciative stares from the men she passed on the sidewalk with her open coat, slinky wrap dress, long legs, and buoyant double Ds. One man had even turned around completely, shouted to get her attention, and was rewarded for all his effort with an eye roll from her just before he stumbled into a parking meter and landed face-first on the sidewalk.

Despite his dark mood, Ricky had to chuckle, watching Mariana in action.

The curvy Latina's physique and attitude had earned her some of the highest tips back when she'd worked for Ricky at Club Majesty. Of course, now that the strip club was closed, thanks to the raids more than two months ago, Mariana didn't work for him anymore. That didn't mean she'd stopped exerting a magnetic power on men that made them go mute and stupid. That's why he'd asked her for her help today.

Ricky watched as Mariana reached his car, pulled the handle to open the passenger-side door, and hopped in, onto the leather seat. When she did, he shifted sideways to look at her. He raised his brows eagerly.

"*So?* How'd it go?" he asked. "Did the cops tell you anything?"

He hadn't had any luck in locating Simone, even though he treated it like a job. It was the only thing he did when he wasn't trying to gather information that the detectives were trying to use against Dolla Dolla.

Simone had shut down her Facebook page and Instagram account. Unable to track her online, Ricky had gone to Simone's empty apartment multiple times to see if she'd come back to pick up something she might have forgotten, since it looked like she'd left in a rush. He'd even tried to pump her neighbors for info, only to be met with silence or outright hostility when he tried to question them.

"I don't care who you are, honey," her elderly neighbor had drawled to him dryly when he'd knocked on her door and told her he was friends with the young woman who'd lived in the basement apartment and didn't know where she had disappeared to. "If that girl wanted you to know where she went, she would've told you. Right?"

He'd even gone to the donut shop he knew Simone had frequented with the other cops at her station, hoping to see her strolling through the door for a coffee and a Danish. But he'd had no success there either.

He'd called her police station, asking for her, but the desk cop had told him she wasn't there and asked if someone else could assist him instead. Ricky had hung up soon after, frustrated and enraged. He had stopped short of going inside the station to look for her himself, tired of playing this stupid game of hide-and-seek with his former lover. But he didn't go.

Not only did he not like the idea of being back inside a

police station so soon after his arrest, but he also didn't know if any of the cops would recognize him and ask him why he was there. It would be just his luck for Detective Ramsey or Detective Dominguez to show up to say hello to one of their buddies. He couldn't take the chance. That's why he'd asked Mariana to do it instead, to take a little trip to the police station for him. If there was anyone who could finesse her way into getting the info that he needed, it would be her.

"I didn't find out a whole lot even though the *pendejo* at the front desk talked my damn head off," Mariana said before tossing her dark hair over her shoulder and settling into her seat. "He told me she don't work there no more though."

"She doesn't work there anymore?" Ricky squinted. "Why the hell not? The police department moved her to another station?"

"No, she don't work there no more! He said she ain't a cop. She quit!"

"Quit?"

Ricky hadn't anticipated that answer. Simone hadn't quit the force because of him, had she?

No, he thought, *she wouldn't do that.* There had to be a backstory here, an element he didn't know about. Simone had harbored so many secrets, he wouldn't be surprised if there was an important part of the story he was missing.

"So I asked the dude where she workin' now," Mariana continued. "He told me he didn't know."

Ricky flopped his head back against the seat cushion, closed his eyes, and exhaled. So he was right back where he'd started.

"The cop said though that he thinks her mom is sick or somethin'. That may have been the reason why she up and quit like that. She might be taking care of her."

Ricky opened his eyes again. "He told you all that?"

Mariana nodded. "He told me her mama lives out in Lanham too. I don't know her name but—"

"I know it," he blurted out, leaning forward in the driver's seat so that he could reach into his back pocket and pull out his cell phone.

Simone had told him her mother's name in passing once. He was now grateful that he remembered.

He opened a search engine phone app and began to type furiously, hoping that he could find her mother's address in an online database.

"So that's it?" Mariana asked. "That's all you need?"

He looked up from his phone screen and nodded. "Yeah, you got a lot more out of them than I could. Thank you, Mari."

He reached into his back pocket again to pull out his wallet and rifle through the bills he had inside, but she stopped him by placing her hand on top of his.

"I told you. You don't have to pay me." Her glossy pink lips curled into a smile. "You know I'd do anything to help you, Ricky. I got your back."

"Thanks, girl." He leaned forward to brush his lips across her pale cheek, but she twisted her head and went for his lips instead, wrapping her arms around him, pulling him close and plunging her tongue inside his mouth.

The kiss caught him off guard, so much so that he lurched back from her in surprise.

Yes, he and Mariana had had a thing last year and hooked up a few times, but then she'd got a man—a mechanic who lived out in Springfield, Virginia—and he'd met Simone. That had ended their late-night trysts at the club, back in his office.

"What? What's wrong?" Mariana now asked, frowning up at him.

"Nothin'," he said, unwinding her hands from around his neck. "I just . . . I just wasn't expecting it."

"I used to kiss you all the time when you weren't expecting it, and you never acted like that before," she said, eyeing him. "So what you got going on for the rest of the day? You busy?"

He was barely listening to her. He'd already returned his attention to his phone and his internet search.

"I said what you got goin' on today, Ricky?" she repeated, slapping his shoulder and making him look at her again. "Damn!"

"Not much," he finally answered.

Since the restaurant and strip club had been shut down, he had been a man of leisure. In fact, he was starting to get a bit stir-crazy, going from juggling two jobs as manager of Reynaud's and Club Majesty to no job at all. He knew he had to get another job soon or start another hustle to pay his bills. Though he had amassed a large savings, he didn't like the idea of blowing through it so quickly without replenishing his money—years in poverty had taught him that. But for now, he would focus on finding Simone. When his thoughts weren't occupied by worries about Dolla Dolla discovering he was an informant, his mind was absorbed with that other central task.

"Then why don't you come by my place," Mariana whispered, running a nail along his jawline, lowering her long lashes. "Stay for a few hours. Let's have some fun like we used to."

He cocked an eyebrow. "Your man won't mind?"

"I broke up with that nigga two weeks ago! Caught him cheatin' on me with some *puta* he met at his garage. I don't have time for that shit! I told him, if he can't appreciate being with a bad bitch like me," she said, pointing to her ample bosom, "then there are plenty of other niggas out there who will!" She bit down on her bottom lip. "So what you think? I got a blindfold . . . ice cubes . . . you name it, *papí*. We can do this."

It was tempting. A roll in the sheets with Mariana might be just the thing he needed to end the dark mood he'd been in since the raids. But something held him back. Desire was there—but the desire to track down Simone was even stronger. If he was in bed with Mariana he couldn't ensure that he'd be focused on her, focused on the sex. He didn't want to waste her time.

"Nah, I can't. Not today." He took her hand and kissed the soft knuckles. "Thanks though, baby."

He then frowned down at his phone screen, seeing three addresses with the name "Nadine Fuller" in the city of Lanham, Maryland. He decided to play it safe and also look up addresses for the last name "Fuller" but only the first initial "N."

"Is it her?" Mariana asked.

"Is what her?" he answered distractedly, typing again, doing another search.

"The *puta* you trying to track down," she said, tapping his screen with her acrylic nail, making him look up at her again. "Is she the reason why you won't come to my place?"

He slowly shook his head again. "Nah! No, she's not the reason. I—"

"You're lyin'." Mariana laughed and wagged a finger at him. "I can always tell when a dude is lyin', Ricky. It's all over your face. So what did she do? Fuck up your shit? Break your heart?"

Both, he wanted to answer, but instead he shrugged.

"Nah! That bitch's man owes me money," he lied, trying his best to sound blasé, "and I'm just trying to collect my shit."

"But what are you gonna do if you can't find her?"

"I'll find her." His jaw clenched. "I'll track them down. I ain't worried."

Mariana loudly exhaled and slapped his knee. "Well, I hope you do, and I hope what I did helped. I gotta go, *mi amor*."

He watched as she pushed open the car door and stepped back onto the sidewalk. She leaned down and winked at him. "Take care, Ricky."

"See you, baby."

After she slammed the door shut, Ricky returned his attention to his phone, copying addresses and saving them. But even as he typed, Mariana's question replayed in his head: What if he didn't find Simone?

What if the cop had gotten it wrong and Simone's mother didn't live in Lanham but in Lorton or Largo or Loudon County? What if he went to every address and discovered all of them were wrong? He didn't have any other leads and didn't have any ideas on how to find them. This whole endeavor could prove to be pointless.

He was starting to feel obsessed, driven by a manic need to see Simone, confront her, and make her pay for what she'd done to him. He even dreamed about it at night—when he could get to sleep.

In some of the dreams he would be shouting, *Why did you do it? How could you betray me like that? I trusted you, bitch!* He'd raise his gun and pull the trigger, always waking up gasping just as the bullet fired.

And sometimes he would dream of them in bed back at her apartment. She would be smiling up at him, running her hands along his face and whispering, *Love you, baby.* She'd then raise her mouth to his for a soul-stirring kiss. And he'd wake up gasping again, but for a very different reason.

It ripped him apart: the not knowing, the lack of closure. He *had* to find her.

Just then his phone began to buzz. A number popped up on his screen that he didn't recognize, so he sent it to voice mail, scrolling through his phone, searching for more addresses. Thirty seconds later, the same number popped up on the screen again. He let out an impatient breath, deciding to answer.

"Hello?" he barked.

No one answered.

"Hello?" he yelled again. "Hello? Who the hell keeps calling?"

He swore he heard breathing on the other end and then a scuffling sound. The caller hung up, leaving him staring at his phone in confusion.

Chapter 9

Jamal

Jamal staggered through the door of the waiting area leading to his office. He approached his assistant's desk.

"Good morning, Sharon," he called to her in a gravelly voice while squinting behind his dark shades. He gave her a haphazard wave as he passed her on the way to his office.

"Rough start to the day, sir?" she asked. She raised her brows at him, eyeing him knowingly.

"Nothing Excedrin and a cup of coffee can't cure."

To illustrate his point, he sipped the store-bought coffee he'd purchased on the way to work.

Jamal was nursing another hangover. This seemed to be happening a lot lately, particularly when he went out with Mayor Johnson. This time it had been a business summit in the city. The mayor and he had gone out for drinks after the event and the rest of the night had been a blur of laughter, women, and alcohol. Jamal had woken up in the bed of some stranger—a blonde who lived in a condo in Adams Morgan. She'd been snoring when he woke up.

He'd sneaked out of her place, wanting to avoid what was likely to be an awkward morning-after encounter.

Hey, you, random person whose bed I just stumbled out of. I can't remember your name and I can barely remember what we did last night, but would you like to have some breakfast together before I walk out the door and we never speak again?

It was the only thing he could imagine saying.

Jamal had at least been relieved to find evidence that he'd worn a condom. In fact, he was *still* wearing it when he'd opened his eyes and raised his head from one of her pillows. It was casual sex, but at least it was "safe" casual sex—thank God. But he knew this had to stop. In the past, he'd never been one for haphazard hookups. That had been more Ricky's MO. He'd always seen that kind of behavior as reckless and irresponsible. It just wasn't him.

Yes, it is, a voice in his head chided. *It's who you are now: a corrupt hedonist who can't even show up to work on time anymore.*

"Mr. Lighty," Sharon called to him. "Mr. Lighty, sir!"

He paused in the doorway of his office and turned around to look at her. "Yeah?"

"Your nine o'clock is still here. He's been waiting for you for the past twenty-five minutes," Sharon said.

Jamal lowered his sunglasses and narrowed bloodshot eyes at her. "Who?"

"Your nine o'clock!" She gestured to the leather sofa on the other side of the waiting area. "You had an interview scheduled with Phillip Seymour at the *Washington Recorder* today." She tilted her head and widened her eyes. "Remember?"

Jamal turned to find the doughy, pale reporter grinning up at him eagerly. Phil pushed his wire-framed glasses up the bridge of his nose with his index finger and waved at Jamal.

"Morning, Deputy Mayor Lighty! I was wondering if we'd have to reschedule our interview. Glad I waited for you."

Jamal barely stifled a groan.

Fuck, he thought.

He had scheduled his interview with Phil last week, back when he wasn't hungover and was just trying to rush Phil off the phone so that he could get to a meeting. Unfortunately, he'd completely forgotten about the interview.

Jamal forced a smile despite his pounding headache. "Actually, Phil, I don't know if we can still do the interview today. I have a meeting I totally blanked out on that starts in thirty minutes. Doesn't it, Sharon?"

"What meeting, sir?"

His smile tightened. "You know the one with that uh . . . uh nonprofit?"

She pursed her lips and loudly sighed. "I'm unaware of what meeting with a nonprofit you're referring to, Mr. Lighty. It's not one I scheduled."

Thanks a lot, Sharon, he thought in exasperation.

He should've known she wouldn't lie for him. Frankly, the no-nonsense woman seemed to be growing tired of his shenanigans, of him stumbling late into the office, bleary-eyed, or him forgetting scheduled meetings and appointments. He suspected she disapproved of the new Jamal as opposed to the boring but punctual old one.

Phil rose from the sofa. "That's not a problem, Mr. Lighty. My interview won't take long. You can still make it to your meeting."

Jamal removed his sunglasses. "Okay, then . . . well . . . uh . . . step inside my office, I . . . I guess."

Phil did as he said, striding across the waiting area into Jamal's office, where he immediately took one of the armchairs facing Jamal's desk.

"Hold all my calls, please, Sharon," he said to his assistant before closing his office door behind them.

He strolled to his desk, setting down his coffee next to his desk calendar and putting his briefcase on the floor.

"So . . . remind me again what this interview is about. You wanted to discuss a housing grant, correct?"

"Uh, no . . . it was about a housing development. Low-income housing, in fact, in Ward 8."

Jamal nodded as he shrugged out of his jacket and tossed it over the back of his chair. "Go on. What questions did you have about it?"

Phil flipped open his notepad and drew out a pen from his jacket pocket. "Well, you see, Mr. Lighty, the development has stalled for the past year. Few if any of the twenty townhomes slated to be built were completed. There's still building materials sitting abandoned under plastic tarps. Workers show up occasionally, but they just sit around and drink coffee, then leave. I was wondering why the project hasn't been completed."

Jamal fell back into his desk chair and stifled a yawn. "Some projects run behind schedule, Phil. Weather can play a part. There are also sometimes issues with the subcontractors. Or it could be—"

"Speaking of contractors," Phil said, flipping pages, "one of them seems to be a pretty good friend of Mayor Johnson. Cedric Morris. He was in several photos with the mayor and his wife."

"All right. So he's friends with the mayor. What does that have to do with anything?"

"I just wonder if the mayor's relationship with Mr. Morris could have anything to do with why the city may be hesitating in holding the builder accountable for his missed deadlines."

Jamal's pounding headache was getting worse. The last

thing he needed was Phil catching on to the mayor's dirty business deals. But he knew from his own experience that the mayor had left a plentiful trail of breadcrumbs for someone to follow. All they had to do was look.

He leaned forward in his chair and braced his elbows on his desktop. "I'm sure that has nothing to do with it, Phil," he lied. "Besides, the entire council had to approve the—"

"And it's not just that development. There are others around the city—I found three more—that Mr. Morris is connected to that have either stalled or seemed to have stopped completely. If this contractor has a history of deserting projects, why does he keep getting awarded contracts? Does the mayor realize the impression this gives?"

Jamal gritted his teeth. "You would have to ask him."

"I tried to ask him, Mr. Lighty, but he won't return my phone calls or emails. I reached out to you because I've interviewed you in the past. I . . . I know you'll be honest with me."

Jamal stilled. *Great*, he thought. Now Phil was guilt-tripping him. But still, he and Mayor Johnson had a deal. He had to keep and protect the mayor's secrets.

Remember who your friends are, Jamal could hear the mayor whisper in his head.

"Look, Phil, if I knew or heard anything about some shady business going on between the mayor and this contractor guy, I would tell you. But I haven't. I'm sure there's a good explanation for all of this."

Phil opened his mouth to speak again, but Jamal held up his hand to stop him.

"I get it. I get it. It may look nefarious on face value, but looks can be deceiving. The mayor is not corrupt. Trust me."

Despite his assurances, Phil stared at him, still looking mistrustful.

"Why don't I do this? Why don't I check into it, if it makes you feel any better?" Jamal asked, throwing him a bone. "Write down the names of the developments and their addresses and I'll see what's going on with them and get back to you."

Phil eagerly nodded. "Thanks, Mr. Lighty! I'd appreciate that."

Jamal watched as the other man scribbled on one of the pages before ripping it out of the notebook and handing it to Jamal. Jamal glanced down at the sheet.

"So are we good now? Did I answer all your questions?"

Phil nodded and rose to his feet. "We're good. If you could give me a call in a week or two and—"

"Don't worry," Jamal said with a chuckle. "I will."

"Okay, thanks again, Mr. Lighty."

He then walked toward Jamal's office door, tucking his pen and notepad into his jacket as he went. He opened the door and stepped back into the waiting area.

"See ya, Sharon!" Jamal heard Phil call out.

"Bye, Phillip!" his assistant answered.

After about a minute, Jamal balled up the paper on which Phil had written the addresses and tossed it into a nearby trash can. He then opened his desk drawer and pulled out a bottle of Excedrin, shaking two into the palm of his hand before tossing them into his mouth and swallowing them dry.

Chapter 10

Derrick

"This was a bad idea."

Derrick paused midway of pushing open the driver's side door. He turned to stare at Melissa, who hadn't opened her door yet. She hadn't even unbuckled her seat belt.

"Huh?" he said, eying her.

"I said this is a bad idea, Dee," Melissa repeated, staring out the car window at the block of row houses. "I never should've agreed to this. What the hell was I thinking? It's gonna be a damn disaster!"

Derrick sighed and closed his door.

They were slated to have dinner at her father and Lucas's place for the first time. Melissa had seemed hesitant when she said yes to her father's offer a couple of weeks ago, but since then the hesitancy had turned into full-on rejection of the idea. That rejection was on display right now.

"Baby, it won't be a disaster. Besides, it'll be a lot worse if we don't go in there. We told them we were coming.

We're already kinda late. It'll look like we stood them up. I bet it'll hurt your dad's feelings."

"And why should I care if I hurt his feelings?" she said through clenched teeth, making it sound almost like a growl. "He didn't care that he hurt my feelings—or Mama's!"

Derrick closed his eyes and tiredly scrubbed his hand over his face. "Lissa, don't start this again. You and your dad talked about this. You had a whole conversation about it. Remember?"

"That doesn't mean everything is cool with us again though, Dee." She turned and glared out the window again. "It doesn't mean that I'm not still pissed or hurt!"

He opened his eyes, reached out, and pushed aside one of her braids before running his index finger along her chin and his thumb along her cheek. This time she leaned her face into the palm of his hand. He turned her face around and leaned over the gear shift so that they could kiss. When he pulled away from her a few seconds later, the anger and stubbornness had left her face. She looked more scared than anything else.

"I know you're still pissed and hurt. I didn't expect you to suddenly be okay with everything. But there's no way you're ever gonna feel better . . . that you're ever gonna stop being pissed or hurt until you *both* make an effort and try again. You reached out to him by inviting him out for coffee. He reached out to you by inviting you to dinner at his place. It's your turn again, baby. We gotta go inside."

She loudly exhaled and rolled her eyes. "I hate it when you do that."

"When I do what?"

"Sound all rational and methodical. It's that damn degree in psychology coming through. I hate it when you use it on me," she said, twisting her mouth ruefully.

He laughed and ran his thumb along her cheek again. "I think it comes in handy, but that's just me."

He watched as she pursed her lips and stared at the façade of her father's row house. The light from the front porch glowed orange and bright in her dark eyes. She sat silently for what felt like a full minute before she finally nodded.

"Fine, I'll go in. I just hope I don't regret this later, Dee."

"For the thousandth time, trust me, bae. You won't."

"There y'all are!" Mr. Theo cried with a smile before opening the door and beckoning them forward. "Lucas was wondering if he would have to reheat the food. Come in! Come in!"

As soon as Mr. Theo cracked open the door, his and Lucas's chocolate-colored Labrador, Otis, came charging onto the screened-in front porch. He leapt straight for Melissa, who let out a squeal when his paws landed on her chest, almost shoving her back a good foot or two. She almost stumbled over a flower pot. She didn't look alarmed as much as caught off guard by the pet.

"Otis! Otis!" her father yelled, reaching for Otis's collar and dragging him back. "Get your brown ass back in here!"

Derrick and Melissa gave each other a bemused side glance as they stepped through the door and found Mr. Theo still struggling to tug the barking and slobbering dog down a hallway that was crowded with plants, stacks of newspapers waiting to be recycled, as well as discarded shoes. Derrick was used to the disarray, but he could tell Melissa was surprised by it.

Mr. Theo's ex-wife, Susan, had kept an orderly home

when he and Susan still lived together. The prim and proper Susan Stone never would have allowed this state of chaos. But Mr. Theo wasn't living with her anymore. That message was loud and clear.

Melissa squinted at her dad as he finally shoved the Labrador into another room, shutting the door behind him. They could still hear Otis's barks and whimpers, even the scratching of his paws against the door.

"I'll take your coats," Mr. Theo said breathlessly, holding out his hand to them.

"You have a dog now?" Melissa asked with raised brows while unbuttoning her jacket.

Her father nodded. "Yeah, we got him from the shelter about a year ago."

"I asked you for years if we could get a dog, Dad," she said, shrugging out of her jacket and handing it to him. "You always told me no. You said that you didn't like dogs."

"I still don't," he answered with a laugh before placing her jacket on a nearby wall hook and taking Derrick's wool coat from him.

"But you got a dog anyway," she persisted.

Her father paused from hanging up Derrick's coat. "Things change, sweetheart. People change."

She glanced at Lucas, who had stepped out of the kitchen and walked down the hall toward them. Lucas's denim apron was stained with a splatter of some kind of sauce. "Yeah, I noticed," she murmured.

"I see you've met Otis," Lucas said.

The smell of the dinner Lucas had cooked wafted down the hall toward them. Derrick noticed that Lucas was wringing a dish towel in his hand while trying to undo the knot in the strings of his apron, before giving up in defeat. He looked nervous. Derrick could understand why.

"Good to see you again, Dee." He nodded at Derrick, then held out his hand to Melissa for a shake. "Hey, Melissa, your father has told me so much about you. I'm excited to . . . well . . . to finally meet you."

Melissa stared down at Lucas's hand. For a few seconds, Derrick wondered if she was going to refuse to shake it, if maybe she was going to turn on her heel, grab her jacket, and head straight back out the door. But, to his relief, she finally shook it and nodded.

"Good meeting you too," she said. "Thanks for having us over."

The rest of the dinner was awkward, but drama-free. Lucas asked Melissa a few questions and she gave short, stilted replies. The dog continued to bay and bark, filling the living room with a strange soundtrack whenever they stopped talking. By the time the dessert had arrived—a caramel apple tart recipe that Lucas had found online—Derrick was relieved the meal was almost over.

He looked up from his dessert plate when Mr. Theo began to snort and hum, to flick his nose with his forefinger. He noticed that everyone else at the table was staring at Mr. Theo too.

"Dad, please stop doing that," Melissa whispered.

"Doin' what?" her father asked as he continued to hum and snort.

"That! It's hard to eat while you're doing it."

Lucas chuckled. "I tell him all the time to just get a tissue," he said before dropping his fork to his empty plate and sipping from his wineglass. "One time he did it in a restaurant. A woman leaned over and asked him if he was in distress and needed his inhaler."

Melissa laughed. It was her first genuine laugh all night. "He did it at my high school graduation too. The valedictorian was giving her speech, and even onstage I could hear my dad snorting like some hog in a barnyard. I was so embarrassed."

"I can't help it if I have allergies!" Mr. Theo lamented. "It's how I clean out my nose!"

Melissa and Lucas laughed even harder and Mr. Theo rose from the table and rolled his eyes.

"Hee-hee-hee. Y'all laugh it up, making fun of a poor ol' man," he said, pretending to be annoyed by their chiding, but Derrick could tell the older man was holding back a grin. He bet Mr. Theo was relieved to see Melissa and his boyfriend finally connecting over something. Theo began to walk around the table, gathering dessert plates and silverware. "I better start on the dishes." He glanced at Derrick. "Can you help me clear the table? Get the wineglasses for me?"

"I'm still working on mine," Lucas said, holding his white wine aloft.

"Me too," Melissa said, reaching for the bottle and pouring herself another glass.

"All right, you slow down with that wine," Derrick joked as he rose from his chair. "I don't want to have to carry you into the elevator and down the hall when we get back home."

"Oh, you're gonna carry me, huh?" She sipped from her glass. "If that's the case, I'm having another one after this!"

Lucas burst into laughter as Derrick followed Mr. Theo from the formal dining room through a door that led to the adjacent galley kitchen. He held his and Mr. Theo's wineglasses in his hands. The door swung closed behind them and he noticed all the general disorder: pots stained with sauces and grease that were stacked next to the sink, potato peels and leftover grated cheese strewn on the butcher block, and trays covered in aluminum foil littering the counter.

He gazed helplessly around them. "Where should I . . . uh . . . set these?" he asked, holding up the glasses.

"You can put them over there," Mr. Theo said, inclining his head to the one empty spot on the counter, near the toaster.

Derrick did as he asked before turning around to head back into the dining room. "I'll grab some more dishes and bring them back—"

Mr. Theo held up his hand. "Nu-uh," he said, shaking his head, dropping his voice to a whisper, "don't go out there yet. Give em a couple minutes to themselves. I wanna see how they do out there without us."

Derrick smiled and nodded. "I got you." He then walked back toward Mr. Theo. "Well, is there anything I can do? Anything you want me to wash or help with?"

Mr. Theo shook his head. "Nope. Just stay in here and keep me company while they talk and I clean up." He then turned on the faucet and dropped a plug into the sink. He grabbed a bottle of liquid soap. "So how you doin', Dee?" he asked a couple of minutes later. "How are things *really* going at the Institute? I know there's always something."

Derrick was half tempted to tell his old mentor the truth, to tell him about Cole and the drugs and the money, about his worries that he had lost control of the Institute entirely. But instead he shrugged. "You know how it is. Same ol' same ol'. The boys are a handful. The staff is good, but hanging on to good people with how little we can pay them is always a challenge."

"So you managed to hang on to that one instructor I

met a couple of months ago? The pretty one with the curly hair?" Mr. Theo asked as he lowered the pans into the soapy water, glancing over his shoulder at him.

Mr. Theo was trying to sound casual but his question had a double meaning, a layer as thick as lead underneath the surface. Derrick could easily detect it.

Mr. Theo was asking about his relationship with Morgan. Theo had met her once when he had stumbled onto her and Derrick having dinner together, one of the many nights that Melissa had thought Derrick was working late or out with friends. Derrick had sworn to Mr. Theo that nothing was going on between him and Morgan, no matter how compromising it may have looked. And there hadn't been anything romantic going on between them—at the time. But Mr. Theo hadn't believed him. It seemed that back then Mr. Theo had understood their "situation" better than Derrick had understood it himself.

"Yeah, Morgan is still working there," Derrick said.

"And you took care of the . . . the issue between you two?"

"There was no issue to take care of," he lied.

Mr. Theo grabbed a scouring pad near the faucet and began to scrub one of the pans in swift strokes, flexing his wiry arm as he did it. "Don't insult my intelligence, son. I was there. I saw how you two were looking at one another, how you acted. I'm old but I'm not blind." He stopped scrubbing and turned to face Derrick. "Is it over? You aren't seeing her behind my baby's back, are you?"

Derrick's jaw tightened. He crossed his arms over his chest. It was a defensive posture he took unwittingly, but he couldn't help himself. He had ended things with Morgan. He had told her point blank that he had made a mistake and Melissa was the woman he really wanted to be with. He didn't deserve to be questioned by Mr. Theo yet again.

"Yes," he answered succinctly, "it's over."

Mr. Theo nodded, then returned to scrubbing his pan. "And I'm guessin' my daughter never found out about it then?"

"No, she didn't. But it was never anything for Melissa to worry about anyway. I wasn't gonna—"

"What should I not worry about?" Melissa called out from behind him.

At the sound of her voice, Derrick startled. He whipped around to find his fiancée standing in a kitchen doorway, staring up at him expectantly.

"Huh?" he uttered, now panicked.

Just how much had she heard?

"I said, what should I not be worried about?" she repeated, stepping farther into the kitchen. "I came in here because Lucas and I are finished with our wine." She held out two glasses and looked between Derrick and her father. "And I heard you guys talking. Sorry! Guess I just . . . barged into your conversation."

"No! No, you didn't barge in. We weren't talking about anything important, baby," Derrick said, forcing a smile and walking toward her. "Just set those on the counter. Your dad said he doesn't want any help for now."

"Oh! Oh, well . . . okay." She did as Derrick ordered, setting the wineglasses next to the two that were already on the laminate countertop. She then looked at her father and Derrick again, squinting. "Are you sure you guys weren't talking about anything important? Anything I should know about?"

Derrick hesitated again. He opened his mouth to answer but her father blurted out, "Can't me and Dee make plans for your birthday without you spoiling it?"

"My birthday? So that's what you're doing? Making plans for my birthday? Well, why didn't you just say that, Dee?" she joked, slapping his arm playfully.

"It wouldn't be a surprise if we did," her father said.

She laughed. "Okay. I wasn't trying to spoil it. Plan away! Don't let me interrupt y'all." She began to back toward the kitchen door.

"No, umm . . . we were done," Derrick said, glancing anxiously at her father. "I was just about to head back out anyway." He then wrapped an arm around her waist and walked with her back into the dining room, giving one last glance over his shoulder at Mr. Theo before he did, hoping that the older man would continue to keep his secret.

"So were you and Dad *really* talking about my birthday?" Melissa asked an hour later. "Be honest!"

They had just left Mr. Theo and Lucas's house and were driving back to their place. Melissa had settled into the seat beside him. Her eyes had taken on that glassy look they sometimes did when she was mildly drunk.

"What do you mean, baby?" He turned onto a side street, pausing at the intersection for a pedestrian who strolled through the crosswalk.

"I mean you guys weren't really talking about planning my birthday, Dee. I could tell!"

Yeah, she's drunk, he thought. Her voice was slightly slurred. He should've told her to slow down tonight; she shouldn't have had that third glass of wine.

"You always get frowny lines right here," she continued, tapping in between her brows with her index finger, "when you lie. You did back in the kitchen. So spit it out!" She beckoned with her hand. "What were you guys *really* talking about?"

He loudly swallowed, wondering why she was bringing

this up now. He'd thought they'd dropped the issue after they walked out of the kitchen and went back into the dining room to share more funny stories with Lucas. She had laughed and talked, even bothered her father for seconds of dessert. He'd thought she'd pushed that whole episode in the kitchen to the back of her mind.

"Come on, Dee. It can't be *that* bad, can it?" She raised her brows. "What? Did Dad tell you that he and Lucas are getting married or somethin'?"

"No!" Derrick adamantly shook his head. "No, nothing like that, bae."

"So what is it? It wasn't about my birthday. So it had to be about something else."

"It was nothing," he said as he drove, wishing she would drop the subject. "It was nothing, Lissa. Really."

She fell silent and eyed him from the passenger seat. The drone of the satellite radio filled the silence.

"It wasn't . . . it wasn't something *you* did, was it?" she asked softly. He could hear the uncertainty in her voice, like she didn't want to know the answer even if he gave it to her.

He choked out a nervous laugh and shifted uncomfortably in the driver's seat. "Why the hell do you think *I* did anything?"

"I don't know," she mumbled before turning to stare out the window.

"You just had too much to drink at dinner, baby." He reached down and absently rubbed her knee. "It's making you paranoid."

"Maybe." She sighed. "Or it could be guilt."

Guilt?

His pulse quickened. She thought he was guilty? So then she must already know about his affair with Morgan.

Was this whole conversation just an elaborate setup to trick him into finally confessing the truth?

"What . . . what do you think I should feel guilty about?" he asked, feeling his throat go dry, feeling his palms dampen on the leather steering wheel.

"Not you, honey. I mean me! *I* feel guilty, and I'm projecting it onto you and it's . . . it's not fair."

He frowned as he pulled to a stop at a light. He turned slightly in the driver's seat and saw that she was blinking back tears. "Why do you feel guilty? What happened?"

She slowly shook her head and sniffed.

"Talk to me, baby!"

"I should . . . I should have told you months ago," she said, almost in a whisper. "I should have told you that night. I didn't want to keep it from you, but I felt so stupid. I was so embarrassed, Dee. I read the whole situation wrong!"

"What situation?"

"After . . . after you and Jay had your big fight, he and I ran into each other again. I didn't tell you but . . . but we kinda started . . . well, we started hanging out."

A horn blared behind them, startling them. Derrick realized the light had changed so he pressed down the accelerator and drove through the intersection. He glanced at Melissa as he drove.

"What do you mean, you started hanging out?"

"I mean we met up a few times. We had lunch. We had coffee together. We talked. We texted."

Derrick's frown deepened. "Wait . . . you were texting and meeting up with him? Why didn't you tell me?"

"Because I was mad at you, Dee! We'd been fighting and you were fighting with Jay too. I had someone to bitch to about you, someone who knew you almost as well as I did. He and I . . . well, we bonded."

Derrick narrowed his eyes, feeling his first spark of anger. "So you bonded over talking shit about me behind my back? Is that what you're saying?"

"Come on, baby! I feel like shit enough as it is! It wasn't like we were plotting your murder. I was just complaining about how you were taking Dad's side, how we couldn't really talk to each other without arguing anymore. And even though he was your friend, I always felt like he was kinda my friend too! What Jay and I were doing was perfectly innocent—at . . . at first." She looked away from him again to stare out the window. "And then one night . . . one night Jay and I hung out. It was the night that Ricky got arrested."

It was also the night that Derrick had told Morgan that he was finally going to break up with Melissa, he silently noted. He had made plans to tell her it was over between them. Little did he know, his fiancée was out that night with Jamal—a dude he used to call his homie, someone he had once considered damn near a brother.

Joke's on you, huh, Dee? Serves you right, a voice in his head mocked.

"He'd just broken up with his girlfriend, Bridget, and I wanted to cheer him up by doing something fun. We went bowling at Lucky Strike. We grabbed dinner at Gallery Place. We went back to his place after, to just . . . just hang out. Or at least, I . . . I thought that's what we went back to his place to do," she whispered.

As she continued to tell her story, Derrick could feel the muscles in his stomach clench. The car compartment suddenly felt a lot hotter. He knew what she was about to say would turn his anger from a spark to full-on flames, but he wanted to hear it. He *had* to hear it. He braced himself for what she would say next.

"I don't know how it happened but . . . but he kissed me, Dee." She closed her eyes. Tears spilled onto her cheeks as she wiped her nose with the back of her hand. "He kissed me and he told me that he . . . he loved me—that he'd always loved me, but he could never say it because you were his boy. He told me that you weren't right for me. That we weren't right for each other. He always knew it."

Derrick blinked, at a loss for words.

"B-b-but it stopped there. It was just one kiss! I pushed him away. I-I swear," she stuttered. "I told him that he was wrong, that it was messed up. I left his apartment and I haven't spoken to him since. But I wanted to tell you. I've felt so guilty about keeping this secret from you! But I thought about it the next day and I figured Jay maybe had one beer too many that night. Maybe . . . maybe he didn't even realize what he'd said, what he'd done. But either way, it didn't feel right hanging out with him anymore. If he really felt that way about me, I didn't want him to get . . . well . . . confused."

Derrick's grip tightened on the steering wheel, imagining that it was Jamal's neck. "He wasn't confused," he said.

"What, baby?"

"I said he wasn't fuckin' confused!" he boomed, making her jump in the passenger seat. "That motherfucka knew exactly what he was doing! I trusted him and he made a move on my girl? What kinda shit is that?"

"Dee, calm down. I already yelled at him . . . cursed him out. It happened *months* ago! Look, it was a mistake. I didn't want to make the rift between you guys even worse over something that didn't really mean anything. Nothing was gonna—"

"It *did* mean somethin', Lissa! He and I were friends for almost twenty years and he betrayed me! I'm not gonna sweep that shit under the rug. And why the hell were you even seeing him on the side like that? You don't expect for a dude to read something into it? To think that you down for whatever, too?"

Her brows knitted together as she pointed at her chest. "Are you really trying to blame *me* for this? Are you saying I led him on?"

"I'm not saying you led him on, baby, but . . . but—"

"But *what*, Dee?"

He told himself to count to ten, to take a deep breath and get his rage under control. He had cheated; Melissa had not. She had confessed about a drunken kiss with Jamal, and he was still keeping his affair with Morgan a secret. He was in no position to make accusations, to point the finger of blame, but that didn't soothe the sting of betrayal. Jamal had betrayed him, after all their years of friendship, after everything Derrick had done for him.

She closed her eyes and turned to face her window. "I shouldn't have told you."

He breathed in and out, over and over again, while staring at the roadway. "No . . . no, you should've told me," he began calmly, relaxing his grip on the wheel. "I'm . . . I'm sorry for shouting at you. I'm sorry if it sounded like I was blaming you. That wasn't what I wanted to do. Because you weren't to blame."

She slowly opened her eyes and turned to face him again.

"You're not in touch with him anymore. Neither am I. So as far as I'm concerned, it's . . . it's nothing we have to worry about. We'll put it in the past. I'll let it go."

"Really, Dee?"

He nodded. "Really."

She leaned over the armrest and gave him a quick peck. "This is why I love you. You're so understanding, baby."

He smiled tightly, feeling it stretch painfully on his face.

Deep down, he wasn't understanding. Deep down, he knew that if he ever crossed paths with his former friend, Jamal Lighty, again, he would beat the hell out of him.

Chapter 11

Ricky

Ricky adjusted the clipboard and box in his arms as he strolled up a concrete walkway neatly bordered by pots of marigolds and chrysanthemums. He glanced around him. The front lawn needed tending. Though the rest of the house's exterior looked pristine, the lawn was now overgrown and needed to be cut, as well as the patches of weeds here and there. As he drew closer, he squinted at the bay window next to the front door, trying to see if he could spot anyone walking past the curtains. But he couldn't. He glanced at the driveway. He didn't see any cars parked there either.

"Shit," Ricky muttered.

It looked like this might be another false lead. He had already been to about three houses in Lanham in the past few days and either found no one was there or no one who lived there had ever heard of Nadine Fuller, or her daughter Simone. He had a couple more addresses on the list that he had to check, but he was starting to worry that his search would prove fruitless.

Ricky climbed the short flight of stairs on the front porch and rang the doorbell. He waited a beat for someone to answer but heard nothing. He rang the doorbell again. Another half minute passed and again there was no answer. He knocked on the door and then strolled to the bay window. He stared between a crack in the curtains. Inside was a living room decorated in cheerful yellow-and-blue furniture. A line of African figurines along with framed pictures sat along the brick fireplace on the other side of the room. Ricky leaned in closer so that his forehead was almost pressed against the cool glass. He was using his 20/20 vision for all it was worth. Among the picture frames, he could swear he spotted a photo of Skylar, Simone's little sister, blowing a kiss at the camera.

"She's not home!" a voice called to him, making him jump back from the window and whip around to face the driveway.

An elderly black woman stood on the other side of the white picket fence in a neighboring yard. She held a set of garden shears in one of her gloved hands and wore a wide-brimmed woven hat. She tilted back her hat and gazed up at him, revealing more of her wrinkled brown face.

"Sorry, honey. I didn't mean to scare you, but I didn't want you to keep wasting your time knocking on the door. She ain't been home in more than a month."

He walked down the steps and strolled toward the fence. "You mean Ms. Nadine Fuller, ma'am?" he asked.

"Yep! I think she's on vacation or somethin'." She flicked her free hand at the house. "But she's been gone for so long, I'm starting to wonder!" She laughed.

So he had hit pay dirt. This was Nadine's home, but unfortunately Nadine had already left.

But that doesn't mean she'll stay away, he thought. Her

furniture was still in the home as well as pictures and knickknacks. She'd have to come back at some point.

Ricky tilted his head and pasted on a charming smile, one that usually worked with the younger demographic, but he wondered if it would have the same appeal with octogenarian women.

"Uh, do you happen to know when she'll be back, ma'am? Any idea? You see, I was supposed to deliver this package to her." He glanced down at the clipboard, pretending to read something on the sheet. "She ordered this and I was scheduled to deliver it today."

"You're a delivery man?" The older woman frowned, staring at his coat, T-shirt, and jeans. "You sure don't look like one! Where's your uniform? Where's your truck?" she inquired incredulously as her eyes shifted to the curb where his Mercedes was parked.

"Well, I'm not *really* a delivery guy," he said with a chuckle. "She had something custom made at our D.C. art studio, and because of the expense, we prefer to deliver it ourselves. A personal touch."

She slowly nodded, turning her eyes away from the curb and back to him. "Well, I guess that makes sense. Nadine is always ordering those dolls and such, but I guess she must have forgot about this one, honey."

He glanced down at the box he held. It was empty, but Nadine's neighbor didn't know that. "That's a shame. She paid a lot of money for this," he lied.

"I see." She held out her hands. "Well, I can take it for her. I could—"

"I am so sorry, ma'am. But that's against our policy. I have to deliver it to her myself. Again . . . the expense."

The older woman nodded thoughtfully. "That makes sense. Well, when she comes back, I'll tell her that you were looking for her and she can set up another delivery time. I guess it escaped her mind. Does she have your number, or do you have a business card that has a number where she can reach you, honey?"

Ricky considered it too risky to leave his real name, but he saw no harm in leaving a number. The Fullers were probably long gone from here anyway and if, by some chance, Simone saw and recognized his number and caught on to the fact he was looking for her, so be it. He'd made her a promise that he'd find her; he'd told her that already.

"No business card unfortunately, but here's my name and number, ma'am." Ricky scribbled on one of the sheets of paper on his clipboard, ripped it off, and handed it to her. "Here you go."

"Well, it was nice to meet you, Malcolm!" she said, staring down at the false name he'd written on the paper. She squinted up at him. "You know . . . you look so much like a man I knew years ago. He was a handsome devil too! You wouldn't happen to be any relation to a Lawrence Doggart, would you?"

He shook his head and chuckled. "No, ma'am."

"Good! He didn't have a dime to his name and was a lyin' S.O.B. who I wouldn't trust to tell me the truth even if I asked him if it was raining outside, but me and Lawrence sure did have some fun together." She stared off wistfully. "That man could make a girl feel special! And what he didn't have in his wallet, he sure did make up for in other areas," she said with a wink. "Let me tell you!"

Ricky's eyes widened in shock at the old woman's frankness. He hadn't expected their conversation to go in this direction.

"I'm Jessie Sawyer, by the way," she said. "I forgot to mention that in all my ramblin'."

"Pleased to . . . uh . . . meet you, Jessie."

"Pleased to meet you too, sweetheart. And I'll pass this along if and when I see Nadine."

"Thank you," he said before turning back toward the lawn. He then strolled to the walkway.

As Ricky neared his car, shaking his head at the bawdy old woman, his phone began to buzz at his hip. He pulled it out of his pocket and glanced at it. He pressed the green button to answer.

"Hello?" he said, just as he opened the car door.

No one answered. He was met with silence. He gritted his teeth.

This was the fifth time this had happened this week. Each time he would get a call from a mystery number—never the same. He'd started to ignore the calls and block the numbers, but they wouldn't stop. Finally, he'd answer and the person wouldn't speak. Sometimes, he swore he could hear breathing or the sound of a television or voices in the background. It was starting to get on his damn nerves.

"Look, whoever the fuck this is, stop calling me! This not talking and hanging up is pissing me off. I don't play that shit!"

And like the previous time, the person hung up. The call ended, and he rolled his eyes in annoyance.

He climbed into the driver's seat, set the empty box on the floor, shut his door, and placed his key in the ignition. He shifted the car into drive just as his cell began to buzz again. He cursed under his breath, removed his cell phone from his cup holder, and stared at the screen. This time he recognized the number, but knowing who was calling him didn't bring him any comfort.

"What do you want?" he answered tersely, slumping back in his seat.

"Where have you been, Ricky?" Detective Ramsey asked.

Ricky grumbled. "Busy. How bout you?"

"Very funny. Look, we want to meet up. Can you meet us near the waterfront in like an hour? We'll pull up in front of the Wharf restaurant and you can hop in. We need to talk for a bit."

Ricky closed his eyes. He didn't know why the detective was putting it in the form of a question. It's not like Ricky had a choice.

"Fine," he snapped. "See you in an hour."

Ricky glanced at his cell phone screen and stared at the curb, watching as a couple passed him arm in arm. The cops were late meeting him. He had been standing there for the past twenty minutes, in front of the restaurant, waiting for them. He worried the maître d' might come outside and harass him, probably thinking he was panhandling. He wondered if this was some power play on the detectives' part: making him wait around for them like some sucker.

Finally, he saw an unmarked Taurus pull up to the curb. The back passenger door flew open and Detective Dominguez leaned out the front passenger window. "Get in!" he yelled over the roadway noise.

Ricky took his sweet time making his way to the vehicle. He climbed inside and didn't get to close the door all the way before the car pulled off, almost giving him whiplash as he slammed back into the seat.

"We haven't heard from you lately, Ricky," Detective Ramsey said as he drove, glancing at Ricky in the rearview mirror. "Why haven't you reached out to us?"

Ricky shrugged. "Dolla's been quiet lately. He knows

what's at stake. He's lying low and he ain't talking about shit as much. That's why I haven't called you."

"But your job is to make him talk!" Detective Dominguez bellowed, glaring at Ricky from the front passenger seat. "What the fuck do you think we brought you in for?"

"Look, I already gave you plenty of info," Ricky argued, irritated at being talked to by Dominguez like he was some idiot. He swore if it wasn't for the fact that Dominguez wore a badge, he would punch him squarely in the face. "I told you Dolla is starting to hunt down the girls who used to work for him. He wants to take them out."

"Yes," Ramsey said, nodding, "we relayed that to the higher-ups. They've got that covered. But that has nothing to do with the investigation we're conducting, Ricky. You're supposed to give us names of Dolla's contacts and—"

"And it's been more than two months, and so far you haven't given us shit!" Dominguez finished for him.

"What the fuck do you expect me to do?" Ricky yelled back. "Dolla's not stupid. Even before all this shit went down, he didn't go blabbing off at the mouth about his suppliers. You really expect him to—"

"We don't expect anything from him," Ramsey said. "But what we expect from *you* is to give us information we need and if you can't do that then, I'm sorry to say, we have a problem, Ricky."

"No, *he* has a problem because the fucking deal is off!" Dominguez shouted. "Your ass is going back to jail!"

"We know you don't want that to happen, do you, Ricky?" Ramsey asked.

Ricky sucked his teeth.

"So you'll try harder to give us what we want, correct?" Ramsey persisted.

"Yeah," Ricky answered sullenly.

A few seconds later, the car skidded to a stop at a street corner Ricky didn't recognize.

"You can hop out here," Ramsey said, gesturing to the sidewalk.

"Y'all ain't even going to take me back? What kinda shit is this? I don't know where the fuck I am."

"You heard the man," Dominguez said, flicking his hand toward the window, not bothering to answer Ricky's questions. "Get out."

Ricky balled his fists in his lap. He slid across the back seat, shoved open the door, and hopped onto the sidewalk. He barely managed to shut the door before the Ford Taurus pulled off with screeching tires.

Chapter 12

Jamal

"And I would like to thank each and every one of you for coming out today in support of such a worthy cause," Mayor Johnson said, leaning toward the podium and bringing his mouth closer to the mike. He then gestured to the line of smiling school children standing to his left, all holding shovels and spades. Many were in hoodies and sweatshirts still covered in dirt from the neighborhood rain garden they had helped build.

"These kids have worked very hard on this community project and they deserve all the attention they are getting today. Let's give them a round of applause, folks! Shall we?"

The small audience that was huddled around them began to clap. Jamal did too. He then pushed up the sleeve of his suit jacket and glanced down at his wristwatch to check the time. If they didn't get a move on, they were going to miss the next event they had scheduled for today. He could try to handle it himself, but Jamal knew how the mayor felt about him taking the lead on things. Jamal sighed as he watched the mayor shake hands and schmooze with the residents and business leaders who had shown up for the rain garden ribbon-cutting ceremony.

"Hey, Mr. Lighty," Jamal heard someone say behind him. "I didn't know you were going to be here!"

He turned to find Phillip from the *Washington Recorder* gazing at him. When he did, he had to fight the urge to grimace.

The last time he had seen Phillip was back at his office at the Wilson Building when the reporter had asked him about some shady housing projects that he was trying to connect back to the mayor. Jamal had hoped Phillip had forgotten about the topic and moved on to something else, but he could tell from the eager gleam in Phillip's eyes that he probably hadn't.

"Uh, h-hey, Phil," he stuttered. "Yeah, I didn't know I was going to be here today either, but the mayor asked me to be on standby to answer questions if . . . you know . . . he needed me." He gave an awkward laugh as he gestured to the mayor, who was now cutting a red ribbon in front of the wrought-iron gate leading to the rain garden.

"Ah, I see! That makes sense." Phillip took a quick glance around them before leaning toward Jamal, dropping his voice to a whisper. "Speaking of questions, Mr. Lighty, I was wondering if maybe you had a chance to follow up on those housing developments that I asked you about a week ago. Remember the list I gave you?"

Jamal nodded before taking another anxious glance at the mayor, who was now posing with a couple of the children and holding a shovel as cameras flashed. He prayed to God that Johnson wasn't overhearing their conversation.

"Actually, I did check on those for you, Phil, and everything is fine," he lied. "Perfectly fine. The projects are just running a little bit behind schedule, but we're aware of the issues insofar as the construction sites, and we're taking steps to rectify them. Our people are on it. We've spoken to the builders. All projects will be completed soon . . . very, *very* soon."

Phillip frowned. "But one project is already a full year behind schedule, Mr. Lighty. That's not exactly 'a little' behind. And when you go to the construction site—"

"Phil, I told you," he began firmly, "there's no reason to worry. The city is keeping an eye on it and we're taking care of it."

"But the mayor's friend . . . the contractor, Mr. Morris—"

Jamal dropped a hand to the reporter's shoulder. "Phil, I can assure you that nothing untoward or inappropriate is happening at those construction sites. You don't have to worry. Okay?"

"Nothing untoward or inappropriate is happening where?" the mayor suddenly asked.

This time Jamal didn't hold back his grimace. He glanced over his shoulder to see Mayor Johnson grinning and strolling toward them. But Jamal wasn't fooled by the mayor's jovial expression. He knew what evil and cunning lurked behind that smile.

"Uh, nothing," Jamal began quickly, shaking his head and dropping his hand from Phil's shoulder. "Nothing that you need to concern your—"

"Hello, Mayor Johnson. I'm Phillip Seymour from the *Washington Recorder*," Phillip said, holding up his press badge and talking over Jamal. "I was asking Mr. Lighty, here, about construction sites where your friend Cedric Morris is the lead contractor. Most of the sites are behind schedule, Mayor Johnson, and it looks like some have been deserted completely. I've been trying to get a comment from you about these sites for quite a while, sir."

Mayor Johnson laughed. "Why on earth would you want a comment from me? Or Jamal, for that matter? Surely, we have folks in our Department of Consumer and Regulatory Affairs who could easily answer your construction questions for your story. Have you tried them?"

"It's not just about the buildings, sir," Phil said. "The article would also address your connection to these sites. The one thing they all have in common is your friend Cedric Morris."

"My friend?"

"Yes, you and Mr. Morris have been acquaintances since law school, I believe, sir. You both were Howard Law, class of 1977."

Shut up. Shut up. Shut up, Jamal thought. *Stop talking, Phil!*

He knew the mayor was not a man you wanted to cross. Phillip was treading onto thin ice.

"And you both have stayed in touch since then," Phillip said, oblivious to Jamal's silent warning. "I found archived articles from several events with photos of you and Mr. Morris posing togeth—"

"Yes, yes," Mayor Johnson said dismissively, "he and I have known each other for a long time and we see each other at parties occasionally, but I still don't know what I have to do with all of this. I don't award building contracts and I certainly don't enforce them. I told you, we have people for that."

Phil nodded again. "I know, sir, but—"

"But nothing. It's faster and more productive to address your questions to the relevant department and appropriate person, wouldn't you agree, Mr. Seymour? If you can't locate that person, I'm sure someone at city hall can find them for you. But you're obviously a resourceful reporter. I'm sure you can do that on your own." The mayor didn't wait for him to reply before he turned his attention to Jamal. "We really should be going, shouldn't we? I believe we have another appearance at three thirty."

Jamal eagerly nodded, now relieved to have an excuse to walk away. "We do, sir. And you're right. We should get going if we want to make it across town on time."

"It was nice meeting you, Mr. Seymour," the mayor said before extending his hand to the reporter for a shake.

Phillip dazedly shook the hand that was offered to him. "Uh, n-nice meeting you too, sir. But if I could just ask—"

"I'm afraid not. We really must be on our way," the mayor insisted before turning and walking toward the curb where a black sedan waited for them. "Jamal, are you coming?" he called over his shoulder.

"Yes, sir!" Jamal paused and slapped Phil's shoulder. "See you, Phil."

"Uh, yeah. See you," Phil said before waving limply.

Jamal settled into the leather seat beside the mayor, shutting the door behind him just as the sedan pulled into traffic.

"That was an interesting discussion," Mayor Johnson said, adjusting his suit jacket and reaching for a binder that sat on the seat between them. He began to flip pages.

"Phil is just a little overeager. I wouldn't worry about it," Jamal said, buckling his seat belt.

"Why shouldn't I? Overeager can also mean persistent." He slowly looked up from his binder and glared at Jamal. "You should've told me about this. I thought you were my eyes and ears. I thought I could depend on you, Jamal."

Jamal nervously cleared his throat. "I didn't tell you because I . . . I didn't think I needed to. I was taking care of it."

"Really? Because it doesn't seem like you've taken care of it if he's still pursuing the story . . . if he asked me questions like that in full view of my constituents and other members of the press."

"Sir, I really will take care of it. Really, I will!"

Jamal watched as the mayor leaned forward and pressed a button to raise the partition between them and the driver. The sound of the droning voice on the car radio abruptly stopped. The only thing Jamal could hear was the soft hum of the car's heater. He swallowed audibly, bracing himself for what the mayor was about to say next.

"I hope you do take care of this, Jamal, because you leave me with only two options if you don't," Johnson said, gazing at him unflinchingly. "Would you like to know what those options are?"

I think I can guess, Jamal thought bleakly, but remained silent.

"I can reach out to my friends, one of whom happens to be our mutual acquaintance, and tell him I'm experiencing a problem with the reporter at the *Washington Recorder* and have him deal with it."

Jamal closed his eyes and cringed. Back to the death threats. He shook his head. "No, sir, please . . . please don't do that. Phil is in his midtwenties. He's barely out of college. He just started working there two years ago. He doesn't . . . he doesn't know any better! He doesn't—"

"And my other option," the mayor continued, pretending like he hadn't heard Jamal's earnest pleas, "is to give our reporter friend something that will distract him . . . a bigger story, shall we say, that he should focus on instead."

Jamal quieted. His eyebrows drew together in confusion and concern. "I'm sorry, sir? What . . . what does that mean?"

"I mean that maybe your friend Phil should be less concerned with housing developments than what's going on right here at city hall, with the behavior of one of the deputy mayors," Johnson said, reclining in the back seat. "Perhaps he would find it interesting that the deputy mayor of planning and economic development has been using the city's tax dollars to frequent prostitutes in New York . . . to get drunk, snort cocaine, and do God knows whatever else. I'm sure he and other reporters would find that to be a juicier story, don't you think? I bet he'd forget about those little housing developments very quickly."

Jamal blanched. "What?"

"You heard me."

"You're really gonna throw me under the bus? Just because he wants to write stories about a housing development?"

The mayor shrugged and smiled. "I told you. I've gotta do what I've gotta do in this situation, Jamal. You've left me with little choice."

"You *took* me to that place," Jamal said through clenched teeth. "I didn't even know where the hell we were going. I didn't know prostitutes were going to be there!"

"And yet you partook of what was available," the mayor said, speaking over him. "I didn't force you, Jay. You did it because you wanted to do it. You certainly enjoyed yourself that night!" He chuckled again.

"You were there too. If Phil finds out about me, you don't think he'd figure out that you were doing God knows what too?" he asked, repeating the mayor's words back to him.

"I'm a member of that establishment. You are not. And I pay a great deal of money for them to protect my secrets. You do not. Besides, I don't have photographic evidence of my . . . activities. Unfortunately, I do of yours, Jamal."

"You . . . you took pictures?"

"*I* didn't take them," the mayor said, pointing at his chest. "One of your companions did. You were very intoxicated that evening. I guess you don't remember her doing it?"

Jamal closed his eyes again, trying desperately to recall all the things he had done that night back in New York. The two prostitutes . . . the threesome . . . the drugs. He could only get flashes, quick snapshots of what had happened, but he couldn't remember many details. If one of the women took pictures of even a small percentage of what they'd done, he'd look awful. He would not only lose his job but also be run out of town, and maybe government and politics entirely.

Had that been the mayor's intention all along? Had he invited Jamal to the brothel just so that he could sucker him into letting down his guard, doing something incredibly stupid, and blackmailing him with the evidence later?

"Jesus," Jamal whispered, opening his eyes and staring at the mayor in disgust. This man really was evil.

"Well, needless to say," Johnson continued, "the photos were . . . very interesting. I'd suggest you do what's necessary so that the only people who are aware of their presence are me, you, and your lovely companions that night. All right?"

Jamal slowly nodded. "All right," he whispered just as the mayor leaned forward again and lowered the partition.

The mayor returned his attention to the binder that still

sat on his lap. "Brian, can you turn up the volume? I wanted to hear that stock report."

"Yes, sir," the driver said with a quick nod. The drone of the radio announcer's voice filled the car again and Jamal turned to the passenger window, now sick to his stomach.

Chapter 13

Derrick

Derrick stared at his laptop screen, willing himself to type the email he had been trying to type for the past half hour. His fingers hovered over the computer keys for a few seconds. He typed one word, then two, then slumped back in his office chair in defeat.

He couldn't concentrate. His mind kept drifting back to the confession that Melissa had made that weekend, the secret that she had been keeping from him for months: Jamal had kissed her. Derrick's former friend had actually made a move on his girl and had tried to break them up.

Of course, Derrick didn't let on to Melissa that he was still obsessing over her revelation. After that intense conversation in the car following dinner with Mr. Theo and Lucas, he and Melissa had woken up the next morning and behaved like the conversation had never happened. They had gone grocery shopping, arguing playfully over what brand of cereal to buy and whether Melissa really needed more bath gel. They went downtown to buy a birthday gift for his mom, came back, watched a movie while eating dinner, made love on the sofa, and fell asleep in one another's arms. It had been a normal Sunday, but in the back of Derrick's mind he could hear an ongoing, whispering dialogue.

She talked shit about you to him, the voice in his head would taunt. *They sat around draggin' you, bruh.*

So! She was just letting off some steam! She was mad at me at the time, he'd reassure himself. *She didn't mean anything by it.*

She met up with him for coffee though . . . for lunch. Is that all they met up for? the voice would ask.

Melissa told me the truth, he'd argue. *She didn't have to tell me even that. She didn't have to tell me anything!*

She said he kissed her, but is that all they did? You've lied to her. Why wouldn't she lie to you? Maybe she isn't telling you the whole truth, the voice would say.

And it was that last thought that always gave him pause. Had Melissa left out part of the story? Had Jamal really kissed her—or had they done a lot more and Melissa had only told Derrick part of the truth to soften the blow?

He wanted to question her again, to grill her on the details. Just how long did Jamal kiss her before she pushed him away? Did he touch her? Did she touch him? Why had she waited so long to tell him what happened?

He knew he had no right to be jealous or suspicious of her; he wasn't innocent himself. He had done his dirt too—a lot worse than her. But it didn't stop the cyclone of emotions from sucking him in. It didn't quiet the voices in his head either. They only seemed to grow louder.

But when it came to Jamal—the offender himself— Derrick didn't have any questions he wanted to ask him. He didn't want to know why someone he had once considered one of his closest friends would not only make a move on his girl, but try to convince her to leave him. He didn't want to know if this was an impulse Jamal had felt, under the influence of a good time and too much alcohol, like Melissa had assured him—or if these were real desires and shady thoughts Jamal had secretly been harboring for years. All he wanted to do was hit him, over and over again. He wanted to stomp him into the ground. He wanted to beat him so bad that even his own mama wouldn't recognize him. If Jamal knew what was good for him, he would stay out of Derrick's vicinity. He wouldn't ever walk in Derrick's line of sight.

Derrick glanced at the clock on his laptop, realizing that it was almost noon. He had already wasted half the day. He shoved back from his desk and pushed himself to his feet. He was supposed to meet Melissa for lunch today. It was part of the effort they were making to get better as a couple by spending more time together. Little did she know he'd probably be focused on questions about her kissing another man during their lunch more than enjoying their couple's time.

He opened the door and strolled down the hall, heading to the stairwell and the floor below, where Melissa was probably waiting for him at the receptionist desk, but he slowed his pace when he noticed the head security guard, Rodney, leaning against a doorjamb. Again, Rodney was having a conversation with Cole, though this time it was with Cole and another student—one of Cole's fawning lackeys.

When Derrick saw them, his anger flared.

Seeing Cole being so chummy with Rodney was yet another reminder of how things were never quite what they seemed. While his fiancée was meeting behind his back with Jamal, maybe Cole was doing the same with Rodney. Hell, maybe all the security guards were under Cole's thumb now, following *his* orders. The suitcases were gone, but who the hell knew what else Cole was conspiring to do at the Institute. Who knew what plans he had in the works or what plans he was carrying out at this very moment.

Derrick stalked toward the trio.

"What are you two doing out here?" he asked, not bothering with the formality or fakeness of a greeting. "Shouldn't you be in class?"

Cole's companion fidgeted nervously, but Cole glanced at Derrick like he was some pesky nuisance he didn't want to deal with right now. "Nah, class just let out. We were headed to the lunch room and just stopped to talk to our boy Rodney, here," he said, thumping Rodney on the shoulder.

Rodney laughed, hooking his thumb in his belt as he continued to lean against the doorway.

"He's not 'your boy.' He's a security officer for the Institute, and one of the things he should be doing is making sure students aren't lingering around in the hallways. We don't pay him to shoot the shit with you two. If you're heading to lunch, then go there."

Rodney frowned. "We were only talking about a minute, sir. The boys were just about to leave. I wasn't—"

"You weren't doing your job," Derrick said, cutting him off.

Rodney glared at him, but Derrick didn't care that he was pissing him off. In Rodney's face, he saw Jamal. He saw Cole. He saw everything that thwarted and undermined him.

"And I can think of a few other times when you weren't doing your job around here, so don't act like this is an isolated incident." He pointed to Cole and his friend. "Now go! I'm not going to say it again."

Rodney shoved himself away from the doorjamb and took a threatening step toward Derrick. "You got a problem with me, Mr. Miller?"

"Yeah, I got a problem with you," Derrick said, not remotely intimidated by the brawny man standing in front of him. Cole and his friend looked on in awe. "I got a problem with what you're doing around my school. And if you're doing what I think you're doing, you gonna have to get the hell up out of here!"

"Man, I don't know what crawled up your ass and died, but you are messin' with the wrong nigga, you hear me?" Rodney yelled, drawing close to Derrick's face. "Don't be comin' at me like that!"

"No," Derrick said, taking a step toward him so that they were almost chest to chest, nose to nose, "don't you come at me like that if you don't want no—"

"Hey! Hey!" someone shouted, placing an arm between the two men. "Stop it! The both of you!"

Derrick looked down, shocked to see Morgan standing in between him and Rodney. She had a hand on his chest and was practically shoving him back.

"What the hell are you doing? Have you two lost your damn minds?" She glared at Derrick then at Rodney and back again. "I heard you shouting all the way in the stairwell. What is going on?"

"Ask him what the fuck is going on," Rodney said, jabbing his finger at him. "He's the one who came over here starting some shit with me. I don't even know what the fuck he's talking about!"

"Don't say 'he' like I'm not your boss, nigga!" Derrick shouted, stepping to him again.

"You don't like it? Then fire me!"

"Fine! You're fired! How about that?"

"Good, because if I'm not working for you no more I got an even better reason to whoop your ass!"

"Then let's go!"

"Stop! Stop it!" Morgan yelled before grabbing Derrick's arm. "Come on! I've got to separate you two because the kids can't see this."

Derrick didn't fight her, though he wanted to. He wanted to tug his arm out of her grasp and start throwing punches at Rodney. He wanted to land blows like he had in the old days, back before he had even arrived at the Institute and served his two years for an assault charge. Back in the old days, Derrick didn't take out his frustrations with words. If someone stepped to him, if someone tried to take what was his, he fought them and he fought hard. He could feel that old version of himself emerging. It was like a pit bull tugging at its leash, growling and baring its teeth.

Morgan had to practically drag him as they walked back down the hall. When they arrived at his office door, she shoved him inside his office and slammed the door shut behind them. She dropped her hands to her slender hips.

"What the hell has gotten into you? Did you really just fire Rodney?" Morgan asked, gesturing over her shoulder to his closed door.

He paced back and forth in front of his desk. Now stuck in his office with Morgan standing in front of his door, preventing his exit, he felt like a caged animal.

"Look, I appreciate you stepping in and everything, but seriously, this doesn't have shit to do with you! Okay?"

"No, it didn't have shit to do with me, but you realize more than a dozen of those boys were standing around watching you two and your dick-swinging contest, right?" Morgan asked. "Those are kids that you care about, Derrick. Kids who look up to you. You really want them seeing you this way? Is this the type of example you want to set for them?"

Derrick stilled. He turned to face her. He could see the

earnest concern on her honey-colored face, in her big green eyes.

"Shit," he muttered.

"Exactly," she said with a nod.

"I'm sorry." He ran his fingers through his dreads, feeling his anger deflate with a *whoosh*. "I don't know what got into me out there but . . . but thanks for coming between us. It could've been worse if you hadn't. I know I'm not your favorite person right now so—"

"Look," she said, holding up her hands and taking a step toward him, "whatever is going on between us is irrelevant, Dee. I may be pissed at you, but I still respect you and what you do for these boys . . . what you mean to this school. I don't know what's going on with you, but whatever it is, you can't flip out on people like that, especially in front of the kids."

"I know it wasn't a good look, but I didn't just flip out on Rodney for no reason. The way I said it wasn't right, but I meant what I said: Rodney hasn't been doing his job and I want to know why."

"What do you mean, he hasn't been doing his job?" Her brows furrowed. "What happened?"

Derrick pursed his lips, contemplating whether he should tell Morgan what had been going on for the last couple of months. Did he really want to drag her into the drama? But maybe she could give him some insight he hadn't considered. Maybe she could offer some advice.

"There's been some . . . some shit going down at the Institute that you don't know about, and it's bad . . . really bad."

"What shit?"

He hesitated again.

"Just spit it out, Derrick!"

So he told her everything. He told her about the drugs

and the money. He told her about Cole, and how the teenager had been behaving in the days since Derrick had found the clandestine suitcases. He explained that he still didn't understand how the suitcases had made it into the Institute without security being aware of them. Cole hadn't really tried to hide them, storing them for anyone to see right under his bunk.

When Derrick finished his story, she stared at him, gaping. She shook her head, sending her curls whipping around her shoulders.

"I don't . . . I don't believe it," she whispered, dumbfounded. "We're talking about the same Cole, right? Chicken-chested, soft-spoken *Cole Humphries*?"

"Yeah, the same one. He's probably been working for Dolla Dolla this whole time. But what I'm not sure about is if Rodney is working for him too. Was Rodney just not paying attention when they brought that shit in here, or was he paid to look the other way? And how do I know for sure that Cole won't do it again . . . that he isn't *still* doing that shit right under my nose? As far as I know, there could be other suitcases stored around here."

He watched as she slumped back against his desk, looking almost dazed. She sighed a few seconds later. "So what do you want to do? Turn Cole over to the cops, then?"

"I would . . . but I've lived in this city long enough to know who the hell Dolla Dolla is," Derrick said, crossing his arms over his chest. "He isn't going to take kindly to me snitching and turning in one of his runners. If I did that, I'd be risking not only my life, but the life of every single boy at the Institute and person who works here."

"So what's the alternative then?" she asked, pushing herself away from his desk. "You're gonna keep picking fights with Rodney? You're gonna keep an eye on Cole forever?"

He gave a half smile. "I was hoping you could suggest somethin'."

"*Me?* Why me?"

He shrugged. "I trust you. You've given me good advice in the past."

At that, her face changed. Her expression softened in a way that it hadn't in months. It was the same look she'd given him back when she used to look at him as they lay in each other's arms. It was that loving look she had right before she used to raise her mouth to his for a searing hot kiss.

She must have realized that she was making that face, because she quickly wiped it away and replaced it with a bland one.

"I think you need to talk to Cole. Ask him point blank what's going on."

"I've tried. And I can't get a straight—"

"But you haven't tried while I'm there. Let me talk to him too. We'll . . . we'll do it together."

He raised his brows in shock. "You'd really do that?"

"I told you . . . no matter what's gone on between us, I still care about the Institute. I even care about Cole, despite the shit he's gotten himself mixed up in. Maybe I can help talk some sense into the kid."

Derrick noticed that she hadn't said that she still cared about him; she didn't list that among the reasons why she was now inserting herself into this drama. But he wouldn't focus on that right now. He would just appreciate her offer of intervention.

"Thanks. I appreciate you doing this. I know you don't have to do it so . . . so . . ." His words drifted off.

She held his gaze for several seconds, both of them not saying a word.

He saw a wellspring of emotion in her eyes and he wondered if it was reflected in his own. Sometimes, he wondered . . . he wondered if he had been a different man, if the circumstances had been different, would he still be with Morgan? Was it possible to love two women simultaneously? He certainly felt like it was possible, because he still had strong feelings for Morgan despite his love for Melissa. He still wanted to hold her, to kiss her, and judging from the way she was looking at him now, she might want him to do it too.

His carnal thoughts were abruptly cut short when he heard a knock at the door. "Dee?" Melissa called out. "Dee, you in there?"

"Uh, yeah!" he said, anxiously clearing his throat. "We were . . . we were . . . um . . . just finishing up, baby. You can come in."

The door eased open and he saw Melissa standing in the doorway, smiling timidly. "I didn't mean to interrupt you. I was waiting for you at the front desk and you didn't show, so I figured I'd come looking for you up here." Her gaze shifted to Morgan. She extended her hand. "I'm sorry. We've never met. Hi, I'm Melissa, Derrick's fiancée."

Derrick was gripped with panic. For a split second, he wondered if Morgan might do something or say something out of pocket or slick to Melissa, like *Hi, I'm the bitch who almost took your man,* or, *Pleased to finally meet you. All the times Derrick said he was out with his friends, he was really kissing up on me.*

But she didn't. Instead, Morgan painted on a polite smile. "Hey, I'm Morgan. I'm one of the teachers here at the Institute."

"Really? What do you teach?"

"Carpentry."

Melissa's eyes widened in amazement. "Wow, that is bomb! A woman carpenter, huh?"

"Yeah," Morgan said with a nod. "And I should probably head out now so I'm not late for my next class." She then glanced over her shoulder at Derrick. "See you later," she whispered before turning away. She then stepped around Melissa and almost ran to his office doorway. He watched as she damn near fled into the hall.

Thankfully, Melissa didn't notice her hasty retreat. She was too concerned with going to lunch. "You ready, baby? I'm starving!" she said.

He nodded and walked toward her. "Yeah, sorry I was late."

"That's fine. You guys were busy. I get it. She seemed nice though."

"She is," he said as they stepped into the hall.

"And pretty," she said just as he shut his door behind them.

"I guess. I hadn't noticed."

"Oh, don't lie," Melissa chided. "She's *very* pretty! And she does carpentry. She's a full package! I wish I did carpentry. I can't even bang a nail without warping it."

He leaned down and kissed her cheek. "I like you just the way you are, baby."

"Really?"

"No doubt."

"Aww, thank you, honey," she said, standing on the balls of her feet to wrap her arms around his shoulders and envelop him in a hug.

Out of the corner of his eye, he saw Morgan lingering at the end of the hall. She was staring at them. When their gazes met, she abruptly turned, opened the steel door leading to the stairwell, and let it bang shut behind her.

Chapter 14

Ricky

"What's up, Dolla? You called me?" Ricky asked as he strolled down the steps into the drug kingpin's sunken living room.

Ricky watched as Dolla Dolla finished his line of blow and slowly raised his bald head to peer up at him from his perch on the sofa. He still had white powder in his mustache. He wiped his nose absently as he nodded at Ricky, smearing the powder on the back of his hand.

"Yeah, I called you. Sit down. Take a load off. You want some of this shit?" Dolla Dolla asked, gesturing to the remaining lines on the glass coffee table.

Ricky sat down in the armchair facing him and shook his head. "Uh, nah, I'm good," he said, waving him off.

"You sure?"

He nodded again. "Yeah."

He hadn't done coke or Molly since the raids and his arrest.

One of the conditions of being an informant was that he had to stay clean. They even made him pee in a cup every couple of weeks to prove he was off the stuff. Ricky had experienced some of the symptoms of withdrawal since then—fatigue and nightmares that left him waking up in a cold sweat, and his mind didn't seem as sharply focused as it used to be. And he still got those cravings on occasion, especially at moments like this when temptation was sitting right in front of him, but at least it wasn't as bad as it had been in the beginning. He hadn't realized how much he'd been hooked on that stuff.

In some ways, he was relieved to finally be rid of it. Like Simone, coke was something in his life that would've eventually come back to bite him in the ass in the end.

Dolla Dolla stared at him for a few more seconds in confusion. Ricky didn't usually turn down taking a hit. He started to wonder if maybe it had been a bad move to decline Dolla Dolla's offer, but finally the kingpin shrugged. "Shit, more for me!" He leaned down and snorted another line. "I'mma need your help with somethin', Pretty Ricky."

Ricky was relieved. Those were the words he had been waiting for weeks to hear.

Detectives Ramsey and Dominguez had been on his ass about not giving them any new information for their investigation. But it wasn't his fault that Dolla Dolla had gone quiet. He had hit up Dolla Dolla anyway. The search for Simone was at a standstill for now, and he wanted to appease the cops and get them off his back. He tried his best to let his former boss know that he was there if he needed him. Based on the call he had gotten today summoning him to Dolla Dolla's Kalorama crib, it looked like Dolla Dolla was finally ready to take him up on his offer.

"You know I'm here for you, Dolla. What you need me to do?"

Dolla Dolla reached for the smoldering cigar sitting in the nearby glass ash tray and brought it to his mouth. "One of my girls reached out to me. She said she ready to come back home to daddy, but I need to know first if she's been talking to the cops, if she told the prosecutor shit she shouldn't have." He took a puff from his cigar and blew out a stream of smoke. "I need you to find out for me."

Ricky frowned. "You want *me* to find out?"

"Yeah, I can't do it. She may be tellin' me the truth, but she may not, and I'm not about to get set up in no entrapment, you feel me? Plus, you a charmin' motherfucka. Talk to her. Work your Pretty Ricky magic. See what she says." Dolla Dolla glanced up at one of his bodyguards who stood off to the side. "Melvin'll take you there."

"Wait. We're leaving *now*?"

"Yeah, you leavin' now, nigga!" Dolla Dolla laughed and took another puff. "You thought I was talking about next week?"

"No, I just thought . . ." Ricky was at a loss for words, thrown off by Dolla Dolla's request and the fact that he wanted it done *right now.* "So I'm just going there to talk? That's all you want me to do?"

Dolla Dolla took another puff from his cigar, blew out smoke, and cocked an eyebrow. "*What?* You plannin' to fuck her too?" He chuckled again. "I know how you are."

"No, I mean . . ." Ricky leaned forward and dropped his voice to a whisper. "You just want me to get info from her and that's it—right? Then me and Melvin dip out of there and I come back here. We tell you what she told me."

Ricky had assumed that when Dolla Dolla said he wanted to track down the girls, it wasn't just to sip tea, eat cookies, and have a conversation with each of them. He thought the whole point was to silence them. Was this going to turn into an ambush for the poor woman? If so, he wanted nothing to do with it. He didn't care what promises he'd made to the detectives. He wouldn't be an accomplice to murder.

Dolla Dolla nodded. "Yeah, what the fuck else you thought I expected you to do?"

"Nothin'. Nothing else." Ricky quickly shook his head and rose to his feet, relieved that he had made the wrong assumption. Maybe Dolla Dolla wasn't as ruthless as he thought. "I'm ready to jet whenever you are, Mel."

The towering bodyguard nodded his dark head, turned, and walked toward the front door, leaving Ricky to trail behind him.

Ricky frowned as Melvin pulled to a stop in front of a rundown building where several children ran around the parched grass of the open courtyard and a group of men played dice on the cement.

"This it?" Ricky asked.

Melvin nodded. "This the address she gave."

The two men climbed out of the Mercedes and strolled up the walkway. When they did, one of the men playing craps glanced up at them and then stared at the glistening black Mercedes now parked along the curb.

"Don't even think about it, bruh," Melvin said in a heavy baritone that sounded harder than granite. He then adjusted his jacket, revealing the Glock tucked in his waistband near his hip.

The man returned his attention to the craps game, like the encounter hadn't even happened. As they drew near the children, Melvin snapped his fingers. "Hey you! High-topped fade. Come over here!"

A lanky boy who looked to be nine or ten years old strolled toward them. He was wearing a stained tank top and cargo shorts, attire that was much too light for the chilly March weather, but Ricky remembered those days when he was a kid and his grandmother only had a limited supply of clothes from Goodwill that she could hand off to him and his little sister, Desireé. You wore what was clean and what fit. Whether it was weather appropriate was sometimes irrelevant.

"Yeah?" the boy asked, tugging up his sagging cargo shorts.

"Look here, I want you to keep an eye on my ride for me," Melvin said, reaching into his back pocket and pulling out his wallet. He handed the boy a hundred-dollar bill. "You see any of these niggas or anybody else even touch that shit, you tell me. You hear me?"

The boy quickly nodded before folding the bill and tucking it into one of the many pockets of his shorts. "I got you."

A few minutes later, Ricky and Melvin climbed the last flight of stairs in the apartment complex, bringing them to the fifth floor. The dimly lit hallway smelled of dirty carpet and vaguely of urine. Melvin stopped in front of one of the maroon doors toward the end of the hall and knocked. When he did, they heard a female voice ask timidly, "Who is it?" on the other side of the door.

"We're friends of Big D. He sent us," Ricky called back. "We came to talk to Tamika."

A few seconds later, the door cracked open only a few inches. He saw hazel eyes peering back at them through the gold door chain. "*Sent you?*" the woman asked. "Why . . . why he ain't come here himself?"

"He wanted us to talk to you first," Ricky explained, painting on a smile. "Are you Tamika?"

She hesitated again. Gradually, she nodded but still didn't remove the door chain.

He held up his hands, showing that they were empty. "Really, you've got nothin' to worry about, sweetheart. We just came here to talk. It's some stuff he couldn't ask you over the phone so he wanted me to do it for him—in person. That's all."

The door slammed shut. Ricky glanced up at Melvin, whose dark face settled into a scowl. The hulking body-guard raised his fist to pound on her door again, but they heard a series of clicks and the door swung open before he could.

In the doorway stood a young petite woman who looked to be in her early twenties. She wore a T-shirt and jeans. Her long hair was pulled back into a ponytail, revealing an almost angelic sienna-hued face with big hazel eyes and rounded cheeks.

"What we need to talk about?" Tamika asked, narrowing those light eyes up at them suspiciously.

"Stuff we really don't want to talk about in the middle of the hallway," Ricky said. "Do you mind if we come in?"

Tamika hesitated again. He could understand why: Two big dudes she had never seen before had shown up to her apartment in the middle of the day, unannounced. He'd be suspicious of them too.

"How about this? Do you mind if just *I* come in? Melvin can wait in the hall. And we can leave the door open if you don't feel safe being alone with me in here."

Ricky could hear Melvin grumbling behind him, but he didn't care. He was trying to earn this woman's trust, to make her feel comfortable. That's what Dolla Dolla had sent him here to do.

She loudly exhaled, making her tiny nostrils flare, and then nodded, gesturing inside the apartment. "Okay. But *just* you! He waits out here and you better keep the door open, or I'm callin' the police."

Ricky nodded before turning to Melvin. "I won't be long."

Melvin grunted before slumping against the door frame.

Ricky followed her down a short hallway into her kitchen. The apartment was filled with only a few pieces of furniture: one stained sofa, a television, a fold-up kitchen table and two chairs that didn't match. A half-full Styrofoam cup of noodles sat on the table along with a can of soda.

"Can I sit down?" Ricky asked, pulling out one of the chairs from the table.

She shrugged and grabbed her cup of noodles. "I don't care. Go ahead," she said before shoving a fork in the cup and continuing to eat. He noticed she didn't take the chair opposite him, but leaned against the counter instead as she ate. That was okay. Again, he knew he had to build her trust.

"So how you been doing, Tamika?" Ricky asked.

"Not too good," she said between slurps, taking a darting glance around the kitchen. She was twitchy, like she couldn't stand still. He wondered if she was nervous—or high. "I'm about to get kicked out of my place, and I need money. That's why I wanna go back to Dolla—if he'll take me back. I wouldn't have left if the cops didn't raid that joint. I know he took care of me. He took better care of me than any other niggas I fuck with," she said with a sneer.

"Did the cops talk to you after the raid? Did they ask you questions?"

She nodded as she ate. "But I didn't tell them shit. I couldn't tell em. I didn't know anything! They kept asking me about who my customers were. They showed me this binder full of pictures of dudes. I didn't know none of them niggas." She dumped the remaining noodles into the already overflowing kitchen sink along with her fork. "They asked me if Dolla made me stay there . . . if he wouldn't let me go. I told them I was there because I fuckin' wanted to be there. He was my man. I stayed with my man. Point blank period!"

Ricky watched as she slouched back against the counter again. He wondered how many girls, like Tamika, may have been forced into prostitution by Dolla Dolla, but had led such horrible lives that they didn't know abuse when they saw it. His sister had been a lot like them and she ended up six feet under before the age of sixteen. But he wasn't here to impart words of wisdom. He wasn't here to tell Tamika that she was better off staying far away from Dolla Dolla and men like him. He was here to save his own ass and that's exactly what he was going to do.

"So what did the cops do when you didn't tell them anything?"

"They tried to threaten me. Kept me there all damn day and night asking the same questions over and over again a hundred different ways." She started pacing. She shoved her hands into her back pockets. "They said they could charge me with soliciting or drug possession, since they found some coke in my bedroom, but I told them they were full of shit. They didn't catch me soliciting nobody, and my bedroom was in Dolla's house. Anybody could've left that coke there. So they let me go. I haven't heard from them since."

Ricky sighed. So she hadn't flipped. This petite young woman with the angel face had held strong during multiple hours of questioning in front of cops, while he had folded like a dinner napkin in less than twenty minutes.

Ain't that some shit, he thought forlornly.

"I didn't tell on him. Let Dolla know that," she insisted. "If that's why he's worried about me coming back, let him know I held him down. I ain't lyin'."

Ricky rose to his feet. "I believe you . . . and I'll tell him. Don't worry."

He then turned, walked out of the kitchen, and stepped back into the hall to find Melvin still waiting for them, looking bored.

"You done?" Melvin asked, raising his thick brows.

Ricky nodded. "We're done. She ain't say nothin' to the cops. We can go."

Melvin pushed himself away from the doorjamb just as Ricky stepped past him into the hall. "I gotta take a piss first." He looked at Tamika. "Where's your bathroom?"

She took a step toward him and pointed down a hallway. "Oh, umm, down that way and to your r—"

She didn't get to finish. Melvin grabbed her wrist and dragged her toward him at lightning speed. It happened so fast that it even caught Ricky off guard. She only got out a squeak of a scream before Melvin clamped a hand over her mouth, twisted her arm behind her back, wrapped an arm around her waist, and yanked her off her feet so that they dangled about six inches above the floor.

"Close the door," Melvin hissed at him.

Ricky stared at him dumbfounded. "Wha-what the fuck are you doin', man?" he whispered. "I thought we were just—"

"I said close the fuckin' door," Melvin repeated, breathing harder as Tamika twisted and kicked in his arms like a fish on a hook. But he kept a viselike hold around her. Pure horror and desperation were in her bulging hazel eyes.

"Do it!" Melvin barked and, almost as a reflex, Ricky shut the apartment door.

He waited in the fifth-floor corridor, listening for the faint sounds coming from inside the apartment. It was a struggle not to run in there and help her, but he knew he couldn't. He couldn't go against Dolla Dolla. He couldn't blow his cover. He was stuck between a rock and a hard place all over again.

He heard tussling. A series of thumps. Another female squeak and then a deafening silence that made his heart sink. A few minutes later, Melvin swung the door open again, making him jump back.

"Let's go," Melvin said, wiping his hands on a wash cloth and tucking it into his pocket.

Ricky would bet a fair amount of money there was blood on that wash cloth. He didn't budge. He felt almost rooted in place by horror at what had happened, at the idea that he had helped entrap that young woman and led her to her death.

"I said let's go. Come on! Dolla's waiting," Melvin ordered, shutting the door behind him and walking down the hall with the calmness of a man who had just taken out a bag of trash, not murdered a young woman in cold blood.

Ricky stared at him for several seconds before gradually putting one foot in front of the other and following him to the stairs.

Chapter 15

Jamal

"Hey, Phil, did I keep you waiting long?" Jamal asked as he walked through the maze of tables filled with federal workers taking their afternoon lunch breaks.

Jamal had called Phillip, the reporter at the *Washington Recorder*, earlier that week and offered to take him out to lunch at one of the nicest restaurants downtown—an upscale tapas joint with high ceilings and an extensive wine list. But Phillip had declined and asked to meet him in one of the federal building food courts instead.

"They've got Chick-fil-A there," he had admitted, almost sheepishly, over the phone. "I really like their sandwiches."

And as he neared the table, Jamal saw that Phillip had gotten the fried chicken sandwich he'd mentioned. When Jamal approached, Phillip lowered the sandwich and waffle fries he'd been double fisting. The younger man smiled as he wiped the smear of ketchup from his lips.

"Hi, Mr. Lighty," Phillip said between chews, spilling a little food from his mouth as he spoke. "No, I haven't been waiting long, but I hope you don't mind that I got started already. I was . . . well . . . I was a little hungry."

"No problem," Jamal said, tossing his suit jacket over the back of one of the metal chairs. "I'll grab a sandwich and a soda and be right back."

Phillip nodded and returned his attention to his waffle fries.

Jamal hadn't invited Phillip today just for a friendly lunch. He'd hoped it could be the chance to finally get Phillip to let go of his whole investigation into those housing developments. After Mayor Johnson's threat, he knew he had to do it or the consequences he faced would be dire.

He returned to the table a few minutes later with a food tray. He pulled out his chair and began to unwrap the paper around his Philly sub. He told himself to ooze charm, to pretend that he was Ricky, one of the most amiable bastards out there when he wanted to be.

"So how you doin' today?" he asked.

"Good!" Phillip said with a nod. It looked like he had almost finished his meal before Jamal had even started his. "I'm busy though. I've got about four stories to file, but I knew you wanted to meet up today and you're a good source, so I was willing to make an allowance for you, Mr. Lighty."

"We've known each other long enough that you can just call me Jamal, Phil . . . or Jay. That's what my friends call me."

Phillip nodded eagerly. "Okay, Jay! Thanks! And you can keep calling me Phil. That's what everyone else calls me . . . well, except my mom, who calls me Danny because my middle name is Daniel, but I . . ." He gave an apprehensive laugh when he realized he was rambling. "Well, anyway, Phil is still fine."

"Awesome," Jamal said, pressing forward and adjusting in his chair. "Because I consider us to be kind of friends, Phil, or at least friendly, right?"

"Sure, sir . . . I-I mean, Mr. Lighty . . . I-I mean, J-Jay!" he stuttered.

"So as a friend, I want to ask you a favor."

Phillip narrowed his eyes as he sucked the last of the ketchup from his plump fingers. "What's that?"

"First, let me say that I think you're an amazing reporter. I truly appreciate your work," Jamal said, hoping he wasn't laying it on too thick. "So I want to offer you the chance to do a great story, to give you more access than what we usually grant other reporters. I'd love you to shadow me for a week or two. Short of coming home with me, I want you there. You can come to every meeting, sit in on every call. When I meet constituents, I want you there. And I'll answer whatever questions you want."

"Really? Wow, because I've been wanting to do something like that. I keep seeing these pieces in the *Post* and I think, if I could just shadow someone and—"

"Great! So we're on the same wavelength. Do you think you could work something like that into your schedule though? I know you said you are busy."

"Sure! Of course I can! When can we do it?"

"As soon as you're available. It all depends on you, my friend. The only thing I ask in exchange . . . the favor I need is that you move on from that whole thing about the housing developments. It's hard to get a real answer with something like that anyway. So many unknowns and all." He shrugged and bit into his sub. "So how does that sound? Would that work for you?"

"Well, uh . . . I'd love to do an immersive profile of you, Jay, but I'd still like to do the housing developments story too. I've got a new lead and I wanted to—"

Jamal quickly shook his head and set his sandwich on

his tray. "No, you see, Phil, how this works is that I do the profile with you and you let go of the other story. You can't do both."

Phil's enthusiasm seemed to evaporate. For the first time, a frown marred his pale, ruddy face. "Why not?"

"Because that's the deal. That's our agreement."

Phillip's frown deepened. "Uh, I'm . . . I'm sorry, Jay, but this is starting to sound . . . well . . ." He pursed his thin lips. "It's starting to sound less like a favor and . . . well, it's kinda starting to sound like a bribe."

"*A bribe?*" Jamal barked out a laugh. "Are you kidding? I'm not handing you a sealed envelope filled with cash, Phil."

Though he had seriously considered doing just that, but he knew a man like Phillip would take one look at the envelope, rush back to his news office, and start typing the story with the headline, "City Official Tries to Squash Report Linking Mayor to Dirty Dealings with a Wad of Cash".

Phillip was wide-eyed and somewhat gullible, but he wasn't stupid. Even Jamal knew that.

"I'm offering you the chance to do one story versus another," Jamal continued. "A *better* story, quite frankly."

"But what difference does it make? Why are you trying to get me to stop writing about the housing developments?" Phillip leaned forward, dropping his voice to a whisper. "Is the mayor really connected to it, like I thought? Is he getting money under the table for it?"

"No, of course he's not."

"Then why won't he answer my questions? If it has nothing to do with him, he can just show me what—"

"He doesn't *have* to show you anything, Phil!" Jamal shouted, now pushed to the brink of his patience. "He's not going to show you! Don't you get it? You're not going to find the answers you're looking for. You're wasting your time. But if you keep butting your nose into stuff you shouldn't butt your nose into, you're gonna regret it in the end."

"What does that mean?"

Jamal rested his elbows on the table and glared down at his sub. He had taken one bite and his appetite was already gone. "It means exactly what I said. Move on to something else."

Their table fell silent even though the clamor around them continued as people ate their lunches, as loud conversations and laughter filled the food court, echoing to the glass ceiling.

"Are you . . . are you threatening me, Jay?" Phillip asked, sounding almost heartbroken.

"I'm not threatening you; I'm warning you because you seem like a good, well-meaning guy who is way . . . *way* out of his depth. And I know what that's like. Take my advice. Take my offer. Do the other story. Please," he said tightly.

He watched as Phillip slowly gathered his food wrappers and napkins and shoved them into his empty paper bag.

Phillip rose to his feet and shook his head. "I'm sorry, but no. No, I won't do the other story. It's not right. This is my job. I'm a reporter. This . . . this is what I do. I'm sorry," he said before turning from their table and walking away. He then tossed his bag into a nearby trash can and shuffled out of the food court.

"Ah, Jamal, there you are!" Mayor Johnson called as Jamal approached one of the Wilson Building's elevators.

Hearing the mayor's voice, Jamal resisted the urge to roll his eyes, only because he knew the mayor would be able to see him do it in the mirror-like surface of the elevator doors.

He had just arrived back from lunch with Phillip and

was still debating on how he was going to break the news to Johnson that Phillip wasn't going to let go of the story. Running smack-dab into the mayor wasn't what he wanted right now.

He winced when he felt Johnson congenially slap him on the shoulder.

"I was just looking for you!" the mayor continued. "But you've been a hard fellow to find all week."

"Yeah, I've had a full calendar," Jamal said, painting on a smile and pressing the up elevator button.

"I know. Your assistant, Sharon, told me you had a busy day today also, which included a lunch with Phillip at the *Washington Recorder*. I was interested in hearing how it went."

Jamal inwardly groaned. He really was going to have to have a conversation with Sharon about blabbing his business to other people, Johnson especially. He hadn't wanted to talk about Phillip this soon. He knew whatever way he said it, the mayor was not going to be happy. He'd hoped he would have at least a couple of days to consider his wording, but it looked like that wasn't going to be the case.

"It went fine," Jamal lied.

"*Fine?* Fine as in he agreed to let go of that little thing we'd been discussing?"

Jamal sighed. "No," he mumbled.

"I'm sorry. I didn't hear you, Jamal. What did you say?"

"I said no. No, he will not let it go."

A bell dinged and suddenly the elevator doors slid open. The compartment was empty. Both men stepped inside.

"Hold the door! Hold the door, please!" an elderly woman called out as she hobbled toward the elevator, bearing her weight on a steel cane.

Jamal reached out to press the button to do so, but the

mayor was faster. Instead, Mayor Johnson pressed the button to slam the doors shut in her face. He then whipped around to face Jamal as the elevator ascended.

"What the hell do you mean he's not going to do it? I thought you talked to him," Johnson barked. His friendly façade had disappeared.

"I did. He got the message, and he said he's still going to write the story."

"You understand what that means, don't you?" Johnson asked, grabbing the lapel of Jamal's suit jacket and yanking him around to face him. "You know you've left me with no choice."

Jamal tore the man's hand from his lapel. "No, you do have a choice. You said it was either Phillip or me, so"— he took a deep breath—"I'm volunteering. Send the pics of me to whoever the hell you want. I don't give a shit, because I'm not going to have that man's fuckin' blood on my hands."

The mayor stilled. "You realize that your career will be over, right? No one will—"

"Yes, I'm not stupid. I know what I'm risking, but frankly, it's worth it."

Just then, the elevator doors opened again, revealing the top floor. Jamal stepped out of the compartment and walked straight to his office. He didn't look back.

Chapter 16

Derrick

Derrick sat behind his desk and glanced up at the clock on his office wall, waiting patiently for it to strike 12:35 p.m. He glanced at Morgan, who sat on the edge of his desk with her legs crossed at the ankles, her arms crossed over her chest, staring at his closed door.

They both waited for Cole Humphries to step through it.

She had agreed to meet Cole with him, to confront him together and finally get to the bottom of whether he was still using the Institute as a way station to smuggle Dolla Dolla's drugs and drug money. They agreed they stood a better chance of an honest answer if she was there. Cole liked and respected her. They both doubted he would lie to her.

Derrick stared at her back, at her slender shoulders in her white T-shirt and her springy curls. He wanted to hug her and kiss her cheek in thanks. She didn't have to help him today. After the way he had treated her, most women wouldn't, but she was here anyway.

"Thanks again for doing this," Derrick whispered.

"Don't mention it," she said, not turning around or even glancing over her shoulder to look at him.

Just then, Derrick's door swung open and Cole stepped through with a broad smile on his face. "What's up, Mr. D? I heard you were lookin' for—"

His words died on his lips when he saw Morgan was in the room too. Cole's confident smile disappeared. His gaze flitted from her to Derrick and back again.

"Hey, Miss Owens," he said. Even his voice changed. It was now an octave higher. "What . . . what are you doing here?"

She glanced down at the armchair facing Derrick's desk. "Have a seat, Cole. Mr. Miller tells me we have a lot to talk about."

Cole squinted suspiciously, still not taking the chair. "So he snitched on me? He told you everything?"

She tilted her head. "He told me enough, but I want to hear the rest from you. Please, have a seat."

Cole finally slumped into the leather armchair. He looked aggravated and every bit of the petulant teenager that he was.

"So," she began, "I've heard you've gotten mixed up in some stuff."

"I'm not 'mixed up.' It's what I want," he said, raising his chin in defiance. "I call the shots."

"Did you call the shots with Rodney? Was he working for you too?" Derrick asked.

"Nah, he wasn't working for me. He did a favor for me like I did favors for him. He wanted tickets to basketball games, so I told him I could probably get the tickets for him if he could help a brother out."

"And by help you out, you mean he would look the other way while you did your dirt? While you moved in the suitcases?" Derrick clarified.

Cole shrugged in response.

That was as good as a yes in Derrick's opinion. Now he didn't feel quite so bad for firing Rodney.

"This is a dangerous game you're playing, Cole," Morgan said. "You think you're calling the shots, but this could easily go left. You could be in way over your head. You are messing around with some bad people."

"They ain't bad," he argued. "Dolla took care of me and my mom when no one else would. He gave me a job. He gave me money. And—"

"And working for him is what landed you in the Institute in the first place," Derrick interjected. "If you keep working for him, you can end up in a place a lot worse—or dead someday."

"Man, I don't wanna hear no preachin' from you," Cole sneered, "you corny-ass nigga! Dolla buys and sells niggas like you!"

Derrick felt his anger perk up at those words, but he fought to get himself under control. He reminded himself that despite Cole's bravado, he was still an angry, scared teenage boy—much like Derrick had been at that age. As he had many times in his life, he channeled the words of his mentor.

Don't give in to the anger, Dee, he heard Mr. Theo say in his head. *Don't be a sucker for that bullshit.*

"And you're just as expendable, Cole," Derrick said calmly. "You're useful to him now, but what's gonna happen when he turns on you, because he will. The only loyalty a dude like Dolla has is to himself."

"I'd like to hear you tell him that shit to his face," Cole said in a whisper that almost sounded like a hiss.

"He doesn't have to," Morgan said, making Cole's gaze snap back to her. "He said it to you—and I'm saying it to you too. That man is using you and wasting your life and all the potential that you have, Cole. And frankly, it pisses me off! I feel stupid and used!"

"*Used?*" Cole looked genuinely taken aback and embarrassed. "I . . . I wasn't trying to use you, Miss Owens."

Derrick knew the boy had feelings for Morgan. If anybody could strike his emotional core under that tough exterior, it had to be her—and that was exactly what she was doing right now.

"You asked me to help you research colleges, to try to find you scholarships. You told me stories about your dreams, about how you wanted to build furniture like me. So were you just running some game on me too? You had the dumb wood-shop teacher thinking that you really gave a shit about getting a degree in design. That folder I gave you is probably sitting in the bottom of a trash can right now, isn't it? Admit it!"

Cole quickly shook his head. "No, Miss Owens. I mean . . . I haven't filled out the applications yet, but I . . . I wasn't running a game on you. I really do want to go to college and study design, but I just . . . I just . . ."

"You just what?" she asked.

"Working for Dolla ain't all about the easy cash. Back in my old neighborhood it was hard for me, you know?" He went sheepish. "I got . . . I got my ass beat a lot. Niggas used to steal my stuff. When these dudes came around saying they could protect me, and all I had to do was a few favors for them every now and then, it seemed like a good deal."

"Does it still seem like one?" Morgan asked.

"Most of the time," he answered softly, then lowered his eyes. "But not today."

Morgan dropped to her knees in front of him, catching both Cole and Derrick off guard. She grabbed his hands, making him meet her eye to eye. "Look, Cole, I need you to listen to me, and listen to me good, okay? You're sixteen and I know that right now you think you understand everything . . . that old-ass people like me don't get it, but I swear to you that I do. And I'm scared for you. I really am. If you keep doing this shit, if you stay mixed up with Dolla, who knows what is going to happen to you. I need you to stop. I need you to stop this shit today."

He shook his head. "I can't, Miss Owens. I can't just—"

"Yes, you can," she insisted. "If it means moving away from here to get away from him, so be it. I'll help you find a college that will take you."

"But my mom . . . my mom can't just move! He'll find her. He'll—"

"If you're worried about your mother, I can talk to some people," Derrick said. "Maybe they can help her with relocation and her expenses. If there's a need, we can make it work."

"So will you stop? No more working for him. No more smuggling suitcases. Make excuses for now to bide your time with him, until we can get you out of here. But please stop this shit, Cole," she pleaded. "You've got to stop."

The young man looked between her and Derrick. "It's not that easy."

"We know. But you're not doing it alone," Derrick said.

After some time, Cole finally nodded. "Okay. I'll stop workin' for him."

"You mean that?" Morgan asked. "You aren't just telling me shit I want to hear just because I want to hear it?"

He shook his head. "No, I mean it. I wouldn't lie to you, Miss Owens."

She smiled and let go of his hands. "Thank you, Cole." She then rose to her feet.

"All right, Cole. Go back to lunch or whatever class you have this period," Derrick said. "We're just going to have to take your word for it."

About a minute later, after Cole had stepped out of Derrick's office, Derrick rose from his chair and rounded his desk.

"I think he really meant what he said in here, believe it or not. He's scared, but I think he's going to try to stop working for Dolla," Derrick said as her gaze drifted back to the door where students now wandered up and down the hall.

"I think so too."

"You did a good job with him."

"So did you. I could tell he got under your skin, but you kept your cool."

"Yeah, it was easy knowing you were doing the heavy lifting. I guess we work well together."

Her eyes drifted from the doorway, back to his face, and again he was filled with regret—for the decisions he made that he knew he had no choice but to make, for what he threw away.

"Look, Morgan"—he stepped around her and closed his office door—"I . . . I know whatever apologies I make will sound empty—"

"Stop, Derrick." She closed her eyes and shook her head. "I don't want to talk about this."

"But I feel like I should explain what happened. Where my mind was at when I—"

"I don't want to talk about it! What part of that do you not understand?"

"But I want you to know that . . . that my feelings for you never changed."

Her eyes shot open.

"I still care about you. I still . . . I still love you."

He could see she was blinking back tears. "If you loved me, then why did you hurt me?" she choked. "You're still with her, Derrick!"

"Because I made a promise to Melissa. She and I have

been together since we were kids. I proposed to her. I was ready to walk away from her, but when . . . when she told me that she wanted to make it work, I felt like I didn't have a choice. I had to stay."

"So you felt obligated to be with her? Is that what you're trying to tell me?"

"Not obligated! It's not like we had some contract. I love her."

She burst into laughter. "Oh, here we go! You love her too! You love her. You love me. You just love fuckin' everybody, huh, Derrick?"

"You know it's not like that. I made her a promise," he repeated. "That means something."

"I understand," she said as the tears spilled onto her cheeks and she wiped them away with the back of her hand. "Your promises to her meant more than the promises you made to me. Got it."

He exhaled and his shoulders sank. "That's not true."

"No, it *is* fucking true! It is true! I told you, I will always be the side chick to guys like you. I will always be the runner-up. You know it, and I know it." She then turned back around to the door, to escape.

"Don't say that," he argued, grabbing her arm, stopping her. "That isn't how I see you. You mean more to me than that!"

"Let go of me!" she shouted, trying futilely to pull away from him. "Get your hands off of me!"

He wanted to let go. He told himself to do it, but he didn't. Instead he tugged her toward him and looped an arm around her waist. He pulled her flat against him. "You mean more than that to me," he whispered, staring down at her.

When he did, all the fight seeped out of her. She looped her arms around his neck and stood on the balls of her feet. He didn't know who had done it first, who had made the first move, but within seconds their lips collided. All the bottled need and desire he'd felt for her came bursting out like a genie from a lamp, and for a while he couldn't tell where his mouth ended and hers began. He shifted her so that she was pressed back against his desk and she clawed at his back as the kiss deepened. They didn't even pause when they heard the knock at the door.

"Dee! Dee, you in there?" Melissa called out as she pushed the door open. "They called an early dismissal at school today so I thought I'd surprise you for lu—"

Her words tapered off as her eyes landed on Derrick and Morgan, mid-embrace.

Derrick released Morgan and tried to ease her away, but the damage was done. Melissa stared at the couple in shock.

Why, of all the days for her to just show up, did it have to be today?

"Lissa," he said just as the fast food bag and soda she held slid from her hands to the linoleum floor, exploding on impact, sending Coke and French fries splattering in all directions. She then turned and stumbled dazedly out the door.

"Lissa!" he shouted, running after her, but he slipped on the soda and collided with the door frame. He landed sprawled on his ass in the pool of Coke. "Lissa, wait!" he yelled after her, but she didn't stop. He watched as she disappeared into the stairwell.

When Derrick arrived home less than forty minutes later, he expected to find the entire apartment destroyed. He thought in a fit of anger and hurt that Melissa might trash the place and all his clothing and belongings would be dangling off their balcony or decorating the bushes in front of the building. But instead, he found the living room and kitchen in the same neat condition that he had left it in that morning. His album collection, stereo, and prized signed Chicago Bulls jersey that hung on their living room wall remained untouched, which actually worried him more.

She was home. He had seen her car parked in their parking garage reserved space. Melissa wasn't one to take something like this—discovering her man kissing another girl—lightly. So what was she doing?

"Lissa?" he called out as he shut the front door behind him and locked it. She didn't answer him, but he heard the sound of drawers being slammed shut in their bedroom. He walked down the hall and found her throwing clothes into a suitcase. Brownie sat on the bedroom floor in his carrier, meowing plaintively.

"Lissa?" he said, walking to their bed, where one of her carry-on suitcases sat open. "What . . . what are you doing?"

"What the fuck does it look like I'm doing, Dee? I'm moving out!" she said as she grabbed a handful of shirts and hurled them into the suitcase. "I left my engagement ring on your dresser. Do whatever the hell you want with it. I don't care."

He cringed. "Don't do this, baby. Can we please talk about this first?"

To his surprise, she paused in her packing to glare at him. She strode around the bed and stood in front of him. "Sure, let's talk about it, Dee. So just how long have you been messing around behind my back? I want to know. And tell me the truth—that is *if* you're even capable of doing that."

He opened his mouth then closed it. He pursed his lips. "It's been . . . It's been a few months. We . . . we started back in November."

"*November?*" she repeated back, sounding shocked.

"You've been cheating on me for damn near six months? You had me crying about kissing Jamal and the whole time you were fuckin' some—"

"I never fucked her!"

"I don't believe you! I don't believe one goddamn word you say, Dee! Everything you've told me has been a lie! Everything you've promised to me—"

"I'm not lying! We never had sex but yes, I did . . . I did cheat. I did see her almost every night. I went to her place more than once. But baby, you and I had hit a rough patch when Morgan and I started . . . started talking. We weren't communicating and things were so . . . so much easier with her."

"So much easier?" She pointed at her chest. "Are you really trying to blame me for your cheating, Dee? You're really going to pull some shit like that?" she shouted.

"No, but you have to admit that things had changed, Lissa! We weren't the same anymore and being with her was like . . . it was like how it used to be between us. But then things got better for us again," he said feebly, "and I . . . and I told her that I wanted to try and make our relationship work so I—"

"So is that what you were doing?" she yelled, shoving him in the chest. "Is that what the fuck you were doing when you had your tongue down her throat? You were trying to make our fuckin' relationship work?"

He stared at her mutely.

"Answer me!" she screamed, slapping him across the cheek. And he accepted her blow as due punishment, as his penance. "Don't just stand there lookin' stupid!"

"I didn't mean for this to happen. I swear to you. I didn't . . . I didn't want to hurt you. I didn't want to hurt her either."

And it was true; he hadn't wanted to hurt either one of them because he cared deeply for them both. But Mr. Theo had told him a while back that when you tried to please everybody, you inevitably would end up disappointing everyone. He now knew what the older man meant.

"You didn't want to hurt *her*?" she repeated in disbelief and then shook her head again bemusedly. "You're . . . you're in love with her, aren't you, Dee?"

A voice in his head told him to lie, to try to salvage whatever feelings Melissa may have left for him. If he lied good enough, fast enough, she might forgive him in the end. But he couldn't lie to her again. She deserved better than that, even if it meant losing her, so he nodded.

"Yes. Yes, I love her. But I love you too."

"Oh, God. Oh, my God," she whimpered, raising her hands to her temples, shaking her head in disbelief.

"I thought I could choose . . . but . . . but I can't. I can't, Lissa."

The tears began to spill then. She angrily wiped them away. "Fuck you, Dee!"

He watched helplessly as she returned to the bed and closed the zipper on her carry-on suitcase. She dropped it to the floor and rolled it past him, shoving him out of the way before she leaned down and grabbed Brownie's carrier.

"You know what? You don't have to choose between us. I've already made the decision for you."

She then walked down the hall to their front door, lugging her suitcase and carrier, and slammed the door shut behind her.

Chapter 17

Ricky

Ricky stared listlessly into his drink, not saying anything. Instead, he settled into the familiarity of the atmosphere. He and Derrick were at Ray's Bar and Lounge—a childhood hangout. It was comforting in some ways to be here tonight and he knew he didn't need to say anything. Derrick would do all the talking. After all, he was the one who had asked to meet up this evening. He wouldn't have done it if he didn't have something to get off of his chest, and judging from the story he'd just told, he had a lot to offload.

"I fucked up, right? I fucked up big, didn't I?" Derrick asked.

Ricky shrugged.

"I tried to talk to her while she was packing up her shit, but it didn't change anything," Derrick conceded as he took a drink from his beer bottle. "She left me. She even took Brownie with her. Took the damn cat. I just don't know where she went. She's not returning my phone calls."

Ricky didn't comment. Instead, he took another sip from his glass.

"I mean . . . I get it. I cheated. I'm in love with someone else, but I'm still in love with her too. I didn't want to lose her! But what do I do? What the hell do I do? I don't even know what . . ." His words drifted off as he squinted at Ricky. "Hey, are you listening?"

"What?" Ricky said absently, raising his eyes from his shot glass.

"I said are you even fuckin' listening? You're sitting over there lookin' bored. My whole world just fell apart and in the thirty minutes we've been here, you haven't said shit!"

Ricky loudly groused and slumped back against the booth cushion. He sucked his teeth. "Dee, your world is *always* fuckin' fallin' apart. You've always had some drama with Melissa. That shit never stops. It doesn't change! As a matter of fact, your fucked-up relationship is yet another reason why I don't *ever* wanna get serious with any broad. Who needs the headache?" Ricky coughed out a cold laugh and took another sip from his glass, letting the burning liquid slide down his throat. "Talkin' about 'I fucked up.' Yeah, you fucked up! You were fuckin' around on her with some other girl, and she found out about it. What do you expect?"

"I wasn't fuckin' around on her," Derrick clarified, twisting up his face. "Morgan and I never hooked up!"

"So you didn't put your dick in it—*yet*. Big damn deal! You told her you were in love with the other broad. That's worse than just fuckin' her! And Lissa caught you kissing her, bruh! The honest truth is that she should've left your ass! You left her with no choice. Shit, as far as I'm concerned, good for her! What was she supposed to do? Say, 'Yeah, Dee, I get you can't make a decision. I guess you can keep your side piece.' See how stupid that sounds? Stop being so goddamn selfish for once!"

"*The honest truth?*" Derrick's face went stony. "Oh, so we just being brutally honest now?"

"You told me to talk. Were you expecting me to just lie to you and tell you whatever the fuck you wanted to hear?"

"No, I didn't expect you to lie. But while we're being all honest, how about I break some shit down for you too?" He tilted his head. "You claim that everything that's happening to you is that chick Simone's fault, but let me tell you as an 'honest' friend—it ain't! You brought this shit on yourself. She was just an excuse! How many times did I tell you that you should've cut ties with Dolla? Huh? How many times did I warn you?"

"Oh, you're pissed about shit you did, so now you want to give me a fuckin' lecture?"

"Everybody knew what you were doin'!" Derrick continued, ignoring him. "We didn't snitch on your ass, but someone else was bound to do it eventually. It was only a matter of time. She just did that shit before anyone else could. So I'm not the only one who's getting what they deserve."

"I knew you were a selfish motherfucka, but I never took you for being a petty bitch-ass nigga too."

"Oh, I'm a bitch-ass nigga now?"

"Yeah!"

"I'm a bitch-ass nigga?"

"Did I stutter?"

"Fuck you, motherfucka!"

"Fuck you too!"

Derrick clenched his fists on the scarred tabletop. He looked like he wanted to punch Ricky in the face and probably would've done it if he'd had enough alcohol in him. In some ways, Ricky wanted his boy to hit him, then he could swing back at him. They could start brawling right here in Ray's, turning over tables, breaking glasses, and bashing Ray's dust-covered jukebox that only played 80s and 90s hits. If they fought, Ricky could finally unleash all the anger and sense of helplessness he'd felt for the past three and a half months. He would finally have an outlet.

But Derrick didn't take a swing. His face abruptly softened. He relaxed his clenched hands.

"Shit. I'm sorry, man." He lowered his head. "I didn't mean to lash out at you like that. I didn't mean that shit about Simone."

"Yes, you did."

"Okay, I meant it. But not in the way I said it. And you're right. I was being selfish . . . I mean, I *am* being selfish. I do make it about me a lot of times and I don't mean to do that. I realize you've been going through shit too, and your shit is a lot bigger than what I'm going through. I know you're worried about your business and your criminal charge, and with Simone going M.I.A., I know it's—"

Ricky let out another cynical laugh and finished off his drink. He slammed the shot glass back on the table, giving a deranged grin as he did it, making his friend go silent. "Dee, believe it or not, that shit is the least of my concerns right now." He wiped his mouth with the back of his hand. "I've got bigger issues, bruh."

Derrick frowned. "What bigger issues?"

Ricky blew air out of his inflated cheeks and glanced around the bar. With the exception of Ray and one elderly man nursing a drink at the counter, he and Derrick were the only people in that joint. No one would hear or care about their conversation. So if he finally told Derrick the truth—all the gory details—he didn't have to worry about it coming back to haunt him. Plus, he had kept his secret for so long, he was getting crushed under the weight of it. When he closed his eyes he still saw Tamika and her panicked, beseeching gaze as she twisted in Melvin's arms. It might give him some relief to finally talk about all of it, to share the burden with someone else.

"Before I start, I'm gonna need a refill," he said, holding his glass in the air and making eye contact with Ray.

Ray paused mid-conversation with the old-timer at the counter to nod. He then grabbed a bottle of Jim Beam bourbon whiskey, walked from behind the counter, and poured some into Ricky's empty glass.

"Thanks, Ray," he murmured.

"No problem," Ray replied before tucking a toothpick into his mouth and walking back to the bar.

"Okay, you've got your drink," Derrick said, pointing to his glass. "What did you wanna tell me?

Ricky raised the glass to his lips and took a drink. "I never told you everything that happened the night and the morning after the raids. I told you that I got arrested. That they took me into some little-ass room for questioning. But I didn't tell you . . . I didn't tell you how I got out of there."

"You said your lawyer got you out."

"He did." Ricky nodded. "But only by working out a deal with the cops. They said they would reduce the charges against me if . . . if I helped them. If I became . . . if I became an informant."

Derrick's eyes widened. He almost spit out his beer, but caught himself. "You're not serious, right?" he asked, choking down his drink.

"You think I'm joking? They want to know who Dolla's suppliers are, who's the next level up from him on the drug totem pole. They want me to find out, but so far, I haven't found out shit—and I don't know if I ever will. Meanwhile, I keep having to prove to Dolla that I'm still on his team, that I've got his back. He made me go to this girl's house to find out some shit for him." Ricky closed his eyes, once again trying to erase the memory of her and that day. "He told me we were only going there to talk to her, Dee. And dumb-ass me, I believed him. I believed him up until one of his men killed her." Ricky opened his eyes again.

"Shit, man." Derrick grimaced. "I thought you had been kinda quiet lately but I had . . . I had no idea why. I never thought . . ." His words drifted off.

"I told the cops what happened," Ricky continued. "I told them he's hunting down all the girls who used to work for him and picking them off one by one. I told them I saw one of the girls get taken out with my own eyes, and you know what those motherfuckas told me?" He took another drink and swallowed. " 'Not my problem.' They said that wasn't their fuckin' problem so it wasn't mine either. They said if those women wanted protection, they should've helped the prosecution so they could get police guards or some shit. They said I should focus on what I'm there for and not worry about those girls." He shook his head. "I can't do this shit anymore, Dee. All this lying, and now I have to just stand there, watching people get killed. This shit is gonna drive me crazy."

Derrick didn't say anything. What could he say? There was no advice he could offer, no way he could tell Ricky how to get out of his situation short of Ricky telling the cops the deal was off and going to jail. But that was pretty much a death sentence. The cops would be sure to tell Dolla Dolla or his men what Ricky had done, how he had been double-crossing him all these months. It would be faster to put a bullet in his own head.

Ricky finished his second glass and shoved it aside. He reached into his back pocket, pulled out his wallet, and put twenty dollars on the table. "Look, man, we should get going. We're both just sitting here feeling sorry for ourselves. We're worrying over shit that we have no control over. What's done is done, right?"

Derrick nodded solemnly. "What's done is done."

Ricky returned to his Mercedes five minutes later. He had a slight buzz but he wasn't drunk. He planned when he got home to drink a lot more, until he blacked out and fell into empty dreams—the only place where he could find true solace. As he pulled on the door handle, his cell began to buzz. He ignored it, opened the door, and climbed onto the driver's seat. As he put his key into the ignition, his phone buzzed again and he pulled it out of his pocket. He stared at the screen and cursed under his breath.

Once again, it was a number he didn't recognize. He wondered if it was the same person who had been calling him for months, breathing on the line, then hanging up.

"Look," he said, pressing the green button, "I'm not up to this shit tonight, so either finally fucking say something or stop calling me!"

"H-hello?" a voice answered fearfully. It sounded like an elderly woman. "I'm sorry, but can I speak to Malcolm?"

"Who the fuck is Malcolm?" Ricky shouted.

So is that the reason he kept getting these damn calls? Because these people were trying to reach a guy named Malcolm?

"I'm so sorry. I must have the wrong number," she said. "I was trying to reach the young man who came a while back to Nadine Fuller's home. He said he was there to deliver a package for a gift she'd ordered, but she wasn't home. This was the number he gave me, but maybe I'm . . . I'm reading it wrong. I . . . I don't have my reading glasses on."

"Ms. Sawyer?" he said, suddenly remembering the woman's name. He recalled her now. She was Nadine Fuller's neighbor, the randy old lady who lived next door.

"Yes! That's me. So . . . so is this Malcolm?" she asked.

"Yeah . . . uh, yeah it is," Ricky said, sitting upright in his seat. "I'm sorry, ma'am. I was a little confused for a second. I was in a crowded restaurant, but I stepped out. I misheard you, but I can hear you clearly now."

"Oh, that's quite all right, honey. I understand. I just called to tell you that I finally heard from Nadine. She came back yesterday to pack up her house and she gave me her address to send the rest of her things that she couldn't take with her in the truck. About an hour after she pulled off, I remembered that you had come looking for her about a month ago. I thought, wouldn't it be a wonderful surprise if you could bring Nadine her package. Do you have a pen so you can write down the address, honey?"

Ricky blinked. After all this time, the trail leading to Simone, which had been cold for months, had finally gotten warm again. No, scratch that. The trail had gotten scorching hot. He quickly forgot about his depression, about his misgivings, and his sense of loss of control. He finally had a sense of purpose again.

"Yes! Yes, ma'am. I have a pen," he said, frantically reaching for his glove compartment. "Go ahead and give me the address."

Chapter 18

Jamal

Jamal knew he was a dead man walking. He had been for the past several days, but only he knew the truth.

The worst part was he felt like he'd had his head stuck in the guillotine all this time, but he still didn't know when the blade would fall. He didn't know on what day he would grab a copy of *The Washington Post* or *Washington Recorder* and find a story about himself in the metro section. He sat down at his office desk each day, waiting for the moment when someone would send an email with a link to a tawdry blog post containing blurry pictures of himself snorting cocaine or having a threesome with AnnaLee and Star.

But each day passed and then the next—and nothing happened. It had been almost a full week, but still there were no salacious news stories. No blog posts.

So he waited. He tried to act normal. He went to meetings and met with constituents and council members. He took phone calls and wrote emails. He kept his distance from the mayor, who seemed to watch him like a hunter would his prey every time they crossed paths, which was more frequent than Jamal would have liked. Jamal wondered what was taking Mayor Johnson so long to do what he'd threatened to do. Why hadn't he exposed him yet? Did the mayor enjoy torturing him, having Jamal endure one sleepless night after the next? Did he take some morbid pleasure in watching him squirm?

Jamal awoke when his alarm clock sounded after yet another night filled with long hours of tossing and turning. He tiredly pushed himself up from his bed and staggered into the bathroom. When he turned on the overhead lights, he winced. He didn't bother to glance at his reflection. He knew there would be bags under his eyes and his face would look almost gaunt with fatigue. He knew that he'd have the look of a man who was enduring hell and had no idea when he would finally be put out of his misery.

Jamal took a shower, brushed his teeth, shaved, and emerged out of the bathroom about thirty minutes later. When he walked into his bedroom, he reached for the remote and turned on the morning news before slipping on a pair of boxer briefs and making his way to his closet to grab one of his suits—a single-breasted gray number he'd worn before. He tossed the suit onto his bed along with a silk tie and walked toward his dresser to find a shirt and a pair of socks. Out of the corner of his eye, he saw a picture flash on the television screen as he yanked open one of the dresser drawers. Jamal paused and turned slightly so that he could get a better view of his flat screen. When he did, his mouth fell open. His socks tumbled from his hand to the bedroom rug.

On the screen was a smiling photo of Phillip Seymour from the *Washington Recorder*, the one that usually ran next to his byline in the newspaper. Below his photo was his name and the caption, "Murder Victim," in stark white letters. Jamal rushed around his bed to grab the remote again and turn up the volume as a news anchor came on-screen.

"The murder occurred soon after Mr. Seymour had arrived home last night, according to police. Neighbors who spoke with Channel 7 news said they heard shouting prior to the gun shots but did not see the assailant. Police are investigating the homicide but still have no leads as to who could have committed the crime."

Then a montage of other photos of Phillip scrolled on-screen. One of him in a T-shirt, wearing a whistle around his neck while standing next to a young boy in a soccer uniform. One of him with his arms thrown around the shoulders of two other men while he smiled almost drunkenly at the camera while wearing an ugly Christmas sweater. One of him kneeling next to a slobbering Saint Bernard.

Jamal struggled to remember if Phillip ever mentioned if he was married. Had he worn a wedding ring? Did he have kids?

"Oh, my God," he whispered.

The anchor appeared on-screen again. His dark face went solemn.

"We at Channel 7, as fellow journalists and colleagues of Mr. Seymour's, would like to offer our sincere condolences to his family and friends. He will be greatly missed."

Jamal fell back onto the mattress, still staring dumbly at the flat-screen TV even as the broadcast gave way to a booming car commercial. He could feel himself going numb.

He sat on the edge of his bed for several minutes, unable to move or articulate a single word.

* * *

When Jamal arrived at the Wilson Building, he didn't stop for coffee or go to his office. Instead, he went straight down the hall to Mayor Johnson's suite.

"Umm, excuse me, Mr. Lighty," Johnson's secretary, Gladys, called to him as he stormed past her desk. "Excuse me, Mr. Lighty, but Mr. Johnson is taking an important call right now. You'll have to—"

"I don't give a shit!" he called over his shoulder.

He didn't look back at her, but he could hear her audibly gasp in response. He didn't care if he'd just upset her delicate sensibilities, nor did he give a damn that he was interrupting the mayor's little phone call; he had to talk to him *right now.*

He turned the knob, shoved open the office door, and found the mayor sitting with his back to the door. The mayor was laughing on the phone and gazing out his office window at the busy city street below. When he heard the door fly open then slam shut, he slowly turned around and faced Jamal.

"Get off the phone," Jamal ordered.

"I really don't know if that would work with the schedule we've been given," Johnson said into his headset, still smiling and keeping a watchful eye on Jamal as he spoke. "A timeline like that would be very aggressive."

"I said," Jamal whispered as he drew closer to the desk, "get off the damn phone. Do it, or I will call the cops, right now!"

"Hey, Bill," Johnson said to whoever was on the other end of the phone line, "can I call you back? Something just popped up . . . No. Nothing serious . . . Give me fifteen minutes . . . Yep! I certainly will . . . Talk to you soon."

He then lowered the headset from his ear and put it back in its cradle. He leaned back in his leather chair, interlocked his fingers, and cocked an eyebrow. "Can I help you?"

"*Can you help me?* Can you fucking help me?" Jamal almost squeaked, cringing even as he repeated the words. He braced his hands on the edge of Johnson's desk and glared down at him. "You killed him, you son of a bitch! You killed him!"

"Killed who? You're acting hysterical, Jamal. I have no idea what you're talking about," the older man said, feigning innocence.

"Stop lying! You know exactly who and what I'm talking about, and you know what you did. I told you . . . I *told* you to leave him out of it! I told you to do whatever you wanted with those pictures of me. That's what I said! Why . . . *why* would you have him killed anyway?" Jamal asked desperately.

The mayor stayed silent for several seconds. Finally, he shrugged. "Because you called my bluff."

"*What?*"

"I said, you called my bluff." The mayor rolled his eyes heavenward. "There were never any pictures, Jamal. I just wanted to make you *think* I had them so you'd have more of a motive to cover your own ass."

"You were bluffing?" Jamal said as the blood drained from his head.

"Yes, and I'm usually very good at bluffing and playing poker, in general. I can figure out what cards my opponent likely holds based on certain tells. So many people are so easy to read and unaware of it, but I misjudged you, Jamal. You seemed like an insecure, shallow, self-aggrandizing young man who would rather die than have his public image tainted, let alone destroyed. I thought you would try even harder to keep that reporter quiet if I made that threat about releasing those photos. But instead, you did the opposite. You were willing to walk away . . . no, you were willing to fall on your own sword in order to save someone else." He tilted his head. "You're more noble than I thought."

Jamal wished there was a chair behind him. He felt as if he might faint, like his knees might buckle underneath him, so he continued to grip the mayor's desk instead.

"It's unfortunate that you were unable to convince your friend to let go of his little story. This is not something I was eager to pursue, Jamal. I take these matters very seriously."

"Fuck you!" Jamal barked. "Fuck you, you psychopath."

The mayor grumbled loudly. "I understand that you're angry, and that's something you'll have to work through. I would be angry too, if I brought a situation like this upon myself and those around me. But eventually, you will have to move on and see the wisdom in what I did. It's one of those hard decisions that a leader must make."

"You didn't have to do it! You could've spared him, and now . . . and now . . ." Jamal said, at a loss for words.

"I told you in the beginning that this is not a game. Mr. Seymour found that out the hard way."

"I quit," Jamal choked, feeling tears of frustration and sorrow well in his eyes. "I quit. And I'm going to the police. I'm going to tell them you're behind this. I'm gonna tell them ev—"

"I don't accept your resignation and you will not go to the police. You can be noble, but don't be stupid. You know what would happen if you did that."

Jamal quieted. His throat tightened. He had wanted this: the power and prestige. He had wanted to stand at Mayor Johnson's right side—and he was getting exactly what he'd asked for and all the burdens that came with it.

"You've learned a hard lesson today. I hope that you fall in line so that you don't have to endure something similar to what Mr. Seymour had to experience. And that, Jamal, is not a bluff—it is a promise."

Jamal was sick to his stomach. He took one unsteady step back from the mayor's desk, then another. He felt like he was sinking into quicksand. When he reached the office door he gripped the door handle with a shaky hand. He turned back around to say something more, but found that the mayor had already picked up his phone again. He was already dialing a number.

"Hey, Bill! I'm back."

The son of a bitch was actually grinning ear to ear.

"Yeah," the mayor continued, "that didn't take as long as I'd expected. Now what were we talking about again?"

Jamal bowed his head, opened the door, and made a hasty retreat.

Chapter 19

Derrick

Derrick arrived back at his apartment, unlocked the door, and gazed inside apprehensively.

He'd tried to be as far away as possible while Melissa packed the last of her things and finished moving out of their apartment. He didn't want to be witness to all the boxes, trash bags, and chaos. Two decades' worth of a relationship and five years of living together would take some time to sort through and haul away. So he had run errands, lingering longer than necessary, giving her all the time he thought she might need. But judging from all the racket he heard from inside their apartment and boxes that were stacked around, she might have needed another hour or two.

"You can put those in there," he heard her say as he stepped inside and quietly shut the door behind him. "Thanks, Mo."

Melissa's best friend, Bina, and Bina's husband, Maurice, were helping her move out. Who knew that the couple they used to double date with would now be bearing witness to the end of their relationship.

Derrick watched Maurice place a stack of bubble-wrapped dishes into a box before taping the lid closed. He hadn't known Melissa was going to take all their dishes, but then again, he wasn't going to stop her either. Whatever she wanted to take, she could have; he wouldn't fight her for it.

Just then, Maurice's son, Melissa's godson, came toddling into the living room, waving one of Melissa's notebooks in the air and letting out high-pitched squeals. The baby had just turned one year old and only started walking about a month ago, but whenever he did it, he seemed to do it at a near run. He was running today too. He ran smack dab into Melissa's leg, making her laugh.

"What are you doing?" she asked, scooping the baby up in her arms, making him squeal even more. "What are you doing, little man? You stealing my stuff? You stealing my stuff?"

At the sight of her holding and tickling her godson, Derrick's heart ached a little. He'd thought that she might be holding their child one day, that after years of promising to start a family, they would finally do it. But that hope was lost now.

Derrick stepped into the foyer and peered into the living room. "Almost done?" he asked, and both Maurice and Melissa whipped around to face him.

Melissa didn't respond. She looked away from Derrick, like she couldn't stand the sight of him. She ignored him and continued to murmur to her godson.

Maurice glanced up at her, then at Derrick. Gradually, he nodded. "Yeah, we almost done. Just a few more boxes

I gotta pack up and load in the truck. We'll be out of here in about a half hour."

Derrick nodded and stood awkwardly in the center of the living room. He shoved his hands into the pockets of his jeans. "Do you . . . do you need any help loading anything?"

"Nope! Not a damn thing," a female voice answered.

Derrick turned and saw Bina striding down the hallway. She was almost the mirror image of Melissa—same height, same show-stopping beauty, and same damn attitude, which was on full display today.

"Hey, Bee," he mumbled.

"Hello, Derrick. I thought you weren't gonna be here," Bina said, tossing her curly hair over her shoulder and cocking an eyebrow.

"Bina," Melissa said warningly, rubbing her godson's back as he babbled.

"*What?*" Bina cried, playing innocent. "I just thought that he'd be scarce today considering everything. I'd think a low-down dirty cheater who broke my girl's heart would have other things to do. Don't you have some chick you could hang out with? Some slipping and sliding you could be doing right now?"

Maurice started to look uncomfortable. "Baby, come on . . ."

"No, it's okay, Mo," Derrick said, holding up his hand. "I deserve it." He then faced Bina again, who was now glaring up at him. "Yes, Bee, I am a low-down dirty cheater, and the truth is, I hadn't planned to be here. Lissa's text said you guys should be done by five so I came back at five thirty."

"Well, you can see we're not done yet so . . . *bye!*" She then pointed to the front door.

His jaw tightened in frustration. Was she really trying to kick him out of his own apartment? His eyes drifted to Melissa. This time she didn't look away from him. Would she insist that he could stay, or did she want him to leave too?

She opened her mouth like she was about to say something, but stopped short when Bina strolled to her and took the baby, propping him on her hip. She then grabbed Melissa's hand.

"Come on, girl," Bina said, "I need your help in the bedroom. We have the last bit of stuff to sort through."

Melissa broke her gaze with his and nodded. She then followed Bina across the living room, walking right past Derrick, not saying a word.

He watched helplessly as both women walked back down the hall to the bedroom, shutting the door behind them. He closed his eyes.

"Sorry, Dee," Maurice said. "I know she was dragging you. Bee's just . . . she's just standing up for her friend, you know?"

"I know." He opened his eyes again. "Look, tell Lissa to text me when y'all are done, okay?"

"Okay," Maurice said.

Derrick turned around, walked back to the front door, and shut it behind him just as Maurice ripped off another strip of tape.

Thirty minutes later, he stepped through the front door of the Institute. It was the weekend and almost evening time. Most of the boys were in the cafeteria, or on the basketball court enjoying what little sun was left before they had to return to the dormitories. He still hadn't gotten the text from Melissa that she had left their apartment, so he figured he'd hang out here until he got the all clear.

Might as well finish up on some work, he thought as he pushed the door open to the stairwell.

As he stepped inside, he heard banging and clanging coming from the basement floor. Instead of heading upstairs, he turned and headed a flight below, in search of the source of the noise. The boys knew they shouldn't be in any of the classrooms afterhours. Whoever was making the noise, he'd have to tell them that whatever they were doing had to stop.

When Derrick entered the basement, he followed the sounds, which led him to the workshop. He looked through the glass window and saw Morgan standing at one of the work tables, banging a sheet of copper with a hammer. He leaned against the door frame, watching for a few minutes as she worked, blissfully unaware of his presence.

"Didn't expect to find you here on a Saturday," he called out to her.

Melissa jumped in surprise. She dropped the hammer, yanked off her protective goggles, and stared at him. "Didn't expect to see you here either."

He strolled into the workshop, inhaling the smell of sawdust and oil stain. "Had to get out of the apartment for a while. Wanted to give Lissa some space."

At the mention of Melissa's name, Morgan's face flushed beet red. She lowered her eyes back to the sheet of metal she'd been working on. "Well, I guess you guys will work it out eventually," she murmured, tugging at her work gloves. "No worries."

"I doubt it. She gave me back my engagement ring. She's moving out. That's why I'm here. She doesn't want me there while she's packing up her stuff."

The workshop fell silent. Morgan bit down on her bottom lip. "I guess you're expecting me to apologize for kissing you, but I'm not. If you two are breaking up, that's on you, Derrick."

"Why should you apologize?" he asked, taking another step forward. "I kissed you too. I didn't tell you no. I'd been wanting to do it for a long time. I've wanted you for a long time, Morgan."

Her eyes shot up from the sheet metal. She quickly shook her head and waved her hand dismissively. "You say that now. But that's only because she's moving out . . . because she's leaving you. You don't have any other choice."

"No, I had another choice. I could've kept lying to her, but I didn't. I finally told Melissa the full truth."

Morgan narrowed her eyes. "Which is?"

"That I'm in love with you, and I couldn't put my feelings for you behind me, even though I wanted to. Even though I knew it might mean the end of a relationship I've had since I was twelve years old."

She stilled. "You told her you're in love with me?"

He nodded and she blanched. She licked her lips and he swore that he wanted to kiss her all over again.

"I don't . . . I don't know what I'm supposed to say to all of this, Derrick."

"You don't have to say anything," he replied with a shrug. "I'm just telling you the truth like I told her the truth. I'm tired of lying."

He could tell he had just hit her with an emotional wallop. It was a lot to take in.

"Look," he said, backing away from her, "I didn't mean to drop all of this on you now—especially out of nowhere. I'll head upstairs and let you get back to your work, okay?"

She didn't respond.

He turned on his heel and headed back toward the workshop door.

"Derrick!" she called out from behind him.

When he turned back around, she leapt at him, pressing her body and her mouth against his, kissing him for dear life.

Chapter 20

Ricky

Ricky sat with his back braced against a fallen tree trunk during the early dawn hours, sipping coffee from his paper cup, gazing at the house twenty yards in front of him. He wondered if he was in the right place. He glanced down at the sheet of paper in his hand, at the address Ms. Sawyer had given him. Then he glanced at the number posted on the wooden sign at the end of the crude gravel driveway. He tucked the sheet of paper back into his pocket and slapped absently at a mosquito buzzing around his ear. The numbers matched.

So this was it. This was the house where Simone likely lived now, though it looked so rustic that he expected some hillbilly with a banjo to amble onto the wooden front porch, not the sophisticated woman who had stolen his heart and betrayed him back in D.C. The house sat in the center of a three-acre property filled with grass, weeds, two-foot-tall shrubs, and even cornstalks on each side. It was set off from the main road about a quarter of a mile. He knew because he had parked along that road, behind a large thicket of bushes that obscured his Mercedes, and walked the rest of the distance to the house.

The two-story home was badly in need of a new coat of paint and the roof looked like it needed some work too. He still found it hard to believe that Simone lived here, of all places, but at around nine a.m. he saw the screen door open and a young woman walked onto the porch. He raised the binoculars he'd brought with him and saw the young woman looked very familiar. It wasn't Simone, but her little sister, Skylar.

The young woman looked a lot better now than when he'd last seen her back at Dolla Dolla's place. She didn't look emaciated anymore; she was back to a healthy weight. Her long, curly hair was shorter, but no longer looked stringy and pasted to her scalp. He bet she'd been to rehab. He bet Simone had done everything in her power to help her sister get better.

She always put her first, he thought bitterly.

He watched as Skylar tugged her oversized sweater tightly around her, then pulled a pack of cigarettes and a lighter from one of the pockets before sitting down in a swing chair. She then began to smoke, staring off in the distance. She did so for a couple minutes before tossing her cigarette off the porch, rising to her feet, and walking back inside, letting the screen door slam behind her.

He wondered how long it would take for him to finally get a glimpse of Simone. After all, it was her he wanted to see, after driving two hundred miles and risking the ire of the Metro Police if they realized he was no longer in town. He wanted to see her. He *had* to see her.

Several hours later, his limbs were stiff from crouching so long behind bushes, and the mosquito bites were itching like crazy. It began to drizzle and Ricky started to rise to his feet and make the quarter-mile trek back to his car when he heard the creak of the screen door as it opened yet again. He instantly dropped to his knees, crouching again on the cold, wet dirt. He zoomed in on the front door through the binocular lenses.

Simone was wearing a billowing poncho and matching galoshes. She'd grown her hair out from the blunt cut he remembered and now let fat curls fall along her brow and ears. She swept one out of her eyes as she walked. She was still gorgeous, but she also looked different for some reason. He didn't know if his anger had skewed his memories of her, but he didn't remember her face being so round and soft. She looked almost radiant. Even her cheeks glowed. He watched as she paused to peer up at the rainy sky.

"Simone," he whispered, expecting to feel a rush of fury now that he was finally seeing her in person after all this time.

This was the person who had ruined his life, who had caused his restaurant and freedom to be taken away. She had left him with no choice but to become a police informant to protect his own hide after she had made him the scapegoat for everything. But at the sight of her, Ricky went numb. He didn't feel rage or sadness or even disappointment. He was in a state of shock, like he was watching a ghost manifest and float in front of him.

Ricky had stayed true to his word; he'd even brought his Glock 43 with him with a loaded magazine. It was tucked into the waistband of his jeans. He'd told himself that he'd come here to use it, to finally take revenge for what she had done to him. But now, he could feel that self-righteous fervor seeping out of him like a deflating balloon.

Did he really want to kill her? Was he ready to pull the trigger? Now was certainly his chance to do it.

He watched as Simone tugged the hood of her brightly colored poncho over her head and strolled to a pickup truck that was parked under a metal carport. All he had to do was rise to his feet again, run the distance between them, aim the gun at her head, and pull the trigger. He could get off a few shots and be back in the dense woods before Skylar or her mother would even realize they'd heard gunshots outside the house. But Ricky stayed frozen; he couldn't move.

Simone reached the pickup and hoisted herself into the driver's seat. She closed the door behind her and turned on the engine. A few seconds later, she drove down the driveway, bumping over mud and gravel. If she had glanced to her left, she would have seen him a few feet away on bended knee, staring up at her, utterly mesmerized.

The entire time, he didn't reach for his gun—not once.

The fuck, he thought with disgust as he watched her truck disappear behind a line of trees, as whatever spell he had been under released its grip on him. *What the fuck is wrong with me?*

He had come here on a mission, and instead he'd stood there with his head up his ass.

Face it. You just don't have it in you to be a killer, my man, a voice in his head taunted.

Derrick had told him that though Ricky had committed many crimes in his life, murder would never be one of them—the main reason being that he wasn't capable of taking a life. Ricky had gotten an inkling of that when he watched Dolla Dolla's bodyguard take out that girl. Now he had a sinking feeling that Derrick was indeed right.

But she deserves this shit, he thought as he trudged back to his car and the drizzle switched to a downpour, making him blink water out of his eyes. Unlike that poor girl whom Melvin had killed, Simone deserved what was about to come to her. And he wouldn't be deterred from what he had to do.

He drove back to town, ate lunch at a rest stop, and lingered before returning to her house at around sunset. He sat in the bushes for hours and waited until well after dark before he decided to make his move. When the clock struck midnight and the lights inside went out, he crept through the woods and around the perimeter of the house until he reached the rear. He waited for the growl of a guard dog or even a motion detection light to come on, but he heard and saw neither.

Not smart, Simone, he thought with an inward shake of the head as he carefully mounted the wooden stairs of the back porch.

For a woman who had packed all her things, abruptly left town, and was obviously trying to stay hidden, she was making a lot of mistakes. But Simone must have assumed if no one had found her and Skylar after all this time, they were safe. Her missteps could work in his favor.

He opened the back screen door a few inches and it loudly creaked, making him wince. He paused and looked up, expecting the shade on one of the back windows to fly open and for either Simone or Skylar to peer down into the dark. But no shade went up. Nothing happened. So he opened the door farther and stepped onto the porch. As he drew near the back entrance of the house, he thought he could hear through one of the open windows the faint sound of a television laugh track.

Had one of them left the television on while she slept, or was someone in the house still awake?

He considered for minute or two whether it would be better to wait until they were fast asleep, and then heard a crack of thunder overhead, signaling that another storm was well on its way. He couldn't stand on the back porch all night, and he didn't want to have to walk in a downpour again. And every hour he stayed in Virginia, the more he felt like he was leaving tracks and traces of himself behind that the police could find later.

No, he had to do it now. If it meant taking them all out, so be it.

You couldn't shoot one when you had the chance, and now you think you're going to kill all of them? Yeah, okay, the voice in his head mocked.

"Shut up," he murmured aloud before reaching for the door handle and turning it. As expected, the handle didn't budge. The door was locked. But he had come prepared. He pulled his lock-pick set from his back pocket, a keepsake from the old days before he had stopped doing odd jobs for Dolla Dolla and had gone full legit. He knelt down in the dim light from upstairs and began to work. It took twenty minutes—much longer than it would've taken in the old days—but he finally got the lock open. He turned the knob and slowly eased the door open. That's when he heard the piercing beep.

"Shit," he muttered.

So Simone hadn't been that stupid, after all. She had an alarm system, even in this rusty glorified shack.

He dropped the door handle, shot to his feet, and turned to make a run for it. He'd made it only three steps when he felt something sharp and metallic jab into the center of his back, and he dropped his lock-picking kit to the grass.

"Don't move. Don't you take another fucking step, or I will fire and you won't be able to walk again!" he heard Simone shout from behind him. "You hear me?"

Ricky followed her order, halting in his steps.

I fucked this up good.

"Now raise your hands into the air—slowly—and turn around to face me! And do it carefully . . . no sudden moves. Don't try anything stupid, because you're messing with the wrong bitch!"

Ricky squinted. Simone was using her "police-officer

voice"; she didn't sound like she knew it was him. Maybe she couldn't see him that well on the dark porch.

Or maybe I'm nothing to her anymore. Out of sight, out of mind.

"What's happening, SeeSee? What's wrong?" Skylar shouted over the sound of the alarm, sounding frightened.

"Stay inside!" Simone yelled.

"What?"

"I said stay inside! Turn off the alarm and call the police, okay?" He heard what he surmised was the cocking of a shotgun. She then roughly jabbed him again in the back a second later. "Didn't you hear me, asshole? I told you to raise your hands and turn the fuck around!"

He slowly raised his hands and turned around to face her. He watched as she reached out and flicked on a switch, lighting up the back porch. When she did, her eyes widened. Her mouth went slack. She dropped her shotgun to her side.

"Ricky?" she squeaked just as the sound of the house alarm finally died. "Oh, my God! What . . . what are you doing here?"

He couldn't respond. His mouth fell open in shock too.

Ricky suddenly realized why Simone's face had looked so much rounder and softer when he'd seen her walking to her truck earlier, why she had practically glowed. He hadn't seen it while she was wearing the big poncho, but he could clearly see it now.

There Simone stood, barefoot, wearing a pale blue cotton tank dress that pulled tight over her full breasts and round stomach. She had to be about five to six months pregnant, based on her protruding belly.

"The fuck," he whispered with furrowed brows, staring down at her.

"SeeSee, I turned off the alarm!" Skylar shouted as she

ran to the back door. "I couldn't hear what you were . . ." Her words drifted off and she skidded to a halt when she spotted Ricky standing on the back porch. "Who's . . . who's that?"

"It's Ricky," Simone said with a smile, glancing over her shoulder at her sister. "He's the one I told you about . . . the one who helped get you out."

Skylar frowned. "*He is?*"

They had met before but she'd been high as a kite each time they'd spoken. He wasn't surprised she didn't recognize him now.

"Ricky," Simone said, setting her shotgun against the door frame and leaping at him, catching him off guard as she wrapped her arms around him. "Damn, I missed you," she whispered against his shoulder, holding him close.

He didn't even attempt to hug her back. He was too astounded to move.

"Have a seat," Simone said, gesturing to one of the chairs at their kitchen table. She then grabbed a sweater off the back of one of the chairs and put it on as she strolled to the refrigerator.

Ricky's eyes kept drifting to the elephant in the room— Simone's swollen stomach that she rubbed absently as she walked. Ricky closed his eyes and slowly opened them again, like her pregnancy was some drug-induced delusion. It must have been, since no one seemed to be acknowledging it, like he was the only one seeing this thing. He watched her swing open the refrigerator door and peer inside.

"Did you want something to drink? Are you hungry?" Simone asked, turning to him.

"Why the hell are you offering him food when you caught him trying to break into our house?" Skylar yelled.

"He wasn't trying to break in, Skylar."

Actually, I was, Ricky thought but didn't say the words aloud. He was still too muddled to speak. He felt like he'd just stumbled into some alternate universe.

How the hell was she pregnant, and why was he just finding out about this? Had she known about this before she moved out of the city? Had she ever planned to tell him? Was the baby even his?

"Yes, he was!" Skylar shouted, snapping his thoughts back to the present. "He'd even gotten the lock open. Why didn't he just knock on the front door if he wasn't trying to break in?"

"I did knock on the front door," he lied, finally snapping out of his malaise, making both women turn toward him.

"I didn't hear any damn door," Skylar snapped.

He shrugged. "You two were asleep."

"I wasn't asleep," Skylar argued. "I was awake, watching TV!"

"Then maybe the TV was too loud, but I *did* knock. That's why I came to the back of the house to knock on that door. I thought you might hear me then."

"You came to the back of the house . . . to knock?" Skylar asked, her face a billboard of incredulity.

He nodded, feeling the lies tumble from his mouth. He knew with a tale this ridiculous, he had to sell it well. "I knocked more than once. I even banged on the window. I tried the door handle and the door was open. I poked my head in and that's when the alarm went off."

"Oh, that's some bullshit! I locked that door before I went to my room! I do every night," Skylar insisted.

"The door was open," he said firmly.

"He's lying, SeeSee!"

Simone's eyes shifted between the two of them. He could see the doubt growing in her. She slowly shut the refrigerator door. She rubbed her stomach again. He wondered how often she did that nowadays.

"It must be some . . . some kind of mistake, some misunderstanding," Simone began. "Ricky tried more than once to *save* you. He wouldn't—"

"Look, I get what he did back then, and I appreciate it. But—"

"You sure as hell aren't acting like you appreciate it," he grumbled.

"But," Skylar repeated, speaking over him, "I don't know why he's here now, or what he planned to do. That's the issue! We should call the police. Remember, there is too much at stake now! We promised each other that we would—"

"I came here to warn you," he interjected. "*That's* the reason I'm here! I came to warn you about Dolla. He's looking for Skylar. He's looking for all the girls. He's already taken out a couple of them, and she's next on his list."

Both women fell silent.

"It took a lot for me to find y'all. It wasn't like I could just look you up online. I drove two hundred miles to do this. I'm risking my life—*again*, and I could go to jail—*again*, if the cops find out I'm here. But I did it anyway." He waited a beat, hoping he was putting on a master performance. "So excuse me for not knocking on the damn door loud enough to get your attention!"

Skylar lowered her eyes. Simone walked toward him.

"I'm sorry, Ricky. I know you're risking a lot by coming here, and thank you for telling us." She glanced back at Skylar. "We'd expected that Dolla would come looking for her. That's why we left . . . why we moved out here to get some . . . some sense of security."

"But *he* found us anyway," Skylar snapped. "Doesn't feel so secure anymore!"

Simone side-eyed her sister. "And excuse Skylar. She doesn't mean to be hostile, but you can understand why she's tense. Right? These have been a hard four months for us."

"Yeah, well . . . it's been a hard four months for me too."

Simone pursed her lips and nodded. For the first time, she looked shamefaced. "I know. I know." She reached out and rubbed his shoulder, touching him and catching him off guard yet again. "Look, it's late. You've probably been on the road for a while and should get some rest. Why don't I show you to one of the rooms?"

"*What?*" Skylar exclaimed. Her eyes snapped up. "He can't sleep here, SeeSee! That's just—"

"Yes, he can and he will," Simone said, glaring at her little sister. "Mom's not home. He can sleep in her room. That is, if . . . if he wants to." She stared up at him.

Ricky considered her offer, marveling at how things had shifted so rapidly in the past half hour. He had come here to kill Simone. Not only had he not done that and probably wouldn't likely do it now, knowing she was pregnant, she was now offering him a room to stay in overnight, like she was throwing a damn sleepover. The whole situation felt so insane that he wanted to turn on his heel and just walk out of this bizarre *Twilight Zone* episode he was obviously starring in. But instead, he shrugged.

"Sure. Whatever. I'll stay," he muttered, making Skylar silently grouse and Simone smile.

"Come on! I'll show you to your room."

Chapter 21

Ricky

Ricky trailed behind Simone down a darkened hallway and watched as she flicked on a light switch and opened up a narrow door, revealing a small closet filled with stacks of towels and blankets.

"We pulled all the sheets and did the laundry today, so I need to grab some fresh sheets for the bed," she said, rifling through a pile, tugging out a few cotton sheets and gathering them in her arms. "I don't think Mom put one on before she left to go visit her sister."

She gave him an awkward smile. Ricky didn't return it.

He was still feeling overwhelmed by a dozen emotions all at once. His brain's synapses were firing a thousand messages and it was a struggle to even understand what she was saying. Meanwhile, she was acting like a damn hostess at a bed and breakfast, like she hadn't been pointing a shotgun at him less than ten minutes ago.

Simone kept walking until she reached the end of the hall and pushed open yet another door, revealing a small bedroom with a cedar night table, single desk lamp, and a queen-size bed. A few cardboard boxes were stacked near the bay window.

Simone walked to the night table and turned on the lamp. She then grabbed the pillows on the bed, putting them into to pillowcases. He watched her as she worked, trying to reconcile the woman standing in front of him with the one he had been envisioning for the past few months. That one had been cold and cunning, strong and calculating. But this woman was none of those things; she was soft and vulnerable, from the wispy hair that curled around her ears to the powder blue, buttoned-up cashmere sweater pulled over her swollen belly. Seeing Simone like this robbed him of his self-righteous anger. It frustrated him all over again.

"You don't have to do that," he mumbled wearily. "I can make my own bed."

"I don't mind. Really," she said as she loudly shook out the sheets, smiling again. "I can have it done in—"

"I said I can do it myself, damn it!" he shouted, stomping toward her and yanking the bedsheets out of her hands.

She stepped back, caught by surprise. "What's wrong?"

"What's wrong? *What's wrong?*" He shook his head in disbelief. "I can't. I can't do this shit with you! I can't stand back and let you act all sweet and nice like you're some . . . some goddamn Claire Huxtable, after all the shit we've been through. After all you fuckin' *put me* through!" He pounded his chest. "You disappeared, Simone. You just pulled up stakes and left town! You quit your job and moved away! You didn't even tell me where the hell you went!"

She lowered her eyes. "I know, and I'm sorry. But I had to, Ricky. I had no choice."

"You wrecked me. Do you know that? I never fell for anybody . . . *anybody* the way I fell for you, and you *used* me! You used me to get to your sister and turned me in to the cops! You left me holding the bag!"

"I'm sorry. I'm sorry! I never . . . I *never* meant to hurt you or betray you. I didn't—"

"No, sorry don't cut it! It don't fuckin' cut it!" He banged the night table, making her jump. "I was arrested! They raided my club . . . my restaurant. I lost *every*thing!"

She closed her eyes and shoved her fingers into her hair.

"I'm an informant now. The cops gave me a choice between turning against Dolla—or telling him how I helped you. So I'm a snitch now . . . a punk-ass snitch! But he's gonna find out. He's gonna find out eventually that I'm working for them, and when he does, I'm a dead man. It's only a matter of time."

She opened her eyes again. When she did, he could see there were tears in her eyes, but he wasn't moved. He'd seen her tears before. She had used them against him in the old days. They used to win him over, but not anymore.

"You robbed me of a lot of shit, but it was my stupidity for trusting your shady ass to begin with! I just don't get how you could rob me of this too," he said, gesturing to her stomach.

She looked down and ran her hand over her bump.

"It's mine. *Right?* Or were you fuckin' some other dude the whole time we were together? Are you even worse than I thought?"

She raised her head to glare at him. "I know that I'm messed up, okay? I may even be shady—as you say—but what kinda question is that? How could you even ask me that, Ricky?"

"Oh, don't act all innocent, like I'm accusing you of

shit you would never do!" he yelled, tossing the sheet onto the bed. "You lied to me from day one. You lied to me about everything!"

"I didn't lie to you about everything! I told you—"

"Yes, you did! Everything out your mouth was lie or a half lie . . . or a *quarter* lie! Why the fuck should I believe you now?"

She threw up her hands in surrender. "Fine. Fine, Ricky. If you want to believe I cheated on you, then okay . . . sure . . . I cheated on you. The baby's not yours. Now you have another reason to hate me. That make you feel better?" She walked toward the open door, looking hurt. A tear finally spilled onto her cheek. "Now if you're finished telling me about how horrible a person I am, and how much I've ruined your life, I'll go back to—"

"Oh, fuck you! Fuck you, you selfish, shady bitch!" he shouted, charging toward her, making her instinctively take a step back. He felt like a pot that had finally bubbled over. "Fuck you and your lies and your fake-ass tears! Fuck you and your—"

"Stop yelling at her!" Skylar shouted, stepping into the doorway. "She didn't want to do it. She didn't want to leave you, but she had to! The cops told her she had to do it, or she'd lose her badge and get thrown in jail, asshole! And she's been crying over you for four goddamn months, so stay off her fuckin' b—"

"Enough!" Simone yelled, sniffing and wiping away her tears with the back of her hand. "Enough! It's okay."

Her sister fell silent, but she still looked pissed. Ricky was pissed too. His chest was heaving.

"Everybody's tired," Simone mumbled. "It's late. We should all . . . you know . . . get some sleep. That's enough shouting for one night. Don't you think so, Ricky?"

He didn't respond. His nostrils flared. His fists were at his sides. He could feel the tendons standing up along his neck. All his rage and hurt had coalesced into something hot and stinging that ran over him like a fever. If he opened his mouth and spoke, he didn't know what words would come out—or if they would be words at all.

He watched as Simone stepped into the hall with her sister. She then quietly shut the door behind them, leaving him alone in her mother's bedroom. He sat on the bare mattress with the sheets balled up beside him, staring at the closed door. He sat for so long that he lost track of time.

Ricky had finally got to yell at her. He'd got to tell her how she had broken his heart, destroyed his life, and betrayed him. He'd told her what he really thought about her. So why didn't he feel any better? Why did he feel *worse*?

He should've known that anything dealing with Simone would leave him feeling helpless and unsatisfied. That woman had had the power even in the beginning of their relationship to twist him into knots, to mess with his head so that he didn't know right from left, or up from down. And it looked like not much had changed since then, but Ricky was going to end things on his terms this time around. He wasn't going to wake up in the morning and leave this house, unsatisfied.

He glanced at the digital clock on the night table and saw that it was almost two a.m. He hopped off the bed, walked across the room, and opened the bedroom door. He strode down the hall. It didn't take him long to find her. Ricky could see through the cracked open door that she was wide awake, despite the late hour and her protestations about being tired. She was sitting in the center of the bed, watching television and rubbing lotion onto her arms and legs. He eased the door open and she turned to look at him, surprised. Her hand hovered over one glossy, brown leg. His eyes drifted to her red-painted toenails.

The first time he'd met her, her toenails had been that same color—that same brassy red.

"Hey," she called out to him. "Can't sleep either?"

He didn't answer her but stepped farther into the room instead, and looked around him. Even if Simone hadn't been in here, he would've known this was her room—from the furniture to the knickknacks. He could remember her old apartment down in Eastern Market. It had been decorated in much the same style. He had spent countless hours in that space, in bed with her, telling her stories about his life, his sister, Desirée, and his Grandma Kay. He had told Simone things he hadn't told anyone else. They'd had an intimacy that he'd thought could only be shared between true lovers, but he knew now it was all a lie.

Smoke and mirrors, he thought.

"Look, Ricky," she began, clearing her throat, "about our . . . umm . . . conversation earlier . . . there's . . . there's something that I have to—"

"Do you know why I came here?" he interrupted as he strolled toward her bed, refusing to be sidetracked from his mission this time.

She halted midsentence and shook her head. "No. Did you need something?"

"I mean do you know why I came here to *this house* tonight?" He sat down on the edge of the bed. "Not just to your room?"

"I thought you came to tell us about Dolla . . . to tell us that he's looking for my sister."

"Yeah, well . . . that was a lie. The real reason why I came here was to kill you."

She squinted and coughed out a laugh. "Wh-what?"

"You heard me! I said I came here to kill you, Simone."

At that, her face changed. If the light had been brighter in the room, he was sure he'd have seen her face go ashen.

"I've wanted to kill you for months. That's how mad I was. I fantasized about that shit. I shot you and stabbed you in my head I don't know how many times. But no matter what the scenario, I decided that before I did it, I was gonna give you every fuckin' reason why you deserved to die. You were gonna hear what I had to say."

Her eyes shifted to the night table. He imagined she had a pistol inside one of the drawers, likely stashed somewhere between her panties and maternity bras. She was probably gauging if she could reach the gun before he reached for her.

"But the moment I saw you, I knew I couldn't do it," he said, making her eyes snap back to his. "Kill you, I mean. I couldn't kill a pregnant woman."

She dropped her hand to her stomach.

"I definitely couldn't kill a woman pregnant with my own damn baby."

"So . . . if I wasn't showing, you're basically saying I'd be a dead woman right now?" she asked, still cradling her belly protectively.

He shook his head. "No, because the baby is only one of the reasons why I couldn't kill you. I realized that too. There's another."

"What's . . . what's the other reason?"

The room fell silent with the exception of her television. He stared down at his hands and gritted his teeth. He had only come to the realization himself not too long ago, but when he had, it'd hit him with a wallop. It made it even harder to say it out loud.

"I'm . . . I'm still in love with you."

She didn't respond. The TV banter continued to fill the silence.

"I'm still in love with your lying, shady ass, even though I know you conned me, even though I know it was all bullshit."

"It wasn't bullshit," she whispered.

He closed his eyes in exasperation. "Simone, don't get it twisted. I may love you, but the con doesn't work anymore. Okay?"

"It isn't a con! It never was! I loved you too, Ricky," she said, easing closer to him. "I *still* do!"

He opened his eyes and let out a cold chuckle. "You love me so much that you got me put in handcuffs and left my ass in jail?"

She dropped her gaze and winced. "I wanted to get Skylar out of there. I got desperate and . . . and I turned on you. It was fucked up. I know that! I went to the captain and told him everything you told me, everything I knew. I broke my promise to you, and I felt awful for doing it. But I swear, Ricky, they told me they were only going to raid Dolla's place!" She reached out and grabbed his arm. "His home in Virginia and his apartment in D.C. . . . that was it! I told them those were the two places where you had seen her for sure. Nowhere else. It wasn't until that night of the raids that I realized what they were really going to do. The captain lied to me. He stood right in my face and lied to me!"

"Betrayal hurts, don't it?" he muttered, making her purse her lips and let go of his arm. "Well, anyway . . . when I called him on it, he blew me off. He said you weren't innocent. As far as he was concerned, you knew who you were working for, so you were just as guilty as Dolla. That's why I called you that night. I wanted to warn you so that maybe you could get out of there before they came in, but it was too late. I knew it probably wouldn't make a difference, but I had to try! I had to try to get you out of there."

Ricky frowned.

At least that part was true. She *had* called him that chaotic night and had warned him about the raid at Club Majesty mere minutes before it all had happened, before the cops burst through the doors. She also had told him to sneak out the back if he could. But how could he know for sure that she hadn't known his club and restaurant would be targets from the very beginning, from the moment she walked into the strip club? How could he know she wasn't lying to him yet again?

"My superiors found out that I'd called you," she continued, oblivious to his doubts about her. "They tore me a new one because they said my call could've jeopardized the raids. They suspended me. They told me they would handle the investigation from that point on without my involvement, but by then I figured out what they really wanted to do. They weren't just going to focus on Dolla. For some reason, they were going after you too, to flip you or prosecute you . . . I wasn't sure. I tried to get a message to you while you were in jail, to let you know what was happening and I . . . I failed. It got back to the captain that I was meddling with the investigation again." She loudly exhaled. "They gave me two options too, Ricky. Either I could get with the program—or I'd have to leave the department. So I . . . I stepped down. I resigned. By then, I was definitely sure I was pregnant, so . . . it felt like the right time to do it anyway."

He stared at her. Her story was so convincing, but again . . . Simone had always been adept at telling a good story. He could feel his hard resolve faltering though. She was chipping away at it, unmasking a layer of sympathy and compassion hidden underneath.

"But I've been out of jail for almost four months now. You had to know that, Simone. If you weren't with the Metro Police anymore, then why the hell haven't I heard from you?"

She gnawed her lower lip, suddenly looking sheepish. "You have. I've called. Quite a few times, actually. I didn't know if the cops were listening in though, so I never said anything. You'd always cuss me out."

Ricky narrowed his eyes. "Wait . . . that was you? *You* were the person who kept calling and hanging up?"

She nodded guiltily. "I knew if they found out I was calling you, they'd say I was still tampering with the investigation. I wasn't an officer anymore; just a regular citizen. I could get arrested too. After a while, I realized how stupid I was being—*again*. Mom and Skylar convinced me that it was too risky to keep doing it, so I finally gave it up. I stopped."

The calls had abruptly stopped about two weeks ago.

"I don't get it. If you weren't going to talk to me . . . if you weren't going to tell me what was going on or where you were, then why the fuck did you keep calling?"

She shook her head. "It's for a dumb reason. Besides, you wouldn't believe me even if I told you. You'd say it was another con."

"I wouldn't have asked if I didn't want to know," he grumbled. "Just tell me the damn truth!"

. . . *for once*, he wanted to add, but didn't.

She sighed and shifted on the bed again, reclining against pillows that were stacked against the headboard. "I called because I wanted to hear your voice. I missed you, Ricky, as cheesy as that sounds." She continued to rub her belly like it was a magic lamp and she was trying to make a genie sprout out of it. "Walking around with a physical reminder of you didn't exactly make you easy to forget. I wondered what was happening to you, if you could ever forgive me for what I did. I thought a lot about you and calling you was . . . well, it was my sad way of reaching out."

She was right. It did sound like a con—a sappy one at that. But that didn't mean he was immune to it.

She's been crying over you for four goddamn months, Skylar had yelled at him.

Ricky could feel another hard layer of his resolve shedding away.

"Look, I know you hate me," Simone continued. "And you have every right to. Frankly, I hate myself too. I messed up your life, and that's not what I wanted. I wanted to save my sister, Ricky. That's it! I didn't want to destroy you. I wasn't out to get you. I hope . . . I hope you can believe that, finally."

He sucked his teeth. "Even if it's not what you meant to do, that's exactly what you fuckin' did. You knew what would happen if you turned on me, and you did it anyway. But in the end, you made out good, right? You didn't lose a damn thing in any of this."

"Yes, I did!"

"You lost your job! *So what?* You can get another one. Am I supposed to give a shit about—"

"I didn't just lose my job! Come on! You really think I care about that? I lost *you*!" She gestured to him. "I lost you! I threw away what we had—and I . . . and I regret it every single damn day."

He fell silent again.

"But I have to remind myself that as much as I screwed up, despite all the mistakes I've made . . . at least something good came out of all of this. It's the only thing that keeps the self-loathing from taking over." She gestured to her stomach again. "I don't regret this. I don't regret our son, even if he's something else I hadn't expected."

"Our son?" he repeated with raised brows.

She nodded. "It's a boy."

A boy, Ricky thought, letting the realization settle in.

So they were going to have a son. He was finally going to have the little boy that his Grandma Kay had mused about when he was a boy himself. *One day, you're gonna have a little one to pass on our name to, Ricky. Make him proud to carry that name*, she'd said.

Simone shifted again, twisting slightly on the bed beside him. "Sorry. I want to keep talking, but . . . I'm gonna have to pause for a bit."

Ricky watched her slowly climb off the bed. "Why? What's wrong?"

"Oh, general pregnancy stuff," she said, placing her hand on the small of her back. "I'm about to start the third trimester and its starting to feel a . . . uh . . . little uncomfortable. He's measuring big and he's heavy as hell."

Ricky smirked. "Any son of mine should be."

"Yeah, well, the pressure on my spine and hips ain't fun; lower back pain is a bitch."

She then began to pace in front of Ricky, kneading her lower back. He squinted at her.

"What the hell are you doin'?"

"Working out the pain. Sometimes walking around and stretching helps."

She then started to do a little wiggle, and Ricky laughed despite himself.

"Don't laugh! This really hurts!" she lamented, giggling and wincing at the same time. She began to knead her side as she shimmied, rocking her hips from side to side.

"Hold still," Ricky ordered.

"Huh?" she asked distractedly, still hopping and rocking.

"I said stop wiggling around like some crazy woman and just hold still!"

She stopped her pacing and dropped her hands to her sides. She then watched in surprise as he reached out and began to firmly rub the spot on her lower back that she had been rubbing seconds earlier.

"That feel better?" he asked.

"A . . . a little," she whispered.

"Turn around," Ricky ordered, and she did so. Without thinking, he raised the hem of her tank dress, revealing her cotton briefs and the bottom of her breasts.

She blinked and gaped.

Nothin' I haven't seen before, sweetheart, he mused as he ran his hand over the soft, warm skin and began to knead her hips.

She moaned softly. "That feels better."

After a while, his eyes drifted to her stomach. He stopped massaging her hips and placed a hand on her belly.

"The doctor said it's too early to feel any kicks on the outside," she whispered, "but he's moving around in there. Trust me."

Ricky wondered if he would ever get to feel his son shifting beneath his palm—a jut or a ripple. Would he know what he was feeling? He bet the sensation would be both weird and wondrous at the same time.

"Hey, lil' man," he said to her stomach. "It's your daddy."

At that moment, he could have sworn he felt a shift beneath his palm, a slight wave. Or maybe it was his imagination.

"I hope the massage helped," he said.

"It did. Thank you."

"Don't mention it." He gave her stomach a light pat.

"I should keep you around," she joked softly, tucking her hair behind her ear.

He looked up at her and their eyes met. His easy smile disappeared.

An old feeling erupted, one he'd thought was not only dormant but had outright died long ago. But here it was again, making his heart beat faster and twisting his stomach into knots. It made his fingertips tingle and his dick harden. He longed to shift his hands from Simone's belly to her hips and her breasts. His gaze drifted to her lips and he was overwhelmed with the desire to kiss her, long and hard. And God help him, he swore he saw desire in her big dark eyes too—an unmasked need that made him want her even more.

But these feelings had betrayed him in the past. They had led him down the path that he now found himself on.

Ricky dropped his hands from her stomach. He lowered his eyes and lowered her dress back into place.

"Well, now that you feel better, I'll let you get some sleep," he muttered, slowly rising from the mattress. "I should get some sleep too. Got a long drive back to D.C. in the morning."

He then eased around her and walked toward her open bedroom door.

"Ricky?" she called to him.

He heard something in her voice that made him stop short. He turned back around to face her. When he did, she leapt at him. Her mouth collided with his before he realized what was happening.

He knew he should pull away from her, and wrench her arms from around him. She'd lied to him, betrayed him, and broken his heart. She was high if she thought he'd ever forgive her, let alone trust her again. But he couldn't deny the longing he felt for Simone, or the desire. Ricky would never believe in her the way he had before that night when the cops stormed into his strip club, but that didn't mean he'd ever stop loving or wanting her.

So instead of pulling away, he drew her closer. Instead of wrenching her arms from around him, he reached behind him and shoved closed her bedroom door. He eased her back onto the bed, never taking his mouth from hers.

In the old days, sex with Simone had been passionate and unhindered, almost rough. He could remember slamming her against a wall quite a few times, or bending her over a chair or table before yanking down her panties. Simone hadn't seemed to mind his roughness though; she'd actually liked it. And she'd been just as rough with him when the mood overtook her.

But he couldn't be rough now. There was no shoving around a five-months-pregnant woman. He didn't want to hurt her or their son. And feeling that hard, round belly press against his abdomen as he kissed her was a big reminder of just how delicate she was, which made him question whether it was safe to have sex with her at all.

Ricky pulled his mouth away and rolled onto his side on the bed, making her stare at him quizzically.

"What?" she asked. "What's wrong?"

"Look, umm . . . I don't . . . I don't know how to work with . . . with all of this," he said, gesturing to her stomach.

She squinted. "All *of what*?"

"I mean . . . are you allowed to . . . you know . . . this far along? I can't hurt him, can I?"

Simone's confused expression was quickly replaced with an amused one. "Yes, I'm allowed to have sex this far along, Ricky. Some women still have sex up to their due date. You can't hurt the baby. Your dick isn't going to be anywhere near him. Don't worry!"

He grimaced. "But there aren't like . . . I don't know . . . rules on what you can do?"

"Well, I probably shouldn't be on my back," she said, easing onto her side and pushing herself up on one elbow. "It cuts off circulation because the baby can sit on a major artery. And"—she slowly straddled him—"I should probably be on top."

"That's better for the baby too?"

"No," she said in a sultry whisper, shaking her head. "I just like to be on top."

She then lowered her mouth to his and within minutes, Ricky was having too much of a good time to remember to be careful of the baby. Simone made sure of that.

Chapter 22

Jamal

"Uh, can I get you anything else, sir?" the barista called out to Jamal.

Jamal shook his head as he took another sip from his ceramic coffee mug. He waved his hand. "No, I'm good. Thank you."

"Are you sure?" the barista asked, running his hand over his gelled hair. "You don't want a refill or a scone or . . . something?"

Jamal nodded, and the young man shrugged as he adjusted his apron. "Okay. Just . . . let me know if you do."

Jamal could understand why the barista had asked if he wanted anything. He had been hanging out in the coffee shop for the past two hours, and in that time, he had only had two cups of coffee and had stared out the window at the people who walked by, at the cars that drove along the roadway.

It was his day off and he had nothing to do. No dates. No plans with friends. But he couldn't stand the prospect of being alone in his apartment with all that silence and his heavy thoughts, so he had come here in the hope of finding some distraction from his inner demons.

He was wearing ratty jeans and a T-shirt. He hadn't shaved. He looked like some hungover grad student.

Jamal flipped to the next page in the newspaper, studiously avoiding the metro section that was folded up on the table. He usually did nowadays. He didn't know what he would do if he stumbled upon an article about Phillip's murder, or if he had to see a picture of him, though at this point it probably wasn't likely. Nearly two months had passed and Phillip's murder remained unsolved. The news of the shooting of the intrepid *Washington Recorder* reporter was likely already forgotten by most who hadn't known Phillip personally, pushed aside for more recent crimes and splashier stories. But Jamal couldn't forget. Every time he thought about Phillip he felt guilt, crippling guilt. And even worse, he knew the truth of what had happened to him and who was behind it—but he couldn't tell anyone.

The door to the coffee shop swung open just as Jamal took another drink from his cup. He glanced up from the article he was reading to see what patron had walked into the shop. When he did, he almost spat out his coffee.

"Hey, what can I get you?" the barista asked with a smile.

Jamal watched as Melissa Stone, of all people, sauntered toward the counter. She was wearing her hair different now. Gone were the long braids that used to hang down her back. They were now replaced by a lion's mane, a twist-out of coiled curls in shades of brown, red, and honey blond that haloed her face. She was wearing a slinky red sundress that hugged her curves and black Converse sneakers. She looked effortlessly urban chic and as beautiful as he remembered.

"Hey, can I get a mocha espresso, please?" she asked before pushing her sunglasses to the crown of her head and digging into her leather hobo bag for her wallet.

Jamal lowered his eyes back to his newspaper and turned slightly in his chair so that his back was now facing her. He hoped she wouldn't notice him.

He vividly remembered the last time they had spoken to one another. The kiss . . . her blistering rejection . . . and how heartbroken and humiliated he had felt after. He was not equipped for a hostile or awkward encounter with her today, not with what he was already experiencing.

A couple of minutes later, the barista handed Melissa her espresso. She nodded her thanks and walked to a table only five feet away from Jamal. He watched from the corner of his eye as she set down her cup, pulled out a chair, and sat down. She began to drink her espresso and scan through her phone, and he was relieved.

Good, he thought. If she was too preoccupied with her phone, she wouldn't notice him. But he must have been projecting some psychic vibes her way because almost instantly, she looked up and locked eyes with his. Jamal turned away in alarm and returned his attention to his coffee. Thankfully, she did the same.

About fifteen minutes later, Melissa rose from her chair. Jamal pretended to be engrossed in his newspaper. He pretended to drink his coffee, even though the cup was practically empty. He was trying his best not to look up when she passed his bistro table and headed toward the counter to drop off her cup. But Melissa did something unexpected; she didn't pass him. Instead she stopped about a foot in front of his table and loudly cleared her throat. He slowly looked up from his paper and stared at her, shocked to see she was smirking.

"I was going to keep pretending like we didn't make

eye contact a few minutes ago, but I figured that was stupid. I should just be a grownup and come over to say hi," she said.

She smelled like citrus and the hair oil she must be using now.

He nodded and laughed nervously. He pushed his glasses up the bridge of his nose. "Hey."

"Hey," she repeated back, shifting her purse on her shoulder. Her smirk morphed into a smile.

Despite his dark mood and what had happened between them, Melissa's smile still had the same effect on him it always did. He found it arresting. It made him want to smile too.

"So how have you been, Jay?"

"Umm, okay. I've . . . uh . . . been okay."

She squinted. "Really? You don't look okay. You look tired—and skinnier. Have you lost weight?"

He shrugged. "Maybe. I don't know."

She glanced at the lone empty seat at his table. "Do you mind if I sit down?"

That caught him by surprise. It was one thing to say hello, make polite conversation, and be on her way. It was a completely different thing to share a table with him. What was going on?

"Uh, sure. I mean, of . . . of course," he said, quickly folding up his newspaper. He watched as she pulled out the chair and took the seat across from him. When she did, she took a sip from her cup, then licked her glossy bottom lip. Desire flared up inside him again, and the emotion felt almost like a betrayal. This woman had pure contempt for him—and he didn't blame her. He had contempt for himself as well. Melissa was being nice now, but he would never forget how she really felt about him.

"So . . . I should tell you that I didn't just come over here to say hi and drink coffee." She paused to look down at her cup. "I . . . I also wanted to come over and . . . well, apologize. I feel like I owe you an apology, Jay."

He blinked in surprise. "*An apology?* For what?"

"For how I behaved that night in December . . . for what I said to you."

He shook his head. "You don't have to apologize, Lissa. You were right; I was in the wrong for kissing you like that. It was out of line."

"Yeah, it was," she said, finally raising her gaze from her cup. "But my reaction . . . all that anger, wasn't necessary. We were friends, and you made a mistake. We had a lot to drink that night and dumb things happened."

He didn't recall them drinking that much, but he wasn't going to correct her. This was obviously something she had wanted to get off her chest for a while. He wouldn't speak again until she finished.

"Besides, I think I was more upset at what you said before you kissed me than the kiss itself. Let's keep it real." She shrugged. "You gave voice to what I'd been secretly thinking all along: that Dee and I weren't right for each other . . . that the reason why we kept breaking up and making up over and over again is because we weren't compatible, but we weren't able to admit it. You said Dee was not the right guy for me—and you were right. I knew in my heart you were right, but I wasn't . . . I wasn't ready to hear it," she said, choking up at the end.

He could see tears in her eyes. He grabbed a napkin from a nearby dispenser and handed it to her. She thanked him and dabbed at her eyelashes, smudging the napkin with mascara. His eyes drifted to her hands, and for the first time he noticed that she was no longer wearing her engagement ring.

"I'm sorry." She sniffed and laughed.

"I told you. You don't have anything to apologize about, Lissa."

"This is not what I came over here to do. I'm so fuckin' sick of cryin'." She blew her nose and bit down on her bottom lip as the tears continued to fall. "It hits me at . . . at odd times. I try not to do it in public though."

"What happened?"

She slowly shook her head and grabbed more napkins. "Ugh, I won't bore you with all the details. But the gist of it is, I found out that Dee cheated on me, and we broke up. I moved out a couple months ago."

Jamal frowned, now stunned. "Dee cheated on you? *Derrick Miller?*"

"I know, right? I never thought he'd be the type to cheat!"

"Shit." He slumped back into his chair. "Me too!"

She burst into laughter even through the tears. "You have no idea how good it makes me feel to hear you say that, Jay! I thought I had been so blind and naïve but . . . but it's good to know you thought that about him too. I wasn't some dumb, clueless chick that he could just manipulate and cheat on."

"You've never been a dumb, clueless chick, Lissa."

She tilted her head and winked. "That's good to know. But enough about me and my screwed-up life." She blew her nose again. "So what have you really been up to? How's work, Mr. Deputy Mayor?"

He started to lie, to tell her that everything was fine and nothing had changed. He'd find the way to quickly segue back to her work and her life, but he stopped himself. He was so tired of lying.

"It's . . . not good," he confessed quietly. "Not good at all."

She lowered the napkin from her nose. Now she was the one frowning. "What do you mean?"

"I mean . . . I've fucked up. I've fucked up royally and now I'm stuck. I have no idea how to fix the mess I've made because all the solutions are horrible. I feel like I'm in a prison and . . . and I can't get out." He ran his hand over his face. "And I don't even recognize myself anymore. I mean . . . I've never really liked myself all that much, but it's a struggle just to look in the mirror some days and not . . . not hate the man staring back at me. I . . . I'm a shitty human being and . . ."

He stopped when she reached across the table, grabbed his hand, and squeezed it.

"You're not a shitty human being, Jay," she whispered. "Please don't say that."

He shook his head again. "You don't know what I've done."

"No, but I know who you are. And I don't think you've done anything you can't come back from."

"You really believe that?" he asked, surprised at how kind she was being, how understanding.

"I wouldn't say it if I didn't believe it, Jay. I'm not fake like that. But," she said, letting go of his hand, "we don't have to talk about that heavy stuff today if you don't want to. Let's talk about something else. Tell me what else is going on with you. Don't tell me anything that makes you sad. I'll do the same."

So they talked. They talked so long that Jamal lost track of time, and for a blissful few hours he forgot about everything that had been worrying him.

Chapter 23

Derrick

Derrick slapped the button on his alarm clock when it sounded, and stared at his bedroom ceiling, watching as the sunlight crept through the window blinds and splashed across the blades of his ceiling fan.

"Damn, is it six thirty already?" Morgan groaned, turning onto her side so that she flopped onto his chest, almost knocking the wind out of him.

He laughed as she snuggled against his neck, rubbing her nose in the stubble along his chin. "Yeah, it's already six thirty. I set the clock fifteen minutes later than I usually do to give you more sleep. Remember?"

"Can't we sleep a bit longer?" she whined. "The bed is so comfy."

"No, we can't sleep longer. We both have to be at work in an hour. We might be able to get away with an hour and fifteen. Maybe."

"A hour and fifteen?" She blew air out of her cheeks, making him laugh again. "Oh, that's plenty of time!"

"Plenty of time for what?"

"For sleeping in," she said as her hand snaked its way

down his bare chest to the waistband of his boxer briefs, "or for a couple other things."

"What other things?" he asked playfully, cocking an eyebrow.

In response, she tugged back his waistband, wrapped her hand around his dick, and gave it a gentle squeeze. "Let me show you, baby," she whispered, before raising her mouth to his for a warm, sultry kiss. Within seconds, he shoved down his boxer briefs to his ankles and was on top of her while she moaned underneath him.

It had been a couple of months since he and Melissa had gone their separate ways, and Morgan was at his place all the time now, so much so that she had moved some of her things into the closets that were once filled with Melissa's clothes. Her body gel was in his shower and some of her hair care products dotted his counter. She even had a toothbrush here right next to his.

It was strange how quickly and fluidly she had melded into his life. He thought the transition would be rockier. After all, he had known Melissa for two decades. There was a level of comfort in a relationship that came with that. He hadn't known Morgan anywhere near as long but something just felt . . . right with her. He could chill with her like she was one of his boys and then make love to her at the end of the night. She didn't mind the long hours he spent at the Institute. He didn't get annoyed calls from her, like he used to get from Melissa, asking when he would finally come home. Hell, some days she stayed later than he did, working with the boys on some project in the workshop.

Sometimes it scared Derrick how right it felt to be with Morgan. Things had seemed perfect with Melissa for years too, before it all went wrong. But he told himself not to think that way, not to wait for the other shoe to drop, so they say. He told himself to just enjoy the moment.

Which was exactly what he was doing right now. Morgan was enjoying the moment too. His head was currently buried between her thighs and she was moaning and groaning beneath him, squirming and panting. He raised his head, licked his lips, and climbed back on top of her, gazing into her eyes. He saw a lot of love and adoration in those green irises and once again, instead of being happy, he was filled with doubt.

Would he disappoint her like he'd disappointed Melissa? Was he just a selfish asshole, like Ricky said, who was bad at relationships and doomed to break her heart in the end?

She must have noticed his hesitation, because she wrapped her legs around him, grabbed his ass, and nudged him forward.

"Don't leave me hangin', baby. Let's do this."

Derrick lowered his mouth to hers just as he thrust forward and she cried out. He did it over and over again and she rocked her hips underneath his, whimpering softly, begging him not to stop. The tempo increased and she unwrapped her legs from around him and spread them wider so that he could go deeper than before.

"Keep going, Derrick. Keep going, baby," she urged breathlessly.

And he did. He braced one hand against the headboard and slammed into her even harder, until they were both moaning and screaming, until her nails dug into his biceps. When he came, his hold on the headboard went slack and he fell against her chest, gulping for air. A few seconds later, she flopped her legs open in exhaustion and wrapped him in her arms, gently kissing his cheek and neck.

Thirty minutes later, Derrick stood in his kitchen in a dress shirt, slacks, and tie. Morgan sauntered into the room, pulling her hair into a ponytail atop her head.

"You're looking mighty dapper and sexy today," she said with a smile before standing on the balls of her feet to kiss his cheek and reaching behind him to give his butt a good squeeze. She walked to the kitchen counter and pulled out a loaf a bread to make toast.

He glanced down at himself and sighed. "Yeah, I had to throw on a tie today. We have someone from the city stopping by to do a tour of the Institute. I'm the one showing them around. I'm hoping they can put in a good word for us to get our grant renewed, but they warned me it doesn't look good. The city's budget is pretty tight this year."

She frowned as she began to load a couple of slices into his toaster before pressing down the lever. "So what does that mean for the Institute? Will you have to cut staff?"

"I hope not." He took a sip from his coffee cup. "But that grant is a lot of money. I don't know how we can operate the way we have been with that much of a shortfall."

She leaned back against the counter. "Can we get money from somewhere else? Can you get another grant?"

"Maybe, but the application process can be a pain in the ass. And a lot of that stuff depends on who you know, and I don't know a lot of rich white folks who run foundations."

She cocked her head. "I do."

Derrick stared at her in disbelief. "What do you mean?"

"I mean exactly what I said—I know someone! Back when I used to make furniture in Bethesda, we had rich people coming through there all the time. In fact, I knew one lady who used to hold some education achievement benefit every year. She and her husband ran a foundation and everything. I can call some of the guys from the cooperative and see if they could dig up her name."

He lowered his coffee mug to the kitchen counter. "Would you really do that for me?"

"Of course, I would! I don't want you to have to let go of any staff or see the kids suffer. Why do you look so surprised?"

For the past four years, the Institute had been a burden he had carried alone. Melissa had even begged him to quit his job as executive director, arguing that he could find better, more well-paid jobs elsewhere. Even when she hadn't been harping on him to quit, he knew she only let the subject drop grudgingly. And it wasn't just her—even friends and old college buddies had offered him jobs, arguing that his talent was being wasted at that place. It was strange to finally have someone being so supportive, someone besides himself not only embracing the Institute, but wanting to see it thrive.

Derrick reached out and grabbed Morgan's hand, catching her off guard.

"What?" she said, laughing nervously as he tugged her toward him. "What?"

He kissed her, long and hard, and basked in the sensation of her leaning against him like she was trying to sink into him.

"Thank you," he whispered.

"Well, that was the nicest thanks I've ever gotten," she said with a chuckle.

"No, I meant it. Thank you. You don't know what something like this means to me."

She raised a hand to her cheek. "I just wanna make you happy, Derrick."

"Of course, you make me happy. Why wouldn't you?"

"I know how hard it is to start all over again. I'm not Melissa but—"

"And I don't want you to be."

She lowered her eyes and he was surprised to see there were tears in them. "You said before that you had a hard time choosing between us, and as weak as it sounds, sometimes I wonder if you . . . you might feel like you made the wrong choice."

But he hadn't made the wrong choice. He hadn't made the choice at all. Melissa had been the one to walk away and he had gone to Morgan, seeking her affection, hoping she would take him back. No wonder she felt like the consolation prize. He had treated her like one.

"I don't want you to feel like you're with the wrong girl," Morgan continued. "I mean, sometimes I feel like . . . like I've got to prove to you that you made the right decision and it makes me feel so . . . so . . . ."

He shook his head and placed a fingertip to her lips. It was finally time to man up, to show her how much she meant to him so that she would harbor no more doubts about how he felt.

"You don't have to prove anything to me. I'm with you because I want to be."

"I know," she said, but still didn't look convinced.

"You know what else? I should start looking for a new place."

"A new place?" she repeated, looking taken aback. "Why?"

"I just wanna start fresh. I've been here for years. It seems like the right time. I was . . . I was wondering if you would come looking with me."

"Sure, baby! I'd love to help you find a new apartment."

"No, I meant . . . I meant, maybe you would want to move in with me. Maybe we could get a place together if you don't think it's . . . it's too soon."

At that she smiled, and in her eyes, instead of tears, he saw pure joy.

"Of course I don't, boy!" she gushed. "I'd love to find a place with you."

"So how about we start looking next week?"

"Sure!" She eagerly nodded and started bouncing on the balls of her feet. "Oh, baby, I'm so excited!"

He laughed. He was excited too.

Chapter 24

Ricky

Ricky stepped out of the shower and wrapped a towel around himself. He grabbed a can from the counter, sprayed shaving foam into the palm of his hand, and began to wipe it on his jawline and cheeks. It was June and getting a lot hotter outside. It seemed like a good time to finally switch from the full beard back to his goatee. He'd just grabbed the razor when he heard his cell phone buzz in his bedroom. He dropped the razor into the sink and rushed out of the bathroom.

In his haste, he almost slipped on the bathroom tile. His towel fell from his waist to his ankles. He reached for his phone on the night table, saw the number on the screen, and smiled. It was the call he'd been waiting for since yesterday, but he didn't answer. When his cell stopped ringing, he tugged open one of the drawers in the night table and pulled out his burner phone. He then dialed the mystery number he'd seen on the screen.

"Hello?" he heard Simone answer timidly above the roadway noise.

"Hey," Ricky said as his smile widened into a full grin.

He didn't think his phone calls were being traced or tracked by the Metro Police, but he and Simone didn't want to take any chances, so they had worked out a method to stay in touch that was nearly untraceable. She would continue to call from an assortment of phones at different locations, and he would call her back from his burner. It was cumbersome, but necessary. He'd told her the morning after he'd spent the night at her place months ago that he didn't want to spend day after day worrying about her and the baby. He understood her absence, but her silence was no longer something he could accept.

"You've got to call me *every* day," he'd told her as he tugged on his jeans and rose from her bed that morning.

"*Every day?*" she'd said with a laugh. "Come on, Ricky!"

"Well, if not every day then I'll settle for at least three days a week." He'd raised his zipper and turned to look at her. "I've got to know that you're okay . . . that the baby's okay. I feel like I should be here . . . like that's my job, but I can't stay here to protect you without putting you two at risk. It pisses me off but—"

"I don't need you to protect me," she'd said, adjusting the pillows behind her as she leaned against the headboard, absently rubbing her swollen belly through the white bedsheet. "Me and the baby will be fine. I promise."

"Don't make promises you can't keep."

"We've been fine so far! No one's found us out here."

"*I* did."

"That's different, Ricky," she'd lamented, rolling her eyes. "You—"

"No, it's not!" he'd shouted, more out of desperation than anger. He wanted to get through to her how important this was to him. "I came here with a gun and I had plenty of chances to take you out . . . to take *all of you* out. I held back. The next dude won't."

Her hand had stilled on her belly and her easy smile had disappeared, and he'd immediately regretted saying what he'd said. He didn't want to make her worry or scare her. A pregnant woman shouldn't have to deal with these things, but he had to tell her the truth. He had so many doubts and fears. He loved her, despite everything she'd done and what she'd put him through. It would be devastating to lose her so soon after they had reunited. It would be even more devastating to lose their unborn son. He didn't know if he could survive if something like that happened.

"Look," he'd said, sitting on the edge of the bed, "I know chances are everything will be fine, but just . . . just keep in touch. Okay? And I mean more than just breathing in the damn phone. Let me know what's going on so I don't have to hop in my car and drive down here every week. Save me the gas mileage."

She'd laughed and nodded. "Okay, I'll stay in touch . . . if it makes you feel better."

"It does," he'd said before leaning down to kiss her goodbye, hoping that the kiss would fortify him for the long, lonely drive back home and the days ahead of him until he heard from her again. Because he knew he couldn't come back, even though he desperately wanted to.

Now Ricky lived for these phone calls, for their mundane conversations and her reassurances that she and the baby were doing fine. He didn't realize how dark his life had gotten these past few months until Simone and his son offered him a glimmer of hope about the future. Things didn't seem quite so bleak anymore.

"Where are you?" he now asked, shouting over the background noise.

"I'm at a gas station about ten miles from home. It's one of the few places that still has a pay phone."

"How's our boy doing? Still giving you trouble?"

She chuckled. "He woke me up at around four a.m. and would not go to sleep. He kept squirming around. He wasn't getting comfortable so I wasn't getting comfortable either, I guess. The doula said he grew another inch. The accommodations are getting pretty tight in there. I can feel it!"

Ricky closed his eyes, remembering the night he'd slept next to her. He had stayed up for hours, even as she snored, staring silently at her with his hand against her belly. He still held on to the precious memory as if it had cost him a million dollars.

"Yeah, at thirty-seven weeks they say women have a hard time sleeping. You might start feeling some contractions too," he continued. "But it's usually just a false alarm. It's just your body getting ready for delivery."

"*What?*" She burst into laughter. "How the hell do you know that?"

"What do you mean how do I know that? I read!"

"Oh, do you?" she asked, now giggling.

The truth was that he now kept a copy of *What to Expect When You're Expecting* in his night table drawer next to her burner phone. He also now had an app on his phone that tracked her weeks and the baby's development during each gestational stage. But he wasn't about to tell her any of that. He could keep secrets too.

"Yeah, I saw it on a web site or TV or somethin', I think," he said casually with a shrug.

"Well, either way, I'm ready for this little guy to come out," she huffed. "Only three more weeks to go! He's getting *heavy*. Sometimes, it's even hard to breathe! And honestly, I just want to hold him in my arms."

Me too, he thought forlornly, but didn't say it aloud.

It was one thing to miss the chance to feel his son kick through her stomach. That was bad enough. But it didn't compare to knowing he may never get the chance to change his son's diapers or to rock him to sleep. Ricky had accepted that he may only ever get to see the baby in photos and videos for the next year or so. As long as Ricky stayed an informant, as long as he continued to work for Dolla Dolla, going back to Virginia to see his son in person was out of the question. He didn't want to put him or Simone at risk.

"I keep marking off the days on my calendar," she said, oblivious to Ricky's growing sadness. "But the doula warned me that sometimes first babies come late. I'm hoping that's not the case. Skylar hopes so too. She can't wait to meet her nephew."

Ricky's jaw tightened at the mention of Skylar's name. It infuriated him that he was keeping his distance from Simone for her and the baby's protection, meanwhile the young woman who had started all this mess and practically had a bull's-eye painted on her back was sleeping down the hall. Skylar's bedroom was even next door to the planned nursery.

"So she's gonna be there during the delivery?" he asked.

"Yep! She and Mom are both going to be there."

Ricky loudly exhaled as he reached down to pick up his fallen towel. He started to wipe away some of the shaving cream on his face as he sat down on the edge of his bed.

"*What?* What's with the sigh?" she asked.

He debated about biting his tongue. He had done it during each of their past phone conversations, but today he just didn't feel like doing it again.

"Is she still going to be living there after the baby is born?"

228 / *Shelly Ellis*

"Uh, yeah," Simone replied, laughing. "Why wouldn't she be?"

"Because it's not safe. *She's* not safe. I told you that Dolla is tracking down all of them, and if he finds her—"

"He won't."

"Can't y'all move her to another place? Hell, I'll give you money to get her an apartment somewhere else. *Any*where else! I don't care how much—"

"I can't desert my sister, Ricky."

"Yeah, I know. I know for a fact you won't desert her," he replied tersely. "I'm facing twenty years in jail because you wouldn't leave her behind. Remember?"

She didn't respond. Again, he heard the background noise of the roadway. He wondered if she was about to hang up. He wondered if he'd pushed her too far by bringing up the past, by showing the bitterness that, despite his best efforts, he couldn't relinquish.

"I'm sorry," she whispered. "I'm sorry. I am sorry, Ricky. I'll say it a thousand times if I have to, but I know I will never be able to make up for what I did to you."

"I didn't say that to put you on some guilt trip," he began softly, trying his best to sound gentle. "I said it because I need to know that you're going to put our son first. I accepted that I was second place to Skylar—"

"Ricky, that's not tru—"

"I accepted that shit," he said, talking over her, pressing forward despite her objections, "but the baby can't be. If shit goes left . . . if it starts to go bad, will you get him out of there? Are you willing to put him first?"

"Yes! Yes, without question!"

He pursed his lips. He wanted to believe her. He desperately hoped he could, but a part of him wasn't sure.

Suddenly, his cell phone began to buzz again—his real

phone. He picked it up, glanced at the screen, and grumbled at the familiar phone number.

"Look, I gotta take this call. I gotta go."

"Okay. I'll try to call you again Wednesday . . . probably in the afternoon."

"I'll be waitin'."

She chuckled. "I know you will."

She then hung up and the line went silent. He took a deep breath and pressed the green button on his phone screen.

"Yeah?" he said.

Detective Dominguez answered in his gruff voice, "We need to talk."

"About what?"

"You haven't been honest with us. I told Ramsey that you're the type to keep secrets. He's disappointed that I was right."

Ricky's face went ashen. His heart sank. Had they found out about this trip to Virginia a couple of months ago? Did they know he was back in touch with Simone?

"T-talk about w-w-what?" he stuttered.

"Meet us in a half hour at the corner of L and Connecticut Avenue. We'll be parked there."

Ricky glanced at his alarm clock and frowned. "*A half hour?* It's eight o'clock in the damn morning and I ain't even dressed yet."

"Then I guess you better throw on some clothes and be out the fuckin' door soon, right?"

Ricky didn't get a chance to reply before Detective Dominguez hung up on him, making Ricky want to throw his phone against the wall.

Thirty-five minutes later Ricky walked up the curb at Connecticut Avenue and L Street. The spot was only a few steps away from the posh Mayflower Hotel, where an old lady with a barking toy poodle was being escorted out the front door by a bellhop. Ricky strolled to the unmarked police vehicle that waited at the curb. Detectives Dominguez and Ramsey sat in the driver's and front passenger seats. When they saw him, they threw open a back door.

"Hop in," Ramsey called to him.

He did as Ramsey ordered, sliding onto the back seat and shutting the door behind him. The car pulled off with a lurch.

"You're late," Dominguez barked as he drove. "Parking is a bitch around here. We had to keep circling the block."

"So what? You want money for gas?" Ricky replied dryly.

"Cute," Dominguez said with a sneer, glaring at him in the rearview mirror. "But I wouldn't have such a smart mouth if I were you. You're in big trouble, Ricky."

At those words, Ricky's balls tightened. His belly flopped. He wondered again if they knew he was back in touch with Simone.

"You should've told us," Ramsey echoed, turning slightly in the passenger seat to face Ricky. His brown face was grave. "We were supposed to have a man on the inside. I don't like hearing stuff secondhand."

Ricky squinted in confusion. "What the hell are y'all talking about? Hearing what secondhand? Just spit it out!"

"We're talking about the heavies that have been coming through Dolla's place for the past couple of weeks. We told you to keep an eye out for some unfamiliar faces. That was the one thing you had to do!" Ramsey charged. "We heard he's planning somethin' big—somethin' real big. But an update like that we wanted to hear from *you*. We *should have* heard it from you."

"You made us look like assholes to our captain, Ricky," Dominguez said. "I don't like that shit!"

"What else are you not telling us?" Ramsey asked.

"Look," Ricky said, holding up his hands, "I don't know what the fuck y'all are talkin' about. I haven't been to Dolla's place in a couple of weeks, and when I was there, I damn sure didn't see any 'heavies' walking around. This is the first I've heard about this."

"What do you mean you haven't been there in a couple of weeks?" Ramsey asked. "It's your job to observe him. Why haven't you been up there?"

"Look, I can't just roll up at his place whenever the hell I want. I come when he calls me. That's how it works. That's how it's always worked!"

"We don't wanna hear that shit! The deal we had is for you to inform us!" Dominguez yelled. "If you can't do that shit then we don't need you!"

"Do you want to go to prison, Ricky?" Ramsey persisted, still glaring at him over the headrest. "Because if you're going to continue to bullshit us and waste our time, that's right where we'll send you."

"Look, stop fucking threatening me! I'm risking my life and trying to give you what you want, but I can't do it if it's not there."

"No more excuses!" Dominguez shouted, pounding his fist into the dashboard. "We want to know everything that you see . . . that you hear. We want to know who comes in and out of there. We want to know what they said. If Dolla gets up to take a piss, we want to know that too. It's been six months! Either you give us the info that we need or the deal is off. Your black ass is going to jail for a long, long time. You hear me?"

The muscles along Ricky's jaw rippled as the car drew to a stop.

"We'll give you a couple more weeks," Ramsey said. "That's it."

Ricky didn't respond. Instead, he just threw open the door and hopped out of the car. At least this time they had left him on a block that looked familiar. But he barely had a chance to shut the door before the Ford Taurus pulled off.

Chapter 25

Jamal

"Look at that view! Just look at it, Jay," Melissa gushed, pausing from sipping her drink and pointing into the distance.

Jamal glanced at the riverbank where a few canoers and families in paddle boats were drifting with the current. He shrugged. "It's okay. It's the same Potomac River that's always been there."

"Oh, come on!" she lamented playfully with a laugh, looping her free arm through his as they strolled along the sandy pebbled walkway, listening to the crunch of their soles on the gravel as they walked. He felt the soft skin of her bare arm rub against his and goosebumps sprouted on his forearm. "It's not just the Potomac River, Jay! It's the breeze . . . the warm weather . . . the sun shining on the—"

"On the trash drifting to shore? On the ducks pooping in the water?" he dryly finished for her before taking a sip of his drink.

She threw back her head and groaned. "Seriously, how can you not love D.C. this time of the year? Nothing compares to it!"

"I'll take your word for it."

He then gently pulled his arm from her grasp and shoved his free hand into his jeans pockets, hoping to keep the tingle he felt all over his body from blossoming into something more, which was usually the case whenever Melissa touched him.

Since they'd run into each other at the coffee shop in Northwest a couple of weeks ago, they'd hung out quite a few times, meeting for coffee or lunch, talking for hours. He usually talked about work but studiously avoided details like Mayor Johnson's corruption and Phillip Seymour's murder. And to her credit, she kept discussions about Derrick to a minimum.

"I don't want to talk about him anymore," she'd told Jamal one afternoon while they both ate pho at a Vietnamese restaurant in Georgetown. "Ain't got time for that shit! I've cried my tears. I've listened to I don't know how many sad love songs. Derrick did his dirt and we're over. As hard as it is to accept it, I have to move on." She'd then leaned down and drunk some of her broth. "And whatever you're holding on to, you need to let go of it, too, homie."

Easier said than done, he'd thought at the time, watching her as she ate.

Some things would always be hard to let go, no matter how much he wanted to do so: the knowledge that he was complicit in Mayor Johnson's crimes, the guilt he felt about Phillip's murder, and the attraction he still had for Melissa, though he tried valiantly to fight it this time around. She had no romantic feelings for him and had made that very plain, but that didn't mean they couldn't be friends. It didn't mean they couldn't find comfort in each other's companionship. He knew he could certainly use her friendship right now.

"I'm tired of walkin'. Let's sit over there," she said abruptly, now pointing to a wooden bench at the edge of the water.

A few seconds later they sat down and stared into the distance, absently drinking frozen coffees they'd bought at one of the food trucks along the National Mall. He watched as she kicked off her sandals and settled her feet into the grass. He tried not to stare at her French-tipped toes, though they were begging to be sucked on.

"So are you finally going to tell me what's bugging you?" she asked, cocking an eyebrow.

He lowered his straw from his mouth. "What do you mean?"

"I mean exactly what I said. Are you finally going to tell me what's up with you? You told me work isn't going well, but whenever I ask you what you mean by that, you change the subject."

"No, I don't." He paused and frowned, lowering his drink to his lap. "Do I?"

She nodded and laughed. "Yes, you do. All the time!" She sipped from her drink again. "I guess I'm a little suspicious because the last man who told me nothing was going on was having an affair with one of his teachers."

Jamal chuckled. "I'm not having an affair with anybody."

"I didn't think so," she said, turning completely around to face him. She crossed her legs and rested her elbow on the back of the bench. She gazed into his eyes and he knew instantly that it would be hard to lie to her. "So fess up."

He shook his head. "It's better that you don't know, Lissa."

"Why? Is somebody gonna take me out? Am I gonna find goons at my door tonight?"

"Maybe," he whispered, turning away from her and

staring at the water, watching as a seagull glided then landed on the river, dunking its head and emerging only seconds later with its prize.

"Are you serious?"

"It could really go bad if someone found out that I told you."

"Who would find out though? Who the hell would I tell? *The ducks?*"

He turned to face her again. "I'm serious, Lissa. I don't want you to get hurt. It's already happened to someone else and I don't know if I could forgive myself if something happened to you."

She quieted. Her smile disappeared. "You're really in some deep shit, aren't you?"

"I told you . . . I've done stuff that I'm not proud of. Johnson isn't . . . he isn't the man everyone thinks he is. He's connected to some shady shit . . . some dangerous folks too. And I've been covering for him. I'm not the person everyone thinks I am either. Not anymore."

"Well . . . and don't take this the wrong way but . . . if you're not proud of what you've done, why do you keep doing it?"

"Because I'm stuck!" he lamented. "I have to do it! If I walk away, Johnson will come after me. He'll—"

"How do you know that?"

"He said he would! He told me if I left, he'd make sure I'd regret it." Jamal grimaced. "The sad part is, Dee warned me."

"Warned you about what?"

"He told me to walk away from Johnson, to quit my job as deputy mayor long ago, back when I still had the chance. But I didn't listen. I said I had too much at stake . . . too much to lose."

She grumbled and turned slightly to face the river again, looking perturbed. "I don't know if I would take life advice from Dee, Jay. And besides, that's all in the past. What's done is done. You can only focus on the present, and right now, as I see it, you have two choices. You can either stay deputy mayor and continue to cover up for this asshole, hating yourself more and more each day. Or you can call his bluff, quit, and leave with your soul intact."

Calling his bluff...

Mayor Johnson had bluffed before. He had lied about the pictures at the brothel to get Jamal to do what he'd wanted. He could very well be lying again.

But he didn't lie about what was going to happen to Phil, Jamal reminded himself. *He'd had him killed just like he said.*

The risks were plentiful and the unknowns were numerous. If he walked away from his job . . . from city hall, he had no idea what awaited him on the other side.

"I'll think about it," he said.

"Really?"

"Yeah, I'll think about it," he repeated, and he would.

"You'll do the right thing. I have faith in you, Jay," she said, slapping his knee.

"You do?"

"Of course, I do!" She slid her sandals back on and rose to her feet. She wiped off the seat of her jeans and tossed her drink into a nearby trash can. "We all make bad decisions. We all face hard choices. There aren't any clear-cut answers. No one's all good. No one's all bad. We just . . . we just *are*, Jay. We're just trying our best. But you've gotta figure out what that 'best' is . . . what version of you that you want to be."

Jamal stared up at her, awestruck by this woman who was simultaneously wise and sexy, beautiful and compassionate. "Dee was out of his fuckin' mind to lose you, to let you walk away. You're amazing, you know that?"

She waved her hand dismissively. "Come on, let's get going. You can tell me how amazing I am while we're walking," she said with a snort.

He rose to his feet and tossed his drink too, before he strolled with her back down the pebbled path.

"So I've been meaning to ask you something else, and it has absolutely nothing to do with work or any of that drama," she began as they continued to walk.

"Go ahead."

"I have this thing Friday evening. It's a fund-raiser for education . . . a big black-tie event and our principal wants some of us teachers to attend and I . . . I need a date. I was wondering if maybe you'd go with me," she said, gnawing her bottom lip.

"Are you asking me out on a date, Miss Stone?"

"Don't be an ass about it, Jay," she said, playfully punching his arm. "I just don't wanna go there alone. Some of those nosy-ass teachers have already asked me when Dee and I are finally going to settle on a wedding date."

"You still haven't told them you guys broke up? Haven't they figured out that you're not wearing your engagement ring anymore?"

"You'd think so, but no . . . and I don't know when I'm gonna tell them the truth. I was with the man for forever! But if I come there with some other dude on my arm, they'll take the hint. Or maybe it'll distract them."

"So I'm just a distraction for your coworkers?" he asked, quirking an eyebrow.

"No, you're not just a distraction! I *want* you there, Jay," she said, looping her arm through his again. This time he didn't pull away from her. "It includes a free dinner and alcohol. And you get to spend the whole night chillin' with *moi*! How could you say no to that?"

The truth was, he couldn't, even though he knew it

wasn't a real date, even though he knew he was still firmly in the friend zone in her eyes. He exhaled and then nodded.

"Fine, I'll go."

"You'll go. *Really?*" She grinned and he felt a warmth spread in his chest.

"Yeah, I'll go. I just gotta clear my busy social calendar first, but it's all good."

She laughed before running her fingers through his tight curls. "And you might think about getting a haircut too, homie. You're getting a bit shaggy up there."

"*What?*" he said, running a hand over his head. "I was trying somethin' different!"

She laughed even harder. "I appreciate the experimentation, but I think it's time to tell your barber to hook you up."

Jamal emerged from the Wilson Building's elevator and his shoulders sank as soon as his shoes touched the carpet. He wanted to cling to the memory of that weekend, of his conversation with Melissa and how positive and reassured she'd made him feel, but he couldn't. Her kind words and laughter faded, and all he could hear was the much louder voice in his head telling himself that he was a fraud and a coward.

He strolled off the elevator and headed toward his office.

"Good morning, Sharon," he said to his assistant as he passed her desk.

She looked up and gave him a polite smile. "Good morning, Mr. Lighty."

He continued on his path to his office but paused when he heard her shout, "Oh! Oh, sir! I forgot to tell you. Mayor Johnson wanted you to attend an event for him today. It's scheduled for eleven a.m."

He turned back around to face her. "What event is it?"

"I forwarded you the email. Gladys sent over the details. They're holding it at the Press Club. It's in honor of Phillip Seymour at the *Washington Recorder*. I think they're dedicating some award to him and they invited the mayor. He wants you to go in his stead if you're available. Turns out your morning is open. You can attend, if you want."

Jamal blinked in astonishment. "What . . . what did you say?"

"I said you can attend it because your morning is op—"

"No, did you just say the mayor wants me to go to a dedication ceremony for an award named after *Phillip Seymour?*"

She nodded as she gazed up at him. "You remember Phil, don't you? He was that nice young man from the *Recorder*. The one who was kill—"

"I know who he is . . . I mean who he *was*. But . . . but why the hell would Johnson ask me to go to that? What the hell was he . . . he even thinking?" he sputtered.

Mayor Johnson was responsible for Phillip's murder and he knew that Jamal was aware of that secret. Neither one of them had any business anywhere near that ceremony. Jamal couldn't shake hands with Phillip's colleagues and his family. He couldn't smile for the cameras. It would be like pissing on poor Phillip's grave. Why would Johnson even suggest this? What kind of sick bastard was he?

Sharon frowned. "Well, I don't know, sir. I guess it's because someone from the city should be there and you knew Phil. I . . . I thought you were even friendly with him," she said, looking more than just a little disconcerted. "I thought you would be happy to support something like this."

Jamal clenched his fists at his sides. This was too much, *way* too much.

"I've had enough of this shit," he whispered to himself before charging back across the waiting area to the door.

"Mr. Lighty?" Sharon called after him. "Mr. Lighty, is everything okay?"

Jamal didn't respond to her question. Instead, he continued on his path down the hall, straight to Mayor Johnson's office at the end of the corridor.

As soon as he stepped into Johnson's waiting room, the mayor's assistant, Gladys, looked up at him.

"He's in a meeting, Mr. Lighty," she said, pulling her phone away from her mouth. "Can you come back—"

"No, I cannot," he said, ignoring her once again as he strode to the mayor's closed door. He turned the doorknob and shoved the door open, only to find the mayor sitting at his desk facing two elderly women in business suits.

"What the hell are you getting at, asking me to go to that dedication ceremony?" Jamal yelled at him. "Why would you even consider asking me to go? Are you out of your damn mind?"

The two older women's mouths fell open, aghast.

The congenial expression that had been on the mayor's face when Jamal entered his office evaporated. He leaned forward in his chair and gestured to him. "Mildred . . . Rosa . . . have you had a chance to meet Jamal Lighty, our deputy mayor of economic development?"

"Uh, n-no," one of them stammered, turning slightly in her armchair to face Jamal. "It's a . . . a pleasure to meet you, Mr. Lighty."

"Don't be put off by his colorful language, ladies," Mayor Johnson said with a chuckle as he rose to his feet and buttoned his jacket. He walked toward Jamal and placed a hand on his shoulder. "Mr. Lighty is actually a very capable deputy mayor. Unfortunately, he accidentally walked into our meeting and—"

"I didn't accidentally do anything," Jamal said, shrugging off the mayor's hand. "I came in here to tell you that I'm not going to Phillip Seymour's award dedication ceremony, you sick son of a bitch! And I'm disgusted you would even suggest that I go. I'm done with you and your bullshit!" he bellowed as the older women continued to stare at him in shock and the mayor glowered at him with barely contained rage. "I'm done with this. I . . . I . . ." His words drifted off. He knew what he had to say; he just had to say it. Jamal took a deep breath. "I quit. I'm done."

He then turned and headed out of the mayor's office, but stopped when he felt a hand clamp around his bicep. He whipped around only to find Johnson glaring up at him.

"Not so fast," the mayor said in a low, menacing voice before painting on a smile again. The entire time he didn't release Jamal's arm. "Would you excuse us, ladies? I need to discuss something with Mr. Lighty. This will only take a few minutes."

The two women nodded and anxiously glanced between the mayor and Jamal. They rose to their feet and walked toward the door, clutching their purses in front of them.

"Gladys, can you get Mildred and Rosa something to drink? Maybe water or tea?" Mayor Johnson called to his secretary, who promptly answered back with a "Yes, sir."

When the two women entered the waiting room, Johnson closed his office door behind them. Jamal yanked his arm out of his grasp.

"Just what the hell do you think you're getting at with that little performance?" Johnson hissed. "What game are you playing?"

"I'm not playing any game. I mean it. I quit!"

Johnson shook his head. "I told you, you can't quit." He pointed a stubby finger into Jamal's chest. "I want to keep you right in front of me so that I can keep an eye on you."

"Don't worry. I'm not going to the cops. I'll still keep your secrets, but I'm not covering for you anymore. I'm not being an accomplice to this!"

"You think it's that simple? You think you can just hand in your letter of resignation and be on your way?" The mayor let out a caustic laugh. "Nothing is that simple, Jamal. If you follow through with this, you are going to pay for it."

Another threat, but this time Jamal really would call his bluff. He pushed the mayor's finger away from his chest. "I'm already paying. I've paid too much."

He then turned, opened the office door, and walked out.

Chapter 26

Ricky

Ricky hesitated briefly, getting into character before knocking on Dolla Dolla's front door. The door sprung open a few seconds later, and by then his "Pretty Ricky" façade was firmly in place.

"What's up, Mel . . ." he began casually, then stopped and blinked, surprised to not find Melvin standing in the doorway, but someone else—another bald-headed bodyguard with an imposing build and height. Melvin was usually the one who answered the door at Dolla Dolla's condo. But he hadn't done it today.

"Why you just standing there? You comin' in or what?" the guard asked with a chuckle, motioning Ricky forward.

Ricky nodded and stepped over the threshold. He watched as the guard shut the door behind him, then pointed to the adjacent wall so that he could pat him down.

"I was just used to seeing Melvin," Ricky said as he pressed his hands against the woven wallpaper. He then leaned forward and spread his legs. He didn't even flinch as the guard's hands went up and down his thighs, as they slid around his waist. The guard then dropped to his knees and raised the hem of Ricky's jeans, checking if he had anything tucked into his socks or strapped around his ankles. The pat-downs were just part of the routine now whenever you visited Dolla Dolla. It was as ordinary as the drink or snort of blow he offered whenever Ricky saw him.

"Where Mel at?" Ricky asked.

"He's busy. Had shit to do for Dolla, I think," the guard said, rising back to his feet and slapping Ricky on his shoulder. "You're good. I'll hold your cell here and give it back to you later."

Ricky frowned as he turned away from the wall.

If Melvin was "busy," he wondered exactly what he was doing for Dolla Dolla. Judging from the last time Ricky had gone on an errand with Melvin, he bet the hulking bodyguard wasn't out picking up milk and a loaf a bread. Had they found another girl? Was Melvin taking her out at this very moment?

Can't focus on that right now, Ricky thought, as he strolled down the hall and headed to the living room, where he knew Dolla Dolla was likely waiting for him. That wasn't what he was here for. He was here to finally get the info that the detectives wanted, that they'd been harassing him about for months.

He had been calling Dolla Dolla a lot more often, reiterating that he was loyal to him, telling him that he was here to do whatever was needed "no matter what." He told him that now, with the restaurant and Club Majesty closed, he was short on cash and needed some new work, and whether that work was illegal was irrelevant to him.

He'd hoped that those reassurances and confessions

would lead to something. Maybe Dolla Dolla would *finally* let him in on the "big things" he was working on that the detectives had heard about. Maybe Dolla Dolla would introduce him to his drug contacts. But so far, neither had happened. And Detectives Ramsey and Dominguez were well past impatient; they were done with their threats and ultimatums. They gave him his final deadline; if he didn't get them the info they wanted this week, the deal was off. He was going back to jail.

That was why Ricky was relieved when he'd gotten the text from Dolla Dolla earlier that day.

Stop at my crib tonite at 7. Got somebody I want U to meet, Dolla Dolla had written, which were the magic words Ricky had been waiting for months to hear.

Now, as he rounded the corner, he wondered exactly who he was meeting. One of Dolla Dolla's suppliers from Miami? One of the pimps Dolla Dolla used to help recruit his girls? But when Ricky saw who was pacing up and down the living room, leaving heavy indentations in the plush rug as he walked, his frown deepened.

"Mayor Johnson?" he murmured.

What the hell was the D.C. mayor doing here—of all places?

"Hey, Pretty Ricky, bring your ass over here!" Dolla Dolla said. He was standing at a nearby bar cart, smoking a blunt and pouring himself a drink. "You want somethin'?"

Ricky slowly shook his head as he descended the stairs into the sunken living room, still stunned that it was the mayor Dolla Dolla had wanted him to meet tonight. He was certain this wasn't the high-level contact the detectives were hoping for.

"Nah, I'm . . . I'm good," Ricky mumbled.

"You want somethin', Vernon? What you old folks drink? A Tom Collins or some shit?" Dolla Dolla asked before bursting into laughter.

The mayor finally stopped pacing, but still looked uncomfortable. "No, I do not want anything to drink, but I would like to know why the hell I'm here!"

Dolla Dolla raised his glass to his lips and strolled to the sofa. He sat down and motioned for Ricky to sit in one of the armchairs. "Take a load off, my nigga. Told you I had somebody I wanted you to meet tonight." He glanced at Mayor Johnson. "You have a seat too."

The mayor shook his head and crossed his arms over his chest. "Not until you finally answer my question. Why am I here?"

Dolla Dolla took a hit from his blunt and set his drink on the glass coffee table. "Man, I ain't gonna tell you but one more time to sit your ass down."

"*Or what?*" the mayor asked, raising his chin defiantly. He buttoned his suit jacket, looking every bit the stately politician Ricky usually saw on TV. "Look, I'm tired of you bossing me around! You might be the H.N.I.C. around here, Dolla, but I think you forget that I am the mayor of this town!" he said, pointing at his chest. "You can't just summon me whenever the hell you . . ."

His words died on his lips when Dolla reached behind him and pulled out his Glock. He then rested it on his knee, keeping his finger on the trigger.

"Keep talkin', motherfucka," he said, nodding. "Tell me again what I can and can't do."

Ricky watched as the mayor's face went slack. The older man looked sick to his stomach.

"Now you two have a seat. We got some talking to do."

Ricky took the armchair as he was ordered. The mayor

still looked a bit stunned, so one of the guards stepped forward, placed a hand on his shoulder, and shoved him down into the other empty chair.

For a split second, the mayor looked like he wanted to buck again, but his eyes drifted to the gun that still rested on Dolla Dolla's knee. He seemed to think better of it and kept his mouth shut.

"This my nigga, Ricky Reynaud," Dolla Dolla said, inclining his head toward Ricky. "He's been tight with me for a long time. He's my business partner. We used to own Club Majesty together."

"It's a . . . a p-p-pleasure to m-meet you," Mayor Johnson stuttered.

"You too," Ricky whispered.

"Ricky, you already know who he is," Dolla said before taking a hit from his blunt.

Ricky nodded again. "Yeah, I know who he is, but I gotta be honest, he ain't who I expected to see today. I'm a little confused."

"I'm confused as well," Mayor Johnson ventured. "Like I've said repeatedly, I have no idea why I'm here. I told you that we can't be seen together. If anyone, especially the press, got wind of the fact that I'm here, I'd be—"

"I don't give a fuck what you told me!" Dolla Dolla boomed. The calm veneer he'd had only seconds ago abruptly disappeared and was replaced with a fiery one. He raised his arm and pointed the gun at the mayor, and Ricky's breath caught in his throat.

He wouldn't shoot him, would he? It had to be an idle threat. Even Dolla Dolla wasn't crazy enough to kill the mayor in his own living room, but Ricky honestly couldn't say for sure anymore.

"You don't give the orders around here," Dolla Dolla said with the blunt still dangling from the side of his mouth.

"I do! You may be the mayor of D.C., but my kingdom goes far and wide, nigga. So keep talkin' shit. Keep doin' it and see what happens! You feel me?"

Gradually, the mayor nodded.

"Good," Dolla Dolla said, before his lazy smile returned and he lowered the gun to the glass coffee table.

Ricky finally released the breath he'd been holding.

"'Cause we got some important shit to talk about . . . important shit for *all* of us." Dolla Dolla then turned to Ricky. "I brought you here to help Ricky. To help us. You see, this nigga got caught up in the shit with me. They took his restaurant away. They took away our club. He needs to be makin' some paper again, so we need to make these charges go away."

The mayor pursed his lips and clutched his hands in front of him. "Look, I want to help, Dolla. I really do. But I told you, I don't appoint circuit court judges. I have no control over—"

"Nuh-uh, I don't wanna hear that shit. You know you got friends in high places," Dolla Dolla said before taking another hit and leaning back against the sofa cushions. "The police chief reports to *you*. I need you to clean this shit up. It's dragged on for too damn long. That's what the fuck I pay you for. You think I gave money to your dumbass campaign . . . that I clean up your messes because we friends? You think my people took out that reporter and I'm about to take care of yet another nigga who crossed you, because we tight? Hell no! I help you so that you can help me, and so far, all I'm hearing is a lot of fuckin' excuses."

"What do you want me to do?" the mayor asked almost pleadingly. "What am I supposed to do, Dolla?"

"Get 'em to drop the case against me and against my boy over here." He leaned forward and slapped Ricky's shoulder. "My lawyers can't do it, so you're gonna have to. The Metro cops are already losing witnesses, right? My people picked off most of them snitches. I got a few more left, but my soldiers are taking care of them. Once they're gone, that should make your job a lot easier." He winked. "Thought they could hide from me. One of them bitches even moved out to the boonies in Virginia, living on a farm and shit." He threw back his head and chuckled and the blood drained from Ricky's head.

He knew immediately who he was talking about; from the description, it had to be Skylar. But how had he found her? How had he tracked her down?

"But she on that shit again," Dolla Dolla continued, answering Ricky's silent question. "I had my people on the lookout for her, because a junkie is a junkie and they don't never change. I figured she'd slip up one day and she did. She thinks she got somebody comin' there to bring her some blow tonight, but I got a surprise for her ass."

"I shouldn't be listening to any of this," the mayor mumbled, shaking his head. "I can't be criminally culpable for—"

"Man, shut the fuck up!" Dolla Dolla snarled. "All your damn complainin' is ruinin' my high!"

Ricky's heart pounded as he listened. He went numb. One of Dolla Dolla's men was already on his way there. He had to talk to Simone. He had to get her out of there and he had to do it now. He shot to his feet, making Dolla Dolla glare up at him. One of the bodyguards took a step forward.

"What you doin'?" Dolla Dolla asked.

"Sorry," Ricky said, forcing a smile, "I gotta use the bathroom. I'll be right back."

He didn't wait for Dolla Dolla to respond. He took a step around the guard, who instantly reached out to stop him.

"Let him go," Dolla Dolla said with a nonchalant wave. "A nigga can pee around here."

Ricky beelined for the bathroom down the hall, shutting the door behind him. When he did, he reached into his jeans pockets for his cell to call Simone and tell her what was happening, but his pockets were empty. He grimaced when he remembered he didn't have his cell. It was still with the guard by the door.

"Shit! Shit! Shit!" he whispered fiercely.

He yanked open the bathroom door again and raced back into the hall.

"I'm sorry, Dolla, but I've gotta go. My stomach is . . . uh . . . real fucked up. I-I don't know what the hell I ate but . . . I'm a mess."

Dolla Dolla squinted from his perch on the sofa. "What?"

"I gotta go," he said again, turning toward the door, not caring that his lie was feeble and he looked conspicuous as hell right now. His bigger concern was getting his phone back. He had to get to Simone before Dolla Dolla's men did. "I'll catch up with you though," he shouted over his shoulder.

He then raced into the foyer. The guard stood in front of the door, barring his exit.

"I need my cell," he said, reaching out to him. "I'm leavin'."

The guard cocked an eyebrow, but he didn't budge.

"I said I need my cell," he repeated, holding out his hand.

The guard's gaze was focused over Ricky's shoulder. Ricky turned around and saw Dolla Dolla standing there. Two guards stood behind Dolla Dolla, blocking the other end of the foyer, closing him in.

"You okay, my nigga?" Dolla Dolla asked, strolling toward him.

"Yeah, umm, I'm fine. I'm just . . . I'm just not feeling well. Like I . . . Like I told you," Ricky said, glancing apprehensively around him, getting the distinct sensation of walls closing in on him.

Dolla Dolla took a step toward him, then another. "Mel told me you was acting funny after that thing with Tamika a while back. He said he didn't think you had the stomach for that shit. You ain't buggin' after what I said about them other girls, are you? Pretty Ricky ain't goin' soft on me, is he?"

Ricky let out a nervous laugh and shook his head. "Nah, it's not that, Dolla. I don't give a damn about those bitches, but I'm not about to shit myself on your leather chair. That's all it is."

Dolla Dolla seemed to regard him for almost a full minute longer. He then finally nodded and gestured to the console where Ricky's cell now sat. "Give him his phone."

The guard finally turned and reached for his cell phone. He handed it to Ricky and Ricky tucked it into his jeans pocket.

"Peace out, bruh," Dolla Dolla said to him as the guard stepped aside and finally unlocked and opened the door.

"Yeah, peace out," Ricky called over his shoulder before striding into the apartment building's hallway.

He waited until the guard finally shut the door behind him before he began to dial Simone's number. When he reached the elevators, he pressed the down button just as her phone rang once . . . twice . . . three times. Finally, he heard her voice message.

"Hey, you know who it is. If you don't, you've dialed the wrong number," she answered cheerfully, making him roll his eyes. "Leave your name and number and I'll hit you back!"

"It's Ricky. Pick up the phone," Ricky said, just as the elevator doors opened and he stepped inside. "They know where you are. They know and they're on their way. Call me back and let me know you got this. I'm on my way there right now," he said as the elevator doors closed behind him.

When he arrived at his car three minutes later, he backed out of the parking space and floored the accelerator, pointing his Mercedes towards Virginia.

Chapter 27

Derrick

Derrick twirled Morgan on the dance floor, feeling more jubilant than he had in months. They were attending the annual Mayhew Student Achievement Benefit and Morgan had already introduced him to the Mayhews, a white-haired couple who lived on Capitol Hill and were third-generation old money but weren't selfish enough to keep it all for themselves. They were the couple who used to buy custom furniture from her. He'd spoken with them for a good half hour, while Morgan had stood by his side, charming them.

"Why don't we stop by the Institute next week and you give us a tour?" Mr. Mayhew had said before taking a sip from his champagne glass. "Doris and I are always looking for new worthy causes to donate to. We'd love to see what you and your staff are doing there."

Derrick had been too stunned by the offer to say yes, so Morgan had said it for him.

"We would love to give you a tour, Mr. Mayhew. Next Tuesday would be perfect if you can schedule it in," she'd said.

Derrick now realized what a good couple he and Morgan were. They were a solid team, and with her help he knew he could do great things not only for the Institute, but in his life in general.

She wants me to succeed. She loves me like crazy, he thought as he wrapped her in his arms as they danced.

As if sensing his thoughts, Morgan wrapped her arms around his shoulders too, and gazed lovingly into his eyes. Derrick allowed himself to be drawn into those two green irises and the deep well of emotions that lay within them. He then let his gaze drift to her sensual smile, those plump cherry-red lips that begged to be nibbled.

He'd been so focused on his past that he'd barely noticed what was standing right in front of him. Admittedly, it was hard after being with Melissa for damn near twenty years to finally let go of her. But he hadn't spoken to Melissa in months, and she'd made no bones about not being able to forgive him for cheating on her. She had obviously moved on. And he was moving on too. He and Morgan were slated to sign the lease on their new apartment tomorrow. He had already given his landlord notice that he was moving out.

Derrick tugged Morgan closer and lowered his mouth to hers, a physical sign that he was finally ready to give her his all. She didn't hesitate before raising her lips to his and meeting him with a warm kiss, lacing her fingers through his dreads. For a few seconds, it seemed as though the rest of the dance floor disappeared and it was only them grinding to the music, kissing in the dark. She abruptly pulled her mouth away.

"Hold up, baby," she whispered breathlessly.

"Why? What's wrong?"

"If that kiss gets any heavier, I think we might have to leave the party."

"We can do that," he said, cupping her bottom. "Makes no difference to me!"

She laughed, rubbing her hands along his broad back. "We can't leave just yet. I don't want the Mayhews to think we came here just to get them to agree to show up to the Institute, then we jet. Besides, there's more people we could meet here. Maybe even more donors, baby."

"Maybe. But I'd rather spend my time kissing up on you instead," he said, lowering his mouth to hers again. She stopped him short by playfully slapping his shoulder.

"Boy, stop!"

"What?" he asked, feeling a little rejected. "I'm just trying to show you how much I love you."

Her face softened. "I love you too, honey. You know that. But you're starting to sound a little tipsy. How many glasses of champagne have you had tonight?"

Four, he thought. *Maybe five*. He couldn't say exactly. He had been having so much fun that he hadn't counted.

"I'm not tipsy! I'm happy. There's a big damn difference. I'm finally thinking clearly now. Things are looking up for me—*for us*! That's all!"

"If you say so, baby." She glanced toward the ballroom's doors. "Look, I'll be right back. I have to go to the ladies' room."

He reluctantly loosened his hold around her. Just then the band finished the slow song and the crowd around them erupted into applause.

"You'll be okay, right?" she asked, staring at him worriedly.

He waved her off. "I'll be fine. I'll be at the bar getting a cup of coffee to sober up some, if it makes you feel any better," he called to her over the sound of clapping and the rising voices.

She nodded and laughed. "Grab two! One for me and

one for you!" she shouted back to him, then headed to the exit with a few of the women departing the parquet dance floor.

Derrick strolled across the ballroom to the bar, where several people were now gathered, some drinking but most casually talking. As he drew closer, he scanned the lacquered counter for an open spot where he could sidle up and get the attention of one of the bartenders. His eyes paused when he spotted a woman leaning against the counter with a wineglass in her hand, talking to a man whose back was facing him. Derrick did a double take as he watched her lower the glass from her plum-colored lips and throw back her head and laugh. Recognizing her instantly, his stomach dropped to his black leather shoes.

There stood his ex, Melissa Stone, in a purple silk gown that clung to her like a second skin, emphasizing every supple curve. She wasn't wearing her long goddess braids anymore. Her hair was golden red now, and in twists that were all braided atop her head like a crown. She had adorned it with two twinkling rhinestones. She looked beautiful, sexy, regal, and . . . happy. She actually looked happy, even though she was standing there without him.

Derrick didn't know what to make of that.

If I'm happy, why shouldn't she be happy, too?

But that didn't stop his faint sense of loss, the sharp pang of heartache at seeing someone he once loved live her best life without him.

He watched as she leaned toward the ear of the man whose back was still facing him. He couldn't see who the man was. She placed a hand on the man's shoulder with a familiarity and intimacy that made Derrick frown. She gave the man a flirty smile.

Was this just a date or her new boyfriend? Had Derrick met this dude before?

Something told him to walk away from the bar. He was with Morgan now. Melissa could date whomever she wanted. It was no concern of his. But he didn't walk away.

Propelled by curiosity and quite a bit of alcohol, Derrick didn't even hesitate before he strolled down the length of the bar toward her. He wouldn't try to talk to her or interfere, he told himself. He just wanted to know who Melissa was talking to.

When he stood a few feet away, she stopped whispering to the mystery guy. Her date finally turned to reach for the glass at his elbow. Derrick could now see him in profile and when he did, he saw red.

It was Jamal—the same man who had professed his love to Melissa, kissed her, and told her to end it with Derrick once and for all . . . the same man whom Derrick had once affectionately called "my boy, Jay," but who had really been the snake lying and waiting in the grass all those years. That son of a bitch was now cuddled up with Derrick's ex at the bar. Jamal even offered his glass to her after he took a drink. She nodded, sipped some of the liquor, made a face, and they both burst into laughter as she handed back Jamal's drink.

Watching them, Derrick couldn't have been more hurt than if someone had shoved a steak knife into his chest.

Melissa must have felt his gaze on her. She turned away from Jamal and glanced in his direction and her smile withered. Her laughter died in her throat.

"Dee?" she said in shock.

His name came out in an exhalation of breath.

Jamal turned to face him. He didn't look alarmed or embarrassed at being caught with Melissa. He actually had the audacity to break into a grin.

"Hey, Dee," he said. "I didn't know you were here. What's up?"

Derrick looked between the two of them. "*What's up?* What's up? No, what's up *with you?*"

Jamal lowered his glass back to the bar top, now looking uncertain. "What?"

"Don't act like you don't know what I'm talking about! What the fuck is this shit?" he shouted, pointing at Jamal and Melissa, while several people turned to look at the trio. Even one of the bartenders stopped, holding the shaker midair, to stare at them.

"Look, Dee . . . chill, man," Jamal began. "I don't know what's—"

"Don't tell me to fuckin' chill, you shady motherfucka! Don't ever come at me like that!" he shouted, feeling the tendons stand out along his neck, feeling his anger boil over. He then glared at Melissa, turning his wrath on her. "So this is the nigga you chose to hook up with after me? *My own boy?* I guess this is your idea of revenge or some shit! You really went that low?"

Melissa sucked her teeth, infuriating Derrick even more. "I'm not even going to dignify that with an answer," she murmured before grabbing her gold clutch from the countertop and linking her arm through Jamal's. "Come on, Jay. He's obviously drunk, and this is stupid."

"I'm not drunk! I wish I fuckin' was! Don't—"

"Yes, you are, Dee," she said tightly, cutting him off. "You've never been a sloppy drunk before. Don't start now. I suggest you sober up quick before you embarrass yourself." She tugged at Jamal's arm insistently. "*Let's go*, Jay."

Jamal paused as if wanting to say more to Derrick, but then he reluctantly nodded, ushering Melissa away from the bar.

"Yeah, go! Go! Run away like the punk-ass nigga that you are!" Derrick bellowed as he trailed after them while they walked back toward the ballroom's entrance.

The crowd began to part like the Dead Sea to allow Jamal and Melissa to pass, giving an angry Derrick a wide berth. He knew from the expressions on everyone's faces that he must look crazy, shouting at the top of his lungs, but he didn't care. He was too hurt, furious, and yes, indeed, drunk, to give a damn.

"You never could own up to your shit, could you, Jay? Always ran away and left me and Ricky to fight your battles for you," he continued, undaunted. "You punk! You bitch! You're as much of a bitch-ass nigga as Ricky said you was!"

Jamal glanced over his shoulder at him as they walked to the exit, but Melissa's eyes stubbornly stayed forward—and it was like waving a red flag in front of Derrick's face. He wanted her to hurt as much as he hurt right now. He wanted her to be angry. He'd be damned if she'd walk away from him like his pain and suffering wasn't worth the time of day.

"I expected some shady shit like this from you, Jay, but I never thought in a million years you would pull something like this, Lissa," he taunted as they stepped through the doors into the hotel lobby, where several couples lingered. "How long did it take for y'all to hook up? Did you dial this nigga as soon as we broke up? You told me you felt nothin' for him, that you pitied his ass! So I guess you pitied him so much you started fuckin' him!"

"Hey!" Jamal said, whipping around to face him and jabbing his finger at him. "Now you know you're out of line for that shit, Dee! Don't talk to her like that!"

"Jay," Melissa said in a warning voice, shaking her head, "don't. It's not worth it." She tugged his arm again. "Let's just go."

"No, don't stop him! He was finally starting to buck up for once. Let him say what the fuck he had to say!" He gave Jay's shoulder a hard shove, sending Jamal back about a foot, making Melissa yelp in outrage. "Say what the fuck you had to say!"

"Dee, stop it!" Melissa yelled. "You're drunk! Just go away and sober the hell up, okay?"

"What's happening?" Morgan asked, jogging across the lobby toward them. "I heard you shouting all the way in the ladies' room, baby."

As she drew close, Morgan's and Melissa's eyes met. Morgan placed a protective hand on Derrick's shoulder. Melissa sucked her teeth again in exasperation.

"Oh, you've got some goddamn nerve coming at me like this, Derrick Miller, when you brought this bitch here," Melissa snarled.

Morgan dropped her hand from Derrick's shoulder to her hip. "*Excuse me?*"

"You heard me!" Melissa yelled back, gesturing to Derrick. "He's your man now, ain't he? That's what you wanted all along. That's what all that sneaking around behind my back was about. You wanted him—now you've got him! Get your man under control!"

"What the hell is she talking about, baby?" Morgan asked, rounding on him. She grabbed his arm. "What's going on?"

He didn't even hear her question. Instead, his gaze stayed squarely focused on Melissa's and Jamal's retreating backs as they continued toward the bank of elevators on the other side of the lobby. He yanked his arm out of Morgan's grasp and went stalking after them.

"Don't walk away from me! Don't you dare walk away, Jay. You stand up and face me, nigga! Face your shit for once!"

Just as Melissa pressed the down elevator button, Derrick charged forward, giving Jamal another hard shove, sending the other man slamming face-first into the gold elevator doors.

"Turn around and face me! Face me, you backstabbin' motherfucka!"

If Jamal wouldn't turn and face him on his own, he would damn well make him do it. He grabbed the collar of Jamal's tuxedo and yanked him around.

"Dee, stop! What are you doing?" Morgan screeched.

Derrick pounced on Jamal before he could gain his footing. He shoved him against the wall next to the elevators, pinning him there.

"Fight me!" Derrick yelled, balling his fist. "Fight me, nigga!"

"I'm not gonna fight you, Dee!" Jamal yelled back, pushing him away. "No matter how much you try to pick a fight with me, I'm not going to do it. I'm tired of fighting! I don't wanna do this shit any—"

His words were stopped short when Derrick punched him squarely in the face. A stream of blood gushed out of Jamal's nose and trickled over his upper lip. A few women in the lobby started screaming. Voices rose in alarm.

Derrick grabbed the front of Jamal's tuxedo shirt and pulled back his arm, ready to punch again.

He thought about all the times he had defended Jamal, all the blows he had taken for his so-called friend over the years. He was going to pay Jamal back for every single one of those hits he'd suffered protecting him from the neighborhood bullies, for every single lie Jamal had told him and double cross Jamal had committed.

But he didn't get to do it. Melissa jumped up and slapped him across his face and alongside his head. She gave him a series of hits, her arms windmilling wildly, and he had to let go of Jamal and grab her hands to stop the blows.

"If you're gonna fight anyone, fight me! Fight me, you son of bitch!" she yelled over and over again. "I'm the one who wants to kick your lyin', cheatin' ass! *Fight me!*"

He blinked and looked down at her in shock. It was like he was snapping out of a spell. He could see that she was crying . . . no, sobbing.

He looked down through his tangled nest of dreads at Jamal, who was now leaning against the wall, holding his bloody nose and gulping for air through a swollen lip.

Derrick released Melissa and staggered back. When he did, she fell to her knees and knelt beside Jamal, touching his face, weeping softly and whispering to him. She then turned and glowered up at Derrick.

"Are you happy now? Do you feel better?" she shouted up at him.

No, he did not feel better. In fact, he felt nothing at all. He turned to find Morgan staring at him. Her face was grim. Her eyes were blank.

Behind her several people huddled in the hotel's foyer. He could see the Mayhews standing in the entryway. Mrs. Mayhew held a hand to her mouth in shock. Mr. Mayhew glared at him.

Derrick guessed they wouldn't be taking that tour of the Institute after all.

"Sir! Sir, are you all right?" a security guard yelled as he raced across the lobby. He was chubby and ruddy cheeked. His blue eyes seemed to almost bulge out of his head as he stood over Jamal. "What happened?" He followed Jamal's and Melissa's wary gazes and looked at Derrick, jabbing the antenna of his walkie-talkie at him. "Did you hit him?"

Derrick didn't respond. He didn't know what to say.

"You stay right there! You hear me?" the guard shouted, pointing a finger at Derrick. Derrick then watched as the guard raised his walkie-talkie to his mouth.

"Hey, John? I'm gonna need some assistance up here. Call 9-1-1 and have them send over—"

"No. No, that isn't necessary," Jamal slurred as blood trickled over his bottom lip. He shook his head and waved his hand dismissively. "I'm fine." He attempted to push himself to his feet but slumped back to the floor. Melissa grabbed his arm and helped ease him to his feet on the second try. He leaned against her slightly before standing upright on his own. "My . . . my friend and I were just . . . just having a little disagreement, and it got heated. That's all. We're cool now though. Don't call the cops."

"A *little disagreement*?" The guard furrowed his brows. He glanced warily at Derrick again. "Umm, sir, I don't know what's going on here, but I'm obligated by the hotel to—"

"I'm fine," Jamal said firmly, reaching into his breast pocket and taking out a handkerchief. He held it against his bloody nose and mouth. "Look . . . Walsh, is it?" he said, glancing at the guard's name tag. "Look, Walsh, the truth is I'm with the mayor's office and I really don't want to bring too much attention to this incident, okay? I certainly don't want a record of tonight in a police report."

The guard continued to glance uneasily between Jamal and Derrick, like he still wasn't quite sure what he wanted to do.

Derrick was also confused. Why was Jamal going to such great lengths to keep him from getting arrested? He'd just punched him in front of a lobby full of people. Everyone had seen what happened. He was willing to pay the price for what he'd done, even if it meant a night in jail.

"I would greatly appreciate it if you could help keep this quiet," Jamal continued. "Can . . . can you do that for me, Walsh?"

The guard seemed to hesitate a bit longer before finally raising the walkie-talkie to his lips. "Hey, John? Forget what I just said. It's taken care of. No need to call 9-1-1. Kay?"

The walkie-talkie filled with static before a voice answered, "Gotcha!"

The guard then pursed his lips and returned his walkie-talkie to his holster. His chubby face creased into a frown. "Again, I don't know what's going on here, but whatever is, I don't want it at this hotel."

"We were leaving. No worries," Jamal said, waving his hand again, still holding the handkerchief to his face.

At that moment, the elevator finally chimed and opened.

"There you go," Jamal said, gesturing to the open elevator doors. He actually smiled despite his cracked upper lip. "You ready, Melissa?"

She nodded weakly before following him into the elevator. She turned to Jamal and he reached out and drew her close. She immediately dropped her head to his shoulder and he rubbed her back. She wrapped her arms around him and clung to him.

They looked like a couple. They looked like they had been together for years. They looked like how he and Melissa used to look months ago. Derrick got the eerie sensation that he was looking at a photo he had been cropped out of, and another man's image had replaced his. Another man had taken his place.

He watched them as the gold elevator doors slowly slid closed.

"What the hell was that, Derrick?" Morgan asked as they walked down the block, back to the parking garage. "Why did you do that?"

Derrick glanced over his shoulder. It was the first time Morgan had spoken to him since the fight. She still looked shell-shocked with her arms clutched around her shoulders, trembling under the street lamp.

Derrick paused and flexed his sore knuckles. "I'm sorry, baby. I don't . . . I don't know what that was. I don't know what happened."

She furiously shook her head, making her curls whip

around her shoulders. "No! No, don't tell me that shit, Dee!" She stomped her high-heeled foot on the cracked cement. "You know . . . you *know* damn well what the hell happened, and what was behind it. You came here to make a good impression . . . to get money for the Institute, and she walks through the door and everything . . . *every*thing fell apart! You completely lost your shit!"

Derrick grimaced. "It wasn't her, baby," he whispered.

"You are full of it! It *was* her!" she said, gulping through her tears. "It was her!"

He reached out and tugged Morgan toward him. He held her against his chest. She cried against his shoulder, letting out ragged sobs that made her shake all over. After a few minutes, she leaned back her head and gazed up at him.

"You told me you loved me. You told me I was the one you wanted to be with."

"I *do* love you. I *do* want to be with you! I said I wanted to live with you. What more can I do to prove it?"

"So why can't you let her go?" she asked as rivulets of mascara slid over her cheeks.

He closed his eyes and dropped his cheek to her crown, not knowing what to say or what lie to tell Morgan to alleviate her pain.

He wanted to love her. He wanted with all his heart to move on. But tonight showed him that he still wasn't ready. He'd feared that he would hurt Morgan in the end. Tonight, his fears had been realized.

"I'm sorry," he whispered against her forehead, brushing his lips over her warm skin. A second later, he felt Morgan squirm restlessly in his arms. She then abruptly shoved back from him.

"Yeah, you *are* sorry!" she shouted, punching his chest. "You're one sorry motherfucka for not appreciating what you got! You were lucky! You were lucky and you didn't even realize it. I loved you and would've done anything for you. We could've been good, Dee. We could've been happy, but you're still pining for a chick who doesn't even fucking *want* you . . . who's already moved on to the next man!" She flapped her arms in defeat. "And now I'm ready to move on too."

He watched helplessly as she turned on her high heel and walked away from him.

"Morgan!" he yelled after her. "Morgan!"

She didn't look back or stop but continued down the block before rounding the corner and disappearing from view.

Chapter 28

Jamal

"Really, Lissa, I'm fine! I don't need any—"

"Just park it on the sofa and wait while I get some ice for that face and peroxide for that lip, sir," Melissa ordered, shutting her apartment door behind them and gesturing with her clutch toward her living room. "I won't say it again."

Jamal sighed and reluctantly nodded, though he had tried more than once during the drive up to her apartment to tell her that he could take care of his wounds himself at home. She wouldn't hear of it. She had badgered him into coming upstairs.

He watched now as she kicked off her stilettoes and strolled down the hall to her bathroom. He walked into her neat and cozy living room, shrugging out of his suit jacket as he did it.

He didn't want to be here. He couldn't believe it, but it was the truth. In the past, Jamal would have been elated for Melissa to invite him upstairs to her place after a night of drinking and dancing, but he just wasn't feeling it tonight.

Not after what we went through, he thought miserably as he gazed down at his bloody handkerchief and the drops of blood on the front of his tuxedo shirt.

He'd thought the ongoing drama that had been his life for the past year had finally come to an end once he'd handed in his resignation to Mayor Johnson, but of course, it couldn't end quietly. It had to do it with an ear-splitting boom. He hadn't expected Derrick to be there tonight. He certainly hadn't expected such a volatile reaction from him, even though Derrick was intoxicated. His former friend could get rowdy when he was drunk; even Jamal could remember that, from back in the day when they used to party as teens and in their early twenties. But Derrick had never gotten angry or violent before. He had never *hit* him.

But worse than Derrick's punches were the words he'd thrown at Jamal. The names hadn't hurt, but his accusations had. He'd said that Jamal could never own up to his own shit, that he'd always run away and left him and Ricky to fight his battles for him. The sad part was it was all true. Jamal had done it their entire friendship—hid behind his friends. And it wasn't until recently, until an innocent man had actually been murdered, that he'd finally owned up to his role in the chaos and took control of his life. But it didn't change the past. That didn't change everything he'd done. His bruised nose and busted lip were a physical reminder of that.

"Okay, I've got the peroxide and unearthed some cotton balls," Melissa called out as she strolled back into her living room, holding a plastic bag and a bottle aloft. She gave him a dimpled grin. "We're in business!"

He wondered how she was doing, how she could be all smiles now when she had been sobbing and slapping around her ex less than an hour ago. He wanted to ask her but was wary of what she might say, of what other truths might come out.

Jamal watched as she sat down beside him and ripped open the bag before twisting off the lid of the bottle. She then doused a few of the cotton balls with peroxide.

"Where's Brownie?" he asked, looking around the living room floor, searching for her cat.

"Locked in my bedroom. I didn't want him to bother us," she said as she dabbed at his split lip. "I'm sorry, by the way. About . . . you know, what happened tonight. You handled it well though," she said as she began to dab at his split lip.

"Doesn't feel like it," he muttered.

"You could've had Dee arrested and you didn't. You didn't hit him back either."

"Yeah, well"—he shrugged—"I didn't have to. You fought that battle for me. I'm a punk-ass nigga, remember?"

She paused. Her face fell. "I didn't fight your battle and you're not a punk-ass nigga. Don't say that."

Sweet, encouraging words from a sweet, encouraging woman. He'd expected as much from her—the babying and the pity. She was doing exactly what Derrick said she would do.

"Thanks, Lissa, but I've got it, okay?" he said tightly as she began to dab at his lip with the cotton ball again.

"Almost done," she said, ignoring him. She sounded a lot like his mother had back in the day when he'd fallen and scraped his knee as a little boy. "Just hold still," she murmured, still dabbing.

"I said I've got it!" he nearly shouted. "Damn!" He pulled his head back.

"*What?*" she asked, lowering the cotton ball from his mouth. "What's wrong?"

"Nothing! It's just . . . I can do this myself. I said that

about a hundred times! I can take care of myself. I don't need your pity. Okay?" he snapped, regretting the word even as it tumbled from his bloody lips.

"I wasn't pitying you, Jay." She sat back, sounding and looking hurt. "I was just trying to help."

That's not what Derrick said, he thought bitterly.

"What? Seriously, what the hell is wrong? Why are you looking at me like that?" she asked, frowning.

"Nothin'." He shook his head and rose to his feet. He reached for his suit jacket, yanking it from the sofa arm. "Nothin'. It's just . . . late. It's been an exhausting, shitty night. I should head home. Thanks for inviting me to that banquet. I'm sorry the night turned out the way it did."

He began to walk out of her living room.

"Jay, come on, don't leave! Talk to me!" She shot to her feet. "What's wrong? It's like you're mad at me or somethin'. Is it about what happened with Dee? You blame me for that?"

He hesitated, unsure if he even wanted to bring up what he was feeling, the doubts he was having. Derrick had intended his words to be as powerful as his jab. He had wanted to hurt Jamal by saying what Melissa really felt about him, but that didn't mean what he'd said wasn't the truth. It didn't mean she hadn't felt that way about Jamal all along.

"I don't blame you," he muttered tiredly. "That shit between Dee and me would have existed regardless of you."

"But I made it worse, right? Because I told him what happened in December? Because he saw us together?"

"He saw us together, but his reaction was out of line. I told you . . . it's not your fault. You and I know there's nothing going on between us. You don't *feel* anything for me."

Not even friendship. He had at least thought she felt that, but it turned out he was wrong there too.

She squinted. "Why do you keep saying that stuff? Why do you keep putting yourself down like that? I never said—"

"Because it's true! You don't feel anything for me. You pity me! That's the only fucking reason why you even started talking to me again. Right? Even Derrick said it."

Her shoulders sank. "So that's why you're acting like this? Dee gets drunk and talks shit, and you actually believe him?"

"Why shouldn't I believe him? That night that I kissed you, you said it yourself! Time passed. Dee broke your heart, so you weren't as angry with me anymore. I was lost and without any real friends or a tether, and you wanted to help me out. That's all it was! It's okay to admit that, Lissa."

"You really think that's it? That you were lost and I felt sorry for you?" She tossed the bloody cotton ball on her coffee table in frustration. "I'm so tired of this shit. I'm so tired of *the both* of you. I swear to God! He's a selfish piece of shit, and you are fucking clueless!"

Jamal stared at her, confused by her outburst. Maybe he was as clueless as she said, because he didn't understand all this anger.

"I didn't start hanging out with you because I felt sorry for you, Jay. I did it because I connected with you! You, of all people, understood what I was going through. You'd seen my relationship with Derrick from the beginning, and you'd damn near broken up with him yourself. I turned to you not out of pity or sympathy or any of that shit, but because . . . because I needed you." She lowered her eyes and fisted the front of her gown in her hands. "And now that I know he's back with that bitch and it's finally, *finally* settled in that it's really over with Dee, I . . . I need you even more. So there you go. I'm . . . I'm the one without a tether. I'm the one who needs help, not you." She slowly raised her eyes. When she did, he could see there were tears in them. "Because I don't know what to do with myself. I'm so confused now . . . and angry and hurt. I thought I was better. I thought I had . . . had moved on! I just . . . I just don't know what to do."

He didn't know either. He felt helpless too.

"I need you, Jay. I know it sounds selfish. I know I'm asking a lot considering what you went through tonight . . . what you've been going through for months, but I need . . . I need you."

She stopped twisting the fabric of her dress, but she still looked vulnerable. He hadn't considered that tonight had knocked her off kilter too, that she was the one who felt lost.

"Please . . . please don't leave. Not yet. Please? I won't . . ."

She broke into tears before she could finish, and he crossed the short expanse between them and held her close. Despite wanting to leave only a minute ago, Jamal quickly settled into the idea of staying the night, and sleeping on the couch if Melissa wanted him to. If she didn't want to be alone with her thoughts and her heartache, he would keep her company. When she tilted back her head, he was prepared for her to ask him to do just that, but he wasn't prepared when she brought her lips to his.

Jamal was so caught off guard by the kiss that he almost pulled his head back in shock. It had to have been an accident. Something they would both laugh about later. But when she moved her warm mouth against his, he realized it was no accident. He drew her closer and let it deepen, wrestling his tongue with hers. He could taste her tears and the dried blood on his wounded lip. He could hear the blood surge in his ears and swore he could even feel the rapid thump of his heart in his chest. He could feel his budding erection and wondered if she could feel it too, pressing urgently against her thighs. She must have, because she reached down and rubbed her hand over his groin, over and over, as they kissed, taking him from half-mast to rock hard.

"I need you, Jay," she whispered plaintively against his lips.

This time he knew what she really meant. What she was really asking, and it was like someone had flicked a match and dropped it into a pool of gasoline. Whatever desire he had been holding back all these months, all these years, caught aflame at that moment.

He lowered the zipper of her gown before tugging the straps off her shoulders. She stepped back and shimmied the top of her gown to her waist, revealing the strapless black lace bra underneath, while he removed his belt and lowered the zipper of his slacks.

Their movements were frenzied and panicked, as though they were on a stop clock, like they didn't want to slow down or stop and consider what they were doing, what they were *about* to do. And the truth was, they didn't.

Jamal didn't want to consider that maybe this was just revenge sex for Melissa. What greater retaliation could she take against a cheating ex than by fucking his former best friend? He didn't want to consider that she was just doing this out of pain and misery and might regret everything in the morning. He just wanted to live for the here and now, and he suspected Melissa did too.

He removed her bra, tossed it to the living room floor, and began to fondle her breasts just as he brought his mouth back to hers. She moaned against his lips, eased back onto the sofa arm, and spread her legs wide. She placed her hands on the small of his back and drew him between her thighs. Jamal removed one hand from her breast, eased up the hem of her gown, and pushed aside the crotch of her thong. He fondled her between the thighs as they kissed, as he licked and sucked her neck and she nibbled his earlobe, making her moan even louder. Hearing those moans, feeling her wetness against his fingertips, he couldn't wait any longer, though he wanted to lengthen the moment as much as possible.

This could be a one-time deal. They could have sex once and never have it again. In the morning, he'd put on his clothes, walk out the door, and they'd see each other the next day and pretend like it had never happened. He could see it even now, meeting up and laughing over coffee, pretending like he hadn't run his thumbs over her nipples or she hadn't shoved her hand into his boxers and wrapped her hand around his dick, stroking him as she kissed him, making him groan. She'd go back to being his buddy Lissa, and he'd go back to just being her boy Jay, but tonight they would be more to each other—a lot more.

Because the moment might be fleeting, he committed everything to memory: the look of her, the feel of her, the quietness of the living room. He made his own mental snapshot before he pushed down his pants and boxer briefs to his knees and entered her with one swift stroke that made her cry out, almost in shock.

Their coupling was fast, ardent, and loud, with neither holding back. She bucked her hips, almost falling off the sofa arm trying to meet him stroke for stroke. He plunged inside her over and over again, holding himself and her steady by bracing one hand against the nearby living room wall and the other on the back of the sofa. This wasn't just sex or a casual encounter. There was more here, some deep well of emotions they were pulling from and pouring into each other with their bodies.

"Oh, God! Oh, God! Oh, God!" she panted against his ear.

When she came, she clawed at his back and shouted out. It sounded almost like a whimper. He screamed her name, then felt his body convulse before he collapsed against her and they both went tumbling back onto the sofa cushions. They lay there for several minutes, catching their breath.

"This may be a bad time for me to ask this but . . . you're on the pill, right?" Jamal whispered as he fluffed the pillow behind his head.

Melissa had just pulled back the bedspread and was about to climb in naked beside him, but paused and cocked an eyebrow at his question.

It turned out that he was indeed spending the night at her place, but not on the couch. After they had made love, she led him down the hall to her bedroom, kicking poor Brownie out into the hall. Even now, Jamal could hear the cat plaintively meowing on the other side of the door.

He had watched in the low light from her lamp on the night table as she'd finished undressing, peeling away the rest of the clothes that he had started to remove only thirty minutes ago, but had stopped when they got caught up in the moment.

Jamal had let his eyes lazily travel over her body as she took off her gown and panties, appreciating every glorious inch and luscious curve. His gaze had fallen on her full breasts and dark nipples, then her flat stomach and her concave navel. When she'd turned around to remove her earrings and place them on her dresser, his eyes rested on the indentation along her lower back and her plump rear end that had a mole on the left cheek. He'd traced the path of her round thighs that had a faint hint of dimples at the back of them. As she'd crawled toward him across the mattress, his gaze had rested on the light triangle of hair between her thighs, a visual reminder that he knew what she felt like on the inside.

Jamal had never thought he'd ever get to see Melissa naked. He had never thought they'd be lying naked in bed together. He had fantasized about it. Hell, he'd dreamed about it a few times in his childhood. But he didn't think it would actually happen—not in a million years. But here they were.

"I have an IUD," she said, her lips curving into a smile that brought that dimple that he loved to her right cheek.

He breathed an inward sigh of relief. *Good*, he thought, then he hadn't got her pregnant tonight. They didn't need that complication and he didn't want to put any more burdens on her.

She climbed onto the mattress and sank beneath the sheets and quilted comforter. He could feel the warmth radiating off of her body like a floor heater, and he instinctively drew closer to her, seeking that warmth.

"What about you?" she asked, resting her elbow on her pillow, reclining on her side. "If we're gonna start asking awkward questions, got any diseases that I should know about?"

He quickly shook his head. "Hell no! Well . . ." He hesitated. "None that I know of."

Her smile disappeared. Her eyebrow shot up again. *"None that you know of?"*

"I mean . . . I got checked out a few months ago and nothing popped up," he assured her. "So I bet everything's okay. Nothing for you to worry about."

After his spate of one-night stands he'd thought it would be smart to go to the doc and get checked out. Though he hadn't used one tonight, he'd used condoms for all of those other encounters, but one could never be too sure. He'd been relieved when the nurse had called him back saying that he didn't test positive for any STDs.

"That's good," Melissa now said as she reached out and cupped his face. "But we should probably use a condom next time to be on the safe side."

He blinked in surprise. "Next time?"

So this wasn't a one-night-only thing? She didn't have sex with him as some temporary salve to ease her pain or to get back at Derrick?

"*What?* You didn't want there to be a next time?" She burst out laughing. "Was the sex that bad?"

"No! No, it was good—*real* good."

"Yeah, I thought so too," she said, running her thumb gently along his cheek, gazing into his eyes.

"I . . . I just thought . . ."

"You just thought what, Jay?"

"Never mind. That came out wrong. I wanna have sex with you again. I'd *love* to have sex with you again."

She laughed, making him realize how overeager he sounded.

"B-but it's not like I'd just be focused on sex. I mean I'm not obsessed with it. I really like—"

"Shhhh," she whispered, cutting off his nervous rambling. She leaned forward and kissed him.

The kiss was sweet and tender and he wanted even more of it, but she pulled back, smirked, and turned her back to him. She turned off the lamp. "Goodnight, Jay."

" 'Night, Lissa," he whispered to the back of her neck, before frowning at the red silk cap she was wearing that was inches from his face. "What is this on your head, by the way?"

"It's a bonnet," she called back to him sleepily in the dark. "Why?"

He frowned. There was a long pause.

"You're telling me you haven't seen a silk bonnet? I wear it to protect my hair at night."

"My mom used to wear one, I think."

She chuckled. "You've been hooking up with too many white girls, Jay. Welcome back to the land of bonnets, head wraps, and scarves, homie."

He burst into laughter and wrapped an arm around her waist. "I love you," he gushed almost drunkenly and kissed the back of her neck, making her laugh too. Because he did. He was drunk in love with her right now and he wasn't ashamed to admit it. He loved Melissa and this moment and he would probably die happy if his life ended today.

She didn't say she loved him back but he felt her clasp his hand, intertwining her fingers with his, making him smile. After a few minutes, they both fell asleep.

Chapter 29

Ricky

The hour-and-forty-five-minute drive to Simone's place in Virginia seemed to crawl at a snail's pace, even though Ricky drove at high speed the entire way, whipping around cars and running the occasional red light. He waited for the police to stop him, to see flashing lights in his rearview mirror and hear the blare of sirens, but no one pulled him over. He kept driving and the whole time his heart was racing. The steering wheel became slick with sweat from his palms. He tried more than once to call Simone as he drove, but never reached her. His calls kept going to voice mail.

The knots in his stomach tightened as he approached the gravel driveway of the Fullers' property, kicking up rocks and dirt in his wake. He squinted at the home's exterior as the car slowed to a stop. The house looked exactly as he remembered it—the wooden porch, the chipped paint on the siding, and the rocking chair perched near the bay window. But this time, he noticed another car in the car port parked next to Simone's pickup truck—a silver

Toyota Camry. He suspected it was Simone's mother's car. A few lights were on inside the house, burning bright in the living room and some of the upstairs bedroom windows. Seeing the house look so serene and ordinary, he breathed a sigh of relief as he tugged his key out of the ignition.

Thank God. I got here in time, he thought. He had made it here before any of Dolla Dolla's goons had.

He threw open the car door, hopped out, and slammed it shut behind him. He raced toward the porch stairs but paused again. He could barely hear it above the incessant chirping of the crickets in the high grass surrounding the house, over the whir of the cicadas in the trees overhead, but he heard it all the same. It was a rhythmic, piercing beep that got louder as he drew near the porch. He immediately recognized it as the house alarm.

"Shit," he muttered before taking the porch stairs two at a time.

"Simone! Simone!" he yelled as he tugged his Glock 43 out of his waistband. He raised his fist and began to bang on the door. He's stomach lurched when the door swung open with a slow creak. Splinters on the floor showed that it had been forced open already. But the door came to a stop abruptly, thumping against something that had fallen on the hardwood.

Ricky looked down and saw a foot, then a jeans-clad leg, then a torso soaked with blood from a gaping wound in the center of the chest. The woman's dark eyes stared up at the living room ceiling. Her mouth was gaping in a permanent scream. Ricky winced when he realized who the woman was. He had seen her posing in pictures back at Simone's old place, but he had never gotten to meet her in person—and now it looked like he never would.

"Nadine," he whispered with a grimace.

It was Simone's mother. She was half slumped on the couch near the door, half on the floor—like she'd been sitting on the sofa and stood up when the door had been kicked open, when she had been taken out by a series of bullets. The poor woman hadn't stood a chance. But if she was dead, did that mean that Simone was dead too, and their baby?

His throat tightened with panic. His heart, already beating fast, seemed to kick into overdrive.

"Simone!" Ricky yelled again, shouting to be heard over the home alarm. He raced into the kitchen and down the hall, gazing into doorways as he ran past the first-floor bathroom and rec room. "Simone, where the hell are you?"

He shoved open the door to a closet, making sure that she wasn't hiding inside, crouched in the fetal position. But she wasn't in there either.

He charged toward the stairs and went clamoring to the top floor, almost tripping over his own feet, screaming her name the whole way.

"*Ricky?*" someone called out.

He knew from the sound of the voice that it wasn't Simone. He whipped around to find Melvin lying on the floor, braced against the wall. His bald head and brow were covered with sweat. He was breathing in and out sharply through his teeth. It came out in bursts and a low whistle. His right hand was clutched over his leg where blood pooled on the carpet underneath him. His gun sat at his side.

"Nigga, what . . . y-you . . . you doin' h-here?" Melvin asked between gasps. Ricky could barely hear him over the beeping alarm. "Dolla sent you?"

Ricky didn't answer his question. Instead he took one menacing step toward Melvin, then another, barely able to contain his rage. "Where is she?" he asked. "Is she dead?"

"Yeah, she dead! One of them bitches shot me though, but I got her ass too. They're in the bedroom down the hall." He gestured with his bloody hand to his right. "I smoked those bitches, but Dolla said to call him when it's done." Melvin winced as he reached for his gun and tried to push himself to his feet. "Call him on your phone. We gotta do it before the cops get—"

Melvin was silenced by a bullet to the head, spraying the wall with a mix of blood, bone, and brain matter. Tears were in Ricky's eyes as Melvin's limp body fell to the floor. Ricky then fired again and again, watching as the body twitched and jumped. In the end, he'd emptied five bullets in him before he lowered his Glock back to his side.

They were all dead. Melvin had said so himself. Simone . . . the baby . . . they were gone.

He closed his eyes and began to silently weep. He slumped to the floor beside Melvin's body.

What else could God take from him? He'd lost his sister and his grandmother before the age of twenty. He'd lost his restaurant and his livelihood and would likely lose his freedom too when he finally went to jail. Simone and their baby were the only precious things he'd had left. Now the few hopes and dreams he'd locked away, had been ripped to shreds.

Ricky gritted his teeth as warm tears slid onto his cheeks and sank into his beard.

If he had killed Melvin the day Melvin had murdered Tamika, this might not have happened. His own cowardice had led to this.

He gazed down the hall at the open bedroom door. He didn't want to see it. He didn't want to see Simone's dead body, but he knew he had to do it. He had to say goodbye before the cops got here. This would be his last chance.

After about a minute, he got himself together enough to push himself back to his feet. He walked down the carpeted corridor and approached the bedroom door. He hesitated before easing the door open, bracing himself for what he was about to see.

A shot fired. Then another. He recoiled when he heard them. One bullet missed his shoulder by only a few inches and instead lodged in the door frame.

"Stay back! Stay the fuck back!" Simone screamed, and Ricky swore it was the most beautiful sound he'd ever heard.

"Baby, it's me!" he said, dropping his gun to the floor, holding up his hands in a mock sign of surrender. "It's me!" he repeated, peeking his head around the doorway.

"*Ricky?*" she squeaked.

He saw her kneeling on the floor beside the queen-size bed with Skylar's head cradled in her lap. Both women were covered in blood, though Skylar seemed much worse off than Simone. The young woman's chest rose and fell as she seemed to fight for every breath. Blood oozed from the corner of her mouth.

Ricky ran toward them and fell to Simone's side.

"I-I tried to stop the b-b-bleeding," she stuttered between sobs. "But it won't . . . it won't stop."

He looked down and saw that she was holding a towel against her sister's stomach. The pink towel was soaked and mostly red now. Skylar's lids were drifting closed as her eyeballs rolled wildly. He could tell Skylar wasn't going to make it.

"Are you shot?" he asked, examining Simone, running his hands over her face and her torso. She was covered in blood but he suspected and hoped it wasn't her own. "Are you okay?"

"Stop it!" She angrily slapped away his hand. "I'm fine!

Stop fucking worrying about me! Worry about her, Ricky! Help me stop the bleeding. Hold this while I call 9-1-1!"

He didn't have the heart to tell her that if the alarm was sounding then the police were already on the way, but no one could possibly get here in time to save her sister. Instead he took the towel, like she directed, and applied pressure.

"It's okay, Sky," she said to her sister as she gently laid her head on the bedroom floor. "It's okay, honey. We'll take care of you. You'll be fine."

She grabbed the edge of the bed and hoisted herself to her feet with a loud grunt, cradling her pregnant belly as she did it. It had gotten even bigger since the last time he'd seen her. She then waddled to her night table and grabbed her cordless phone and began to dial just as Skylar took her last shaky breath, as the young woman's eyes went blank. Ricky shifted and placed two fingers along her throat, checking for a pulse. He felt nothing.

"Hello!" Simone shouted behind him. "Hello, yes, I have an emergency."

"She's gone," he said, removing the towel.

"What?" she shouted back to him, frowning as she returned her attention to the dispatcher. "Yes, my sister has been shot. We need help!"

"I said she's gone. Skylar's gone, baby. She's dead."

She turned back around to face him and dropped the phone from her hands. She shoved him aside and cupped Skylar's face.

"*Sky?* Sky!" she screamed.

Ricky placed his hands on her shoulders. "We need to go."

"No! No!" she howled, grabbing her sister and cradling her head against her chest. "I'm not . . . I'm not leaving her! I'm not leaving her!"

"She's dead, baby. I'm sorry, but she's gone. We have to go," he said in a firmer voice, reaching for the phone and hanging it up. "Melvin didn't call Dolla. He's gonna figure out something went wrong, and if the cops get here and he finds out you're still alive and I'm here, we'll *all* be dead. We have to go!"

"I said no!" She continued to shake her head and weep, to cling to her sister's body fiercely, like a wolf mother who refuses to abandon her dead cub.

"Think about the baby," he said to her. "Think about our son. You promised me you wouldn't sacrifice him, that you'd protect him. Don't do this!"

She slowly opened her eyes and looked up at him. Her gaze was so desolate, so tortured. But he must have finally gotten through to her because she slowly eased her little sister back to the floor. With shaky limbs, she slid back across the bloody floor. He helped Simone to her feet and he could feel her trembling in his arms. She dropped her head to his shoulder and sobbed as he eased her down the hall. They stepped over Melvin's legs like they would a piece of fallen furniture before they made their way to the staircase.

When they reached the first floor and the living room, Simone started screaming all over again.

"Mom! Mom! Oh, God! Mommy!" she screeched as they passed her mother's body. She stopped and reached down to the floor as if to grab her mother's hand, but he roughly yanked her back.

"No!" she yelled when she realized he was pulling her away from the body. "Please, Ricky! Please, I can't just—"

"I said we have to go," he repeated firmly, wrapping his arms around her, almost carrying her out the front door.

It wasn't easy but he got her to his car. When he swung

the passenger door open she nearly fell into the seat, sobbing uncontrollably, saying words that were nearly unintelligible. He slammed the car door shut behind her and walked around to the driver's side, before taking one last glance at the house, climbing inside, and pulling off with no idea where they were headed next.

Keep an eye out for more from
The Branch Avenue Boys
And be sure to read
IN THESE STREETS
Available now from
Shelly Ellis
and
Dafina Books
Wherever books are sold

KNOW YOUR PLACE

Shelly Ellis

ABOUT THIS GUIDE

The suggested questions are included
to enhance your group's reading of
Shelly Ellis's *Know Your Place*.

DISCUSSION QUESTIONS

1. Do you think Derrick made the right decision not to go to the police when he discovered the suitcases under Cole's bed?

2. Ricky decides to become an informant for the Metro Police out of fear that Dolla Dolla will find out he was the reason behind the raids. Would you have flipped under similar circumstances, or would you have just taken the fall?

3. Ricky decides to track down Simone after he is arrested. Do you think he's only motivated by revenge, like he says?

4. Jamal is faced with the choice of protecting his own reputation or protecting the reporter Phillip's life. He offers himself to Mayor Johnson as a sacrifice. Were you surprised by Jamal's decision? What does that say about how he's evolved as a character since the previous book?

5. Derrick admits that he is in love with both Melissa and Morgan. Do you think this is true? Can a man really love two women equally—or does he just want to have his cake and eat it too?

6. Ricky knows that he can never again really trust or believe Simone, but decides to rekindle their secret relationship. Could you be involved romantically with someone you couldn't trust would always tell you the truth?

7. Jamal decides to quit working for Mayor Johnson, despite the risk. Do you think the mayor really is bluffing with his threat again, or does he mean it this time around?

8. Jamal and Melissa finally start the romantic relationship he always wanted. Do you think he is the rebound guy or are they legitimately falling for each other?

9. Ricky once again places himself in the line of fire to help Simone. Do you think he is right in his motivations, or is he once again making a grave mistake?

Connect with Us

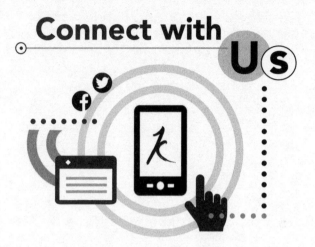

Visit us online at
KensingtonBooks.com
to read more from your favorite authors, see books
by series, view reading group guides, and more.

for sneak peeks, chances to win books and prize packs,
and to share your thoughts with other readers.

**facebook.com/kensingtonpublishing
twitter.com/kensingtonbooks**

Tell us what you think!

To share your thoughts, submit a review,
or sign up for our eNewsletters, please visit:
KensingtonBooks.com/TellUs.